To Christine
Enjoy the adventures of
Andy + Carey
Sandra Farris

CAN YOU HEAR THE MUSIC?

CAN YOU HEAR THE MUSIC?

By
Sandra Farris

iUniverse, Inc.
New York Lincoln Shanghai

Can You Hear The Music?

All Rights Reserved © 2003 by Sandra Farris

No part of this book may be reproduced or transmitted in any form or by any means, graphic, electronic, or mechanical, including photocopying, recording, taping, or by any information storage retrieval system, without the written permission of the publisher.

iUniverse, Inc.

For information address:
iUniverse, Inc.
2021 Pine Lake Road, Suite 100
Lincoln, NE 68512
www.iuniverse.com

ISBN: 0-595-30268-8 (pbk)
ISBN: 0-595-66144-0 (cloth)

Printed in the United States of America

This book is dedicated to my family and to the newest members: Carina Zarate-Farris, Hayden and Elise.

Also to my friends and coworkers at Marana Municipal Court and Pima County Justice Court. To Norma Stout and Dr. Katherine Hatch, PHD

Have you ever listened
To the sounds that God has given
The sounds of children as they play
Or the gentle breeze of a summer's day
The sound of thunder on a rainy night
Or the wind as she blows with all her might
A train that whistles from far away,
A haunting sound, some might say
The ocean waves as they crash on shore
A bird's sweet song, and so much more?
It's truly a symphony of sounds
That we can hear from all around.
Just close your eyes and give in to it
Now stop and listen…can you hear the music?

—Darlene McKeen

Acknowledgments

The spring poem in Andy's chapter is by Esther Russell, my mother. The opening poem is by Darlene McKeen, my sister and co-author of *Wind Dancers,* ISBN:0-595-25781-X (Pbk), ISBN:0-595-65329-4 (Cloth)

Cover: Photo Illustration by Dennis Farris
Model: Amanda Mockbee

Prologue

November 1919

Henry and Janine James pushed their way through the revelers in the hotel banquet room, grasping hands firmly to keep from getting separated. Merchants had traveled from all parts of the South and Midwest for the three-day convention and display of new spring merchandise for 1920. Now that it was over, Henry and Janine had only one thing on their minds…to get a good night's sleep and return home to their daughter as quickly as possible.

As they climbed the stairs and started down the corridor, a child cried out from behind a door and they could hear a woman's voice soothing away the nightmare. A veil of distress fell across Janine's face and did not go undetected by her husband. He knew she was thinking of their little Corey.

"Let's go home tonight. It's only eighty miles and we can be there when Corey wakes up in the morning," Henry proposed, grinning sheepishly.

"I thought you'd never ask," laughed Janine.

This trip had been a combination second honeymoon, after twenty years of marriage, and doctor's orders to take time off from work. Janine couldn't refuse to accompany her husband, but now she was ready to go home to her daughter.

The day had been tiring for both of them, but as Henry looked at the peaceful form of his wife sleeping beside him, he knew the drive was worth the exhaustion he felt. Another thirty miles and they would be home! He shifted in his seat, trying to dispel the pain in his chest and arm. *Probably got a cramp from sitting in one place too long*, he thought, peering through the light drizzle starting to fall.

Suddenly, a more intense pain tore through his chest and down his arm until it was unbearable. His foot jammed on the accelerator. Pinpoints of light ringed the darkness as he stared ahead trying to see the road. His mouth opened to call out to Janine, but he heard only the fading sound of the car engine. A warm black wave of unconsciousness swept over him as the speeding automobile careened out of control over the embankment.

CHAPTER 1

Corey James stood beneath the bleak November sky and took one last look at her home. It was the final door to be closed on the only world she had known the past nine years. Her chin quivered and her body trembled uncontrollably as she savored every familiar detail. Only two weeks before she had stood on this very spot, watching as the black Maxwell disappeared down the street and she could no longer see the white handkerchief her mother waved. Now, she looked down the same street, wishing with all her strength for this to be a horrible nightmare from which she would awaken and see her parents returning.

"It's time to go, Corey," her uncle George James said gently.

Corey clung desperately to Mrs. McPhearson's hand, a silent plea in her eyes since she could not summon the words.

"Please, Corey, you have to be brave for me." Mrs. McPhearson stooped down as she struggled against her own tears. "Your uncle is flesh and blood kinfolk, and he is taking you to your new home." The rest of her words were lost as the child grabbed her around the neck, burying her face in the housekeeper's shoulder. Silently, the old woman prayed for the strength to send the girl on her way without breaking down completely.

"Mrs. McPhearson, I'm sorry, but we really have to go," George James implored.

Ellie McPhearson stood up, took a deep breath, and broke Corey's strong grip. "Corey, dear, there is nothing for you here, child, and the sooner you leave, the better. Now pull yourself up straight and tall, no more tears, and go with your uncle." The last words she managed with a forced sternness.

A tear glistened among Corey's thick, black eyelashes, and Mrs. McPhearson wiped it away. Corey was a miniature of her mother. Her black hair framed her round, cherubic face and beneath her tightly closed eyes were saucer-like discs of deep blue. How many times those twinkling eyes had melted Ellie's resistance as she tried to reprimand the girl for some wrongdoing. Not that Corey was a bad child, she had been pure pleasure; but like most children, she needed occasional prodding.

Mrs. McPhearson bent over Corey once again and placed a loving kiss on her forehead before gently turning her over to Mr. James. Lest there be any further protests, she hurried back to the house, knowing if she turned for a last look it would be her undoing.

George James rubbed circles on his temples as he replayed the confrontation with his wife while he placed the child in the taxi.

❦   ❦   ❦

"My brother and his wife were killed in an automobile crash last night." He hesitated long enough for her to comprehend what he had said. "I have to go to Oklahoma and tie up all the loose ends." Pausing again, he moved over to the bed and sat beside his wife. "Lizzie, I will be bringing my niece back to live with us." He sat with his head bowed, waiting for the storm.

"A child? That's right, they had a child!" Lizzie exclaimed. "But, George, we're not prepared for a child! *I'm* not prepared for a child. Can't she go someplace else? Do *we* have to take her?" she screeched.

"You know there are no other relatives. She's my brother's child, Lizzie. I can't turn my back on her." There was a hint of pleading in his voice.

"And how are you going to feed and clothe another person on your salary? We barely make ends meet as it is," she snapped. "Who's going to be the one stuck with her all day while you're at work? I'll tell you who…me!"

George knew the topic of money would come into this discussion. Lizzie never missed a chance to let him know how unsuccessful he was, but this time he was prepared. "My brother left the child well provided for. It won't be that bad. It's not like she is a baby; she's nine years old."

A light flickered in Lizzie's gray eyes. Of course, she had momentarily forgotten about her brother-in-law's business. Maybe it wouldn't be so bad after all. The girl was old enough to take care of herself and she could help around the house. Yes, she smiled to herself, things were going to be all right.

"You are right, dear, we can't shirk our responsibilities," she cooed, patting George on the hand. "Of course, we will take the child."

🍁   🍁   🍁

George shook his head to clear his mind and followed Corey into the waiting cab.

CHAPTER 2

April 1920

Corey James stood above the opening in the pantry floor, her breath coming in quick gulps as she fought back the suffocating feeling that enveloped her. A musty, earthen odor lingered in the air. It was as though she was standing above the two graves again, watching as the earth reclaimed her parents. She had had nightmares of being buried alive since that day and the cellar, opening at her feet, brought them vividly to life.

"Corey James, you get down those steps and fetch that jar up here right now! I'll have none of your foolishness, child," Lizzie ordered as she loomed above Corey, her huge form blocking the light from the trapdoor. The thunder in her voice shook the girl to the core of her being; it was a tossup which was more frightening…her aunt or the cellar.

Corey tightened her grip on the wooden railing, her large blue eyes filling with tears. "Please, Aunt Lizzie, couldn't we wait for Uncle George to come home?" she begged.

"Fear is an unbecoming trait, young lady, and you are going to overcome it right now," Lizzie smirked, slamming the trapdoor shut behind Corey.

"Please, Aunt Lizzie, let me out of here!" Corey screamed, pounding on the door.

"You will stay down there until you learn there is nothing to be scared of!"

Corey eased down the ladder and stood at the bottom until her eyes adjusted to the darkness. Terrible thoughts began to fill her head. What if Aunt Lizzie left her down here? Would it be like the nightmares with the air slowly being shut off until she could no longer draw a breath? Tears filled her eyes and she gulped the heavy air. No one would miss her, she thought, and she recalled the conversation with her aunt the first day she had come to Naples, Texas.

❦   ❦   ❦

"You'll always be an outsider looking in," Aunt Lizzie had sneered. "As soon as you face that fact, the better off you'll be. Nobody cares about you."

"My folks cared about me…and Mrs. Mc—" Corey had cried in protest.

"Let's set the record straight, Miss High-and-Mighty. Your folks put up with you because they had no choice. If they had wanted a child, they would have had one long ago. Think about it…do any other children have parents old enough to be their grandparents? You're nothing but a mistake and a bothersome one at that."

❦   ❦   ❦

Corey winced sharply as the words echoed in her head. It wasn't true! But why had her parents waited so long to have a child? Did they really love her, or were they just "putting up with her" as Aunt Lizzie had said? And what about her new friend, Tommy Rice? Was he really her friend or was he just being nice? How could she tell the difference?

Then there was Muffin. How she loved her little dog! Thinking about him warmed her heart, and in spite of the panic, she felt a smile tug at her lips. She let her mind drift back to the day he had come into her life…

❦   ❦   ❦

Uncle George called Corey in from the garden, excitement coloring his voice for the first time since she had met him.

"Get that thing out of my house right now, George," Lizzie yelled as Corey entered the house.

Corey didn't know whether to laugh or cry when she saw the puppy scurrying around Uncle George's feet, trying to get away from Lizzie's fury. She bent down and picked up the trembling white ball of fur and held it tightly while she murmured soothingly in its ear.

"Where did you get him, Uncle George? Is he really mine?" the words tumbled out in disbelief.

"My boss thought you might like to have a dog. He says all children should have a pet of their own. Of course," George laughed, "he said that because his dog had a litter of puppies and this was the last one. It seems he was having trouble getting someone to take him because he is the runt of the litter. Still I thought it was very kind of him to think of you, so perhaps you could stop by the bank after school tomorrow and thank him."

"We're two of a kind," Corey whispered into the dog's ear. "Two outcasts nobody wants. Well, no more. We have each other now."

Lizzie consented to keep the dog, only after George suggested that getting rid of him would offend the vice president of the bank, George's boss. and with the condition the dog remain outside. Should he cause any trouble, he would have to go.

For a time, life became more bearable for Corey. When she was troubled, she could bury her face in Muffin's fur and speak openly of the frustrations and fears she had previously kept hidden. She felt loved and wanted again, but that wasn't to last, however. As Corey's fondness for the animal grew stronger, so did Lizzie's jealousy of the child's bond with the puppy. Lizzie became more vindictive, lashing out at the child at every opportunity.

🍁   🍁   🍁

"I haven't got all day, young lady. Are you listening to me? Fetch that jam up here right now," Lizzie shrieked, jolting Corey back to the present.

As she strained to see in the darkness, the black shapes of the ham and bacon hanging from the ceiling added to the eerie atmosphere. Past the meat, shelves lined the wall. That was where the jam was kept, along with *a candle and matches!*

Eagerly, Corey started across the room, her breath still coming in short gasps. In her haste to find the candle, Corey brushed against the box of matches, sending the wooden sticks scattering across the floor. On her hands and knees, she groped until she located a match and struck it across the wooden beam. At first, it was a blinding light as the flame danced on the end of the stick, but when she touched it to the candle, a warm light began to push back some of the dreaded darkness.

Corey stood for a moment reveling in the soft glow before she grabbed a jar from its place on the shelf and tucked it under her arm. Slowly, she made her way back to the foot of the stairs, shielding her precious flame so it wouldn't go out.

"Aunt Lizzie, I have the jam," Corey called out, and trying to keep the terror from her voice, she lied, "I'm not afraid of the dark anymore, either."

"See, now don't you feel better?" Lizzie asked as she opened the door, somewhat disappointed the child had recovered so quickly.

"Yes, ma'am," Corey answered, focusing on her aunt's topknot of twisted hair, afraid that if she looked into Lizzie's eyes, her aunt would see the fear in her own. Now she had to get outside where there was air and lots of light.

"Not so fast, Corey," Lizzie said as she grabbed the child by the arm. "I want you to take the clothes out and hang them on the line for me."

"Yes, ma'am." Corey's voice quaked as she started for the door.

"I'm not finished, young lady," Lizzie sneered, then I want you to get cleaned up and serve tea when Grace comes over. You could use some lessons in social manners."

Corey was in no mood to face that terrible gossip, the widow Canfield, or to see the greedy eagerness with which her aunt awaited every mean tale that came from the old woman's mouth.

"Please, Aunt Lizzie, may I be excused? I really feel sick to my stomach," Corey moaned.

Lizzie whirled Corey around and slapped her hard across the face. "You sniveling brat, there is nothing wrong with you. You're just sulking because I shut you in the cellar. You will do as you're told and that's that!"

Corey ran from the house holding a hand over her mouth, fighting back the nausea. Her face stung and a lump was forming on her cheek where Lizzie's ring had bruised the skin.

"Hey, Corey, whatcha doin'?"

She watched in desperation as Tommy came across the yard. She didn't want him to see her like this, but it was too late to run back into the house.

"I was fishin' and caught two—" he started. "Whew! What happened to your face?"

"I don't want to talk about it," Corey answered, as she turned away from his inspection.

"Your aunt again?" He sighed and tenderly touched the bump on Corey's cheek, wincing as he imagined the pain. "Oh, Corey, if I was old enough I would marry you and we could go away where you would be safe."

"Thanks, Tommy, but I can't wait that long to get away from here."

"What are you going to do?" he asked fearfully.

Before Corey could reply, Lizzie came out the back door with a basket of laundry. "You get on with hanging up this wash. You don't have the time to be visiting with the likes of him," Lizzie glared down her nose at the boy.

Tommy scooped up his pole and started quickly for home. Having gone a short distance, he turned around with the strong urge to stick his tongue out at Lizzie, but she gave him such an evil look he was too frightened to do anything but run. *Mean old woman anyway,* he thought, kicking angrily at a tuft of grass.

As Corey snatched the clothes from the basket one by one, she began to develop a plan. She would serve tea for her aunt and think of a reason to be excused. She needed to think of something that would allow her enough time to slip out the window and get a good start before she was missed. A contented smile crept across her face. She could even be on her best behavior, knowing what was to come, and Lizzie would never suspect a thing. Since Lizzie would have company to keep her occupied, Corey could easily fool her.

Setting the tea tray on the table beside Lizzie, Corey carefully inspected it to make sure she hadn't forgotten something.

"Aunt Lizzie, will you be wanting anything else?" Corey smiled pleasantly at her aunt and Mrs. Canfield.

"No, I think that will be all for now." Lizzie shook her head, her topknot jiggling precariously. She was puzzled at Corey's behavior, but she pushed aside the thought in her haste to hear what Grace Canfield was about to tell her. A good slapping around was all that child had needed.

"Then, if you don't need anything else, will it be all right if I take a nap?"

"Yes, fine, fine," Lizzie agreed, not really listening to what Corey had asked. She was annoyed the child was still in the room.

Corey closed the door to her bedroom and leaned against it until her heart stopped pounding. Had Aunt Lizzie suspected anything? Had she behaved strangely back there in the parlor? She eased the door open a crack and the sound of the two women chattering happily assured Corey that all was well. Quickly, she crossed the room to her dresser and picked up the brooch that had belonged to her mother. There was no time to pack cloth, but she could not leave her prized possession.

Her finger pressed against the small trigger and the face of the pin sprung open, revealing the smiling faces of a man, woman, and child. The picture had been taken on Corey's sixth birthday, the year she had begun school. She remembered the tears in her mother's eyes that morning as she had started for school, feeling so proud and important. How could she have known life would change so drastically in just three short years?

Why had this happened to her? Why, why? she cried. But there were no answers, and she slipped the brooch carefully into her pocket, tucking the questions away with it. There were more pressing things to consider right now.

Muffin bolted around the corner of the house in answer to his mistress's soft whistle. Corey scooped the little dog into her arms and started across the back yard toward town. She would stop by the grocery store and use her errand money to get some food. She patted her pocket to make sure the money was still there. There was enough for one day's worth of supplies. After that, she didn't know what she would do, nor did she care at this point. She would face things as they happened.

Corey tucked the package containing the soda crackers and a slab of cheese under her arm and slowed her quick steps to a more carefree amble so she wouldn't attract undue attention. She could see the end of Main Street and her freedom ahead and she had to fight the urge to run.

"Corey, could you take this prescription over to the feed store? My delivery boy is off this afternoon, and Mr. Harrington can't leave the store right now to come after it. Thanks," Mr. Rodgers, the pharmacist, shoved the medicine into her hand.

Corey didn't want to be delayed any longer, but she had been unable to answer the man before he turned and went back inside the drugstore. Oh well, it was on her way and how long could it take to drop off medicine?

The delivery took fifteen minutes, ten of which she spent waiting for Mr. Harrington to finish with a customer. Her tension was somewhat relieved when he gave her a whole quarter for her trouble. It was more than she had ever gotten before for errands. Happily, she went out the back door, turned the corner of the feed store and called to Muffin. "Here, boy, here..." The rest of the words froze on her lips as Grace Canfield seized her by the arm.

"Corey, child, your aunt is worried sick. You really should have told her you were leaving the house," she purred smugly. "Come, dear, I'll see that you get home safely."

"That's all right, Mrs. Canfield, I can walk from here," Corey said, a note of pleading creeping into her voice.

"Nonsense, your aunt would never forgive me if I just left you here after she's been looking everywhere for you. Now, get in," she ordered, holding the door open.

Corey crawled into the backseat, trembling with fear at what would be awaiting her when she returned to Lizzie's house. Even Muffin sensed something was wrong and he lay against her, very still and quiet.

Lizzie had seen the car pull up and met them on the porch, her eyes liquid fire, searing Corey under their gaze.

"Thank you, Grace," she said stonily. Then turning to Corey, she grabbed her by the shoulder, pushing her into the house.

"I should've known you were up to something when you were being so goody-goody, you little brat! If you hadn't been so preoccupied with running away with *that boy,* you would've remembered the spoon for the preserves and I wouldn't have discovered your little plan," Lizzie yelled. "You picked the wrong time for your games. You've embarrassed me in front of my friend, and I won't let you get away with it," she fumed. "Whether you like it or not, young lady, you're not to leave this house again unless I say so."

Corey glanced pleadingly at her uncle, who had just returned from work, but he just shrugged his shoulders and blinked nervously behind the thick eyeglasses that made his eyes look much too large for his thin face. He ran long fingers through his thinning hair in a gesture of helplessness. He, too, was afraid of Lizzie and, rather than risk having her rage directed at him, he took up the newspaper and blocked the scene from his view.

"Get out of my sight before I really let you have it!" Lizzie screamed. "I don't want to see your face again today."

CHAPTER 3

❀

Corey awoke gasping for breath, her nightgown soaked with perspiration. A little over two months had passed since the incident in the cellar, but the nightmares had not diminished. The hall clock struck five…another hour before her aunt and uncle got up. Afraid to go back to sleep for fear the nightmare would return, she dressed and stripped the sheets from her bed, replacing them with clean ones.

The next hour she washed the kitchen floor on her hands and knees and started the laundry, then gathered the eggs. At six o'clock, she put the kettle on for Lizzie's tea and laid out the breakfast dishes, along with the tray to take the tea to her aunt. After breakfast she would wash the dishes, hang up the laundry, feed the dog, and dust the furniture. The rest of Saturday would be hers until suppertime.

Corey looked around the gleaming kitchen for one last inspection before Lizzie came out. Satisfied, she picked up the tray.

"Aunt Lizzie, I have most of my chores done already and I thought I could go fishing with Tommy, if it's okay with you," she asked all in one breath, as she set the tray on the bedside table.

"I'll have to see about that, Corey. I'm sure you can wait until I've gotten out of bed for your answer," Lizzie answered, sipping her tea slowly.

Corey sat silently through breakfast, anxiously waiting for Lizzie to give her answer regarding the fishing trip. Summer was almost half over, and she was could hardly wait until school started. It had been a long summer, having spent so much time with her aunt.

Breakfast was over and Lizzie still had given no response. Corey finished her chores before she meekly asked again for permission to go fishing.

"Let's see what you've done first," Lizzie stalled, checking the furniture for dust. "Hmm, the windows could be washed, and how about the kitchen floor? You did say you washed it?"

Corey followed her aunt back into the kitchen and then, to her horror, she watched as Lizzie deliberately poured her cup of tea on the floor.

"Oh, now look what I have done," she leered. "and it has splattered all over your clean floor. *Tsk, tsk,* you will have the whole thing to do over again, I'm afraid—" she took the scrub brush with the pail from the porch, and shoved them at Corey—"the whole floor."

"You weren't going to let me go at all, were you? You didn't have to do this. All you had to do was say no. I worked hard on this floor."

"Watch you tongue, missy, or I'll slap it right out of your mouth. Now get on with it and no more of this nonsense of going fishing."

Corey scrubbed the floor with a fury as she tried to fight back the tears. She was not going to give her aunt the satisfaction of seeing her cry.

Lizzie smugly watched Corey's struggle, her arms folded across her chest, until Corey had finished the floor and she pushed a pan into her hands. "Pick the beans in the garden. When you're finished there, I'll find something else for you to do," she ordered.

As Corey moved among the rows of green bean vines, she saw Tommy coming across the yard.

"Hello, Tommy. Goin' fishin' or just coming back?"

"Coming back. I've been fishing since seven this morning, then went swimming with Johnny Peters, and there wasn't nothing left to do. Boy, I'm glad school starts next month. I've run out of things to do."

"Not me," Corey sighed, "I've got a passel of chores to do today. Did you catch anything?" she asked, changing the subject.

"Just a bunch of chiggers and an ole crawdad…"

"Corey James, what are you doing out there?" Lizzie yelled from the porch.

"Talking to Tommy, Aunt Lizzie."

Lizzie approached the youngsters, hands on her hips as she glared at them. "Haven't you got enough to do, or shall I give you more? You get on with picking those beans or I'll take a switch to you."

Tommy fled without so much as a good-bye, and as Corey watched him disappear, her eyes filled with tears of humiliation. Why did her aunt continually embarrass her in front of her friends? She fought desperately to keep from lashing out, knowing from the smirk on the old woman's face she was waiting for exactly that reaction. *One day,* Corey thought, *one day.*

Corey finished picking the beans and started for the house where she was greeted enthusiastically by Muffin. He had seen the pan in her hands and, thinking there was food in it for him, sat perched on his hind legs, begging.

"Oh, you poor thing, I forgot to feed you this morning. Wait here while I get your food," she cooed to the dog.

Muffin was still sitting up when Corey returned with the scraps she had saved from breakfast. She set the dish down, and he devoured its contents almost instantly. Little round black eyes peeked from beneath shaggy white hair, as he begged for more. Corey bent down, drawing the dog to her, and scratched the top of his head.

"That's all there is, Muffin. You'll have to wait until this evening for more. You shouldn't have eaten so fast. Don't you know that will make you sick?" She gave him a loving hug and set him down on the porch.

"All right, young lady, I've had enough of your loafing." Lizzie yelled and began slapping Corey. She hated that dog and seeing Corey with him instead of working had sent her into a rage.

Muffin heard Corey's cries, grabbed the hem of Lizzie's long dress, and ripped a hole as he did so. Immediately, the woman grabbed the broom from beside the door and began swinging at Muffin, breaking the broomstick on the ground in the process.

"Run, Muffin," Corey screamed. Turning to her aunt, she saw the fire dancing in her eyes and shuddered in fear.

Lizzie walked into the house in a deadly silence and returned with the razor strap. Corey could hear the singing sound as her aunt swung the strap through the air. The child felt its stinging bite each time it slapped across her legs.

"Now, missy," Lizzie commanded through clenched teeth, "you go to your room and I don't want you to leave it until you're told! As for that flea-bitten mutt, if he ever comes around here again, I'll kill him."

Corey lay across the tiny cot choking back the tears. "I will not cry anymore. I will not cry anymore," she swore into the patchwork quilt. Her legs throbbed as she slowly eased lengthwise onto the bed. It was the third time this week Lizzie had taken the strap to her and Corey silently vowed it would be the last. She would not take it any longer.

Poor Muffin, he was only trying to protect me. Now he had run away and she would probably never see him again. But Corey, too, was planning to run away…as far away from this terrible place as she could go. This time, though, she would have a plan. If she were to succeed, she first had to work out every detail.

A ten-year-old girl traveling alone would be easy to spot. This was the problem she'd think about. Corey closed her eyes tightly, studying the situation. What if she were to have a disguise? A young boy wandering the countryside didn't attract much attention; boys were always fishing or hunting. But where would she get the clothes? She had no dungarees or shirts; girls just didn't wear those things.

There was Johnny Peters...no, it would have to be someone she could trust and Johnny would surely tell her aunt. It would have to be Tommy. As much as she hated to involve her friend, he was the only one she could trust with her secret. Besides, he had a pair of pants his mother had been trying to get rid of for weeks. They would be perfect.

Good, Corey thought, *that wasn't so difficult.* The next step was to wait until her guardians went to bed and then, freedom! Comforted by the thought, she drifted into a peaceful sleep.

Sometime later Corey was awakened by a scratching noise. She lay motionless, waiting for the sound again. There, it was coming from the window! Slowly, painfully, she made her way across the room and peered outside where she saw a familiar form in the moonlight.

Corey opened the window and spoke in hushed tones to the waiting dog. "Quiet, Muffin. You'll wake everybody up. Wait there for me. Stay!"

Listening intently for any sounds in the house, Corey felt her heart skip a beat as the clock boomed in the hall. Ten o'clock. Good, her aunt and uncle would have been in bed for an hour. It was a rare occasion when they didn't go to bed at nine.

Corey sought out the loose section of the baseboard along the floor and, using her comb, pried it open. Here the floor hadn't been extended over the rough subflooring, and that provided a space large enough for the flat tin box that held her treasures: a small, heart-shaped locket Tommy had given her on her tenth birthday, her mother's brooch, a little money she had put away, and two red-and-white striped bows the dressmaker had given her for her hair. Her hair! There was another problem she had overlooked.

Corey turned on the lamp and sighed at the long black curls reflected in the mirror. She would have to cut it, but if she started prowling around now looking for scissors, she would take a big chance on getting caught. This chore would have to be done at Tommy's, too.

Returning to her task, Corey put the box of treasures carefully on the bed. Then, taking a scarf from the dresser, she spread it beside the box. Next, ever so quietly, she made her way down the hall to the kitchen where she collected two apples, half a loaf of Lizzie's freshly baked bread, a couple of pieces of leftover chicken, and a small wedge of cheese. Back in her room she folded the food in her scarf, picked up the treasures, and slipped through the window into the night.

"Come, Muffin," Corey whispered. "We're leaving this bad ol' place. You must be very quiet and not wake up anyone." The little ball of white fur looked up at his mistress and wagged his tail as if he understood.

The moon was directly overhead and so bright you could almost read by it. The large oak trees that lined the street cast lacy dark shadows upon the ground. The cool, powdery dirt felt good to Corey's bare feet as she walked down the middle of the street, her shoes flung across her shoulder.

Tommy lived at the end of the street, four houses from Corey's. It was a short walk, but painful because her legs were sore and stiff from the whipping. When she reached Tommy's at last, she circled the house looking for his bedroom. She gathered some gravel and tossed one pebble at a time against the window. Presently, the boy stuck his head out, rubbing the sleep from his eyes.

"Who's that?" he called.

"Sh-h-h, don't be so loud. Can you come down for a minute?" Corey whispered.

"Is that you, Corey?" Then, "I'll be right down."

Corey watched the other windows to make sure no one else heard. If Tommy's parents knew she was here they would send her home, but no lights appeared and she felt reassured. Just then Corey felt a tap on her shoulder and she whirled around in panic.

"What's up, Corey? How come you're out so late?"

"Good grief, Tommy, did you have to scare me to death?"

"Well, you said to be quiet. What's up?" he repeated.

"Come over here and I'll tell you." Corey led Tommy a safe distance from the house. "I need a favor. You know those old pants of yours, the ones with the holes in the knees? Well, I need them and a shirt and a pair of scissors. Can you get them without waking your parents?"

"Sure, but why do you need all that stuff? You still haven't told me what you're doing?"

"If you must know, I'm leaving home. Aunt Lizzie got mad at Muffin and me this afternoon and gave me a hard lickin' with the strap. She said she would kill Muffin 'cause he tore her dumb ol' dress when she hit me."

"But what do you need the stuff for?"

When she told him her plan, he stood for a minute thinking about what she had said, and his eyes widened. "I don't know, Corey, the clothes are one thing, but your hair…"

"Are you my friend or not? I haven't got all night to stand here talking. Please, Tommy, you've got to help me."

"I—I guess so, but if my mother finds out, you won't be the only one who got a lickin'. Wait here for me."

Tommy opened the screen door quietly and entered the summer porch where the dirty laundry was kept. The pants he was looking for still lay across the basket where he had left them after his fishing trip. He grabbed the pants and a shirt beneath them. Next, he had to go into the parlor where his mother kept the sewing basket. Tiptoeing, he crept through the kitchen, past the dining room, and across the hall to the parlor. Just inside, he paused for a moment to make sure he had not been heard. The only sound was the *tick-tock* of the grandfather clock in the hall.

Slowly, he searched in the darkness for the basket. *It's over here somewhere*, he thought. Then he struck his toe against the corner of the rocking chair. "Ouch!" he yelled. Quickly, Tommy put his hand over his mouth and listened once more. There! He heard the creaking of his parents' bed. Someone had heard.

"Tommy, is that you? What are you doing down there?" his mother called.

He hobbled to the steps and answered, "It's okay, Mother, I just came down for a drink of water and stubbed my toe. Sorry I woke you."

"Turn on a light, honey, don't go wandering around in the dark like that."

"Whew! That was close," he exclaimed, listening to his mother get back into bed.

Tommy grabbed the scissors and returned to the backyard, but Corey was nowhere in sight. Thinking she had been frightened off, he shrugged his shoulders and turned to go back inside when he heard, "*Ps-s-t,* over here," from behind the lilac bush.

"Here's the pants and shirt. I have to get back inside before my mother gets up again. When you've finished with the scissors, put them under the porch. I'll sneak them back in the morning. Good luck," he whispered and, before Corey could speak, he ran toward the house.

"Now, how am I going to do this, Muffin? I can't see where I'm cutting." Muffin looked up at his mistress and turned his head from side to side. "I guess I'll have to do the best I can."

Corey parted her hair down the back with her fingers, held one section in her hand, and started cutting with the other. The scissors chewed their way through the long, thick hair. It was a slow process, but at last she'd finished. She hid the scissors under the porch as Tommy had instructed. She then dug a small hole at the base of the lilac bush and buried the clippings from her hair. In the darkness she changed into the pants and shirt, bundling her dress to be left along the way where it would not be found so easily. Then, Corey and Muffin were finally on their way.

Tommy stared wistfully out the window at the two figures walking away from his house. He would miss his friend and hoped she'd be all right out there alone. As he turned from the window, he wiped a tear from his eyes, knowing it would be acceptable to shed a tear for a friend he might never see again. Besides, no one was looking.

CHAPTER 4

It was a beautiful July night and the big silver moon lighted their way. As Muffin and Corey walked, it seemed to move with them. A soft breeze stirred from its sleep and carried the sweet scent of magnolia blossoms. Frogs called to one another from the pond where Corey had fished with Tommy when she could sneak away. How she would miss her friend!

Corey and Muffin had walked for what seemed hours when she began to feel the pangs of hunger. It had been some time since she had eaten, having been sent to bed long before supper.

"Are you hungry, fella?"

Muffin sat up and barked excitedly as Corey took a piece of chicken from her scarf. She tore off strips of meat and piled them on the ground, along with bits of cheese and bread. When this was done, she took out more for herself and ate it with great enthusiasm.

After they had eaten, Corey wrapped the remaining food in her scarf for later and tied it securely to her belt loop. She took the treasures from the tin box and stuffed them into her pockets so she would not have to carry anything. It was still dark, but she could see the beginning of daybreak along the horizon. Soon her aunt and uncle would discover her absence and start looking for her. She had to put as much distance between them and herself as she could.

As they walked, Corey and Muffin passed farmhouses with the soft glow of light shining from their windows. The farmers were already up, starting their day. The houses were closer together now, and Corey realized they were nearing a town. The gray dawn was giving way to a reddish-gold light as the sun peeked over the horizon, allowing her to see buildings ahead. As she stood wondering what to do, a familiar sound reached her ears.

A train! Many times she had watched the trains come through, waving to the engineers and counting the open boxcars as they passed. She had even imagined what fun it would be to climb into one and ride to some faraway place. She could do it now and really get far away, fast. Best of all, it would be free. Corey saw the train was stopped, which gave her an excellent opportunity to climb aboard.

"Run, Muffin, we're gonna catch a train," Corey called, and began running across the field following the hissing sound from the steam engine. She could see the train between the bushes and breathed a sigh of relief. She had forgotten her aching legs in the excitement and was running easily across the distance when a hand seized her by the arm, almost jerking her off her feet. Muffin began barking angrily and snapping at the intruder.

"Keep thet dog quiet 're I'll have him fer my supper tonight," ordered a gruff voice. "Sit down here and gimme thet bundle you're carryin'."

Corey peered around to see the bewhiskered man who had grabbed her shoulder. His clothing was so dirty and faded she couldn't tell what the original color had been. A dingy gray had all but obscured his once-auburn hair, and bushy eyebrows of the same color framed bright gray eyes that twinkled mischievously at Corey. Constant exposure to the outdoors had etched deep lines into the man's face, making him look far older than his fifty-two years.

Weatherworn and dirt-streaked hands tore eagerly at the scarf and a grunt of satisfaction rumbled from his throat when he saw the food. He had not eaten in a couple of days and this was an unexpected treat.

"Gonna take a lil' pleasure ride on thet train, wuz you, boy?" he asked after finishing the food.

Corey had had time to settle down, and she felt anger overtaking her fear. This hobo had scared the wits out of her, eaten her food, and now was prying into something that was none of his business.

"What's it to you?" she asked.

"Right spunky kid, ain'tcha? I shoulda let you git caught. Serve you right."

"What do you mean…get caught?" she snapped.

"C'mere," the hobo growled, pulling her to the edge of the bushes. "See them men over yonder? Them's railroad dicks looking fer kids like you. Know what they do if'n they ketch 'em? They put chains 'round their ankles and make 'em work in th' cotton fields, then whup 'em with long strips o' leather till the blood runs down their backs."

Corey shrank back into the bushes, trembling at the tale. When she was able to control her voice, she turned to the hobo, "Thanks, mister, I didn't think…" but the rest was lost in tears. She was tired, scared, and felt so alone.

The hobo studied Corey with pity. He had not meant to scare the child so badly. The boy was quite obviously a runaway; it was written all over his face. He'd only meant to scare him enough to send him packing for home.

"What's yore name, boy? Whatcha doin' out here all alone?"

"Cor-. Corey," she stammered. "Muffin and I are going home and I thought it would be quicker if we could get on that train."

"Where's home and how d'ya know this here train goes there? Where're ya comin' from?" he asked, eyeing her suspiciously, playing her game.

Corey shuffled her feet uneasily, "Back there. We were visiting my aunt and it was time to go home."

"'Pears to me thet aunt o' yours would be a mite worried 'bout lettin' a youngun strike out all by hisself." Then, throwing back his head, the man laughed softly. "I know you be a runaway. Tell me, boy, where you be runnin' to? Gonna join th' circus?" Again he laughed, bringing a fresh set of tears to Corey's eyes. "Aw, don't start blubberin' agin. If'n you want to run away, ain't no skin off'n my nose. Here, wipe yer face." He handed her the empty scarf in which her food had been wrapped.

"Thanks," she sniffed and blew her nose, while the hobo sat watching her.

"You know, kid," he continued, the lines in his face softening, "can't nuthin' be as bad at home as whut you're gonna have out here in this world by yerself. You think that story I told you 'bout them railroad dicks is scary? Well, thet's a picnic up agin whut's waitin' out there fer th' likes o' you."

Corey sighed, telling him her story, and, remembering the last whipping, the pain surged through her legs, causing her to wince sharply.

"Here, kid, let's have a look-see."

The hobo helped Corey pull the pant leg up and whistled low under his breath. "Land, child, ain't no lickin' you got, wuz a downright beatin'. Thet thar aunt o' yours outta have th' strap taken to her fer this." He shook his head as he looked at the ugly blue stripes that had now formed welts from the back of Corey's knees almost down to her ankles. Traces of blood were still crusted there.

"Will you help me get on that train, mister? I'd be ever so beholden to you. I have to get away from her fast, or she will be looking for me real soon."

"I'd sure like to help, kid, but it'd be too risky, 'specially with thet dog. If'n you'd leave him here, mebbe I could see thet you got on all right, but after thet you'd be on your own. Ain't never been no babysitter, 'n I ain't gonna start now."

"Oh, no, I can't leave Muffin. He goes where I go. He'll be quiet, I promise he will. Please, mister?" Corey begged.

"Thet mutt can't go. Them's my conditions, take 'em or leave 'em."

"I won't leave Muffin behind. We made it this far without your help and we can go on without it," Corey answered defiantly.

"Fine by me. I don't need no whimperin' kid on my hands neither. Lots o' luck." He turned and started through the bushes, muttering, "Durn fool kid, ain't nuthin' to me if'n he makes it or not. Kids can be a heap o' trouble." Still, he turned and looked back in Corey's direction once more as he left.

Suddenly, it was as though he were looking back forty years at himself, orphaned and lost with the same determination written upon his face. "Nope, ain't gonna git involved," and he lumbered through the brush, trying to put some distance between Corey and himself.

Exhausted and frustrated, Corey lay down upon the ground with an arm wrapped around her dog. "We'll be all right, Muffin. We'll just rest for a while, then we'll go on." She had barely gotten the words out before she fell asleep.

It was dark again when Corey was awakened by Muffin's growl, seconds before a hand clasped across her mouth.

"C'mon, kid, it's time to go. Don't make no sound," came a familiar voice as the hand released her.

Corey got up without a word and followed the dark form moving ahead of her. *So, he came back*, she thought.

"You'll hafta carry thet dog 'n keep him quiet. We missed one train and we gotta be quick if'n we want to git on this one. Be a while 'fore another'n comes along."

Corey could hear the train screeching and bumping as it started pulling away, then she felt herself being picked up and pushed through the open door of the boxcar. She clutched Muffin protectively, straining her eyes to see if her new friend had made it, too. The train was picking up speed and she heard the grunt as the hobo landed beside her.

"Here, kid, I picked some peaches. Thoughtcha might be hungry since I et you're food 'n all," the man offered apologetically. "'N I got some salve from th' doc in thet thar town fer your legs."

"Thanks…" Corey began, "I don't even know your name."

"Andy. Andy Curruthers at your service."

"Thanks, Andy!" Corey gratefully took the peach and wiped it on the tail of her shirt before eating it.

Andy felt about in the darkness, spreading the salve on Corey's legs the best he could, his hands surprisingly gentle.

"You didn't steal that, did you, Andy?" Corey asked, hoping he had done nothing dishonest on her behalf.

Andy chuckled, "Gonna be my conscience, too, are ya? Don't fret, I never steal nuthin'. I work fer whut I git. Chopped some kindlin' fer a widder lady so's she could boil her wash, then I fixed and painted her fence. Thet's where I got th' money. Now, you git some rest while you kin."

The train was at a steady run, and Corey could see the dark forms of trees whipping past the open door. The wheels beat a hypnotic rhythm against the rails. Soon she would be far away from Aunt Lizzie. Comforted by the thought, she lay back down upon the straw bed Andy had made for her and drifted once again into a deep, healing sleep.

Light was creeping into the horizon when Corey opened her eyes. Muffin was still asleep at her side and Andy was sitting in the open doorway, his head partway out, looking up the line. He felt more than he heard, the slight movement as Corey sat up. He spoke to her, still watching out the door.

"We're gonna git off soon. There's a town ahead 'n with it gittin' light we can't take the chanct o' stayin' on. Thet there town be a purty fair size, 'n like as not they'll have them railroad bulls snoopin' 'round. I wantcha to be ready to jump off when I tell you."

Corey looked at the ground flying past in a blur. "Can't we wait until the train stops?" she asked uneasily.

"No," Andy snapped. "Do whut I tell you."

Saying no more, Corey picked up the dog and silently watched Andy for his signal. The train began to slow and the ground came into focus. Andy peered into the distance, finally standing as the train slowed even more.

"Gimme thet dog 'n git ready to jump. I'll be takin' this feller off with me."

Corey obediently handed Muffin over and looked down once more. It felt as though someone was beating a drum inside her head and her heart was keeping time with the beat. Her hands, wet with perspiration, trembled as she held the doorway and prepared to jump.

"Okay, kid, now!" Andy commanded.

Corey stood frozen as she looked down at the ground whipping past.

"C'mon, kid, jump! We've waited longer'n we shoulda. Jump!"

The story Andy had told earlier about the railroad detectives came vividly to her mind. Corey summoned all her strength, took a deep breath, and jumped from the moving train. Landing on her feet in a crouched position, she rolled as Andy had instructed. She thought she would never stop. The sand bit into her arms and a branch from a bush caught her across the cheek, stinging like Aunt Lizzie's switch. When at last Corey stopped rolling, she lay upon the swirling ground and waited for the dizziness to subside.

A short distance away, she could hear Muffin's excited bark and angry voices. Pushing herself slowly off the ground, she looked in the direction of the commotion. A man held Andy firmly by the arm and shouted to someone she could not see from where she was hidden. Keeping low under the cover of the bushes, she crept closer, all the while trying to think of some way to help Andy. After all, she was responsible for his predicament. If she had not waited so long to jump, he wouldn't be in this mess.

So far, so good. The man's unseen partner had not joined them yet. She had to get Andy's attention without being seen and let him know she was there to help.

Andy had been watching for Corey and nodded slightly in recognition as he spotted her moving through the small clearing. He worked his captor around so the man's back was to Corey and edged closer to the clump of bushes where she sat. As quietly as possible Corey crawled on her hands and knees from the cover, waiting for them to get closer.

Muffin, too busy with the detective to notice Corey before, suddenly spotted her. He released the man's pant leg and started toward her. As the man turned to see what brought the sudden change in the dog, Andy gave him a big push, sending him tumbling completely over Corey. He landed flat on his back on the ground, momentarily stunned.

Andy grabbed Corey by the hand and pulled her to her feet. They started running, Muffin close at their heels. Corey didn't dare look back for fear the man would be there ready to grab them. Ahead was a heavily wooded area where they might be able to elude the detective among the trees.

They had run a short distance into the woods when Andy stopped and indicated a thick growth of brush for Corey to hide in while he climbed a tree to get a better vantage point of the trail behind them. She strained to hear above the beating of her heart and gasped for her breath to return. It seemed hours before Andy finally came down and assured her they were safe.

"You did me right proud, kid. I thought fer sure I wuz a goner. Did ya see the look on thet feller's face when he bit th' dust?" Andy slapped his knee, letting go a laugh that rang through the woods, causing birds to take flight. A squirrel in a nearby tree chattered in scorn as he scampered high into the trees. Corey started laughing, too, and it felt good to release the tension of their narrow escape.

"C'mon, kid, we'd best git movin'. See if'n we kin find us some grub. The dog o' yours looks like he could use some water, too." Andy grinned at the heavily panting Muffin.

The trio hadn't walked far when they came upon a clearing and the most beautiful lake Corey had ever seen. The crystal blue water caught and reflected the bright rays of the sun, almost blinding her as she stood marveling at such a place.

Corey followed Muffin down to the shore. Bending over to take a drink, she saw in the water's surface a stranger staring back at her. This was the first time she had seen her reflection since her transformation, and she was quite surprised at the difference the boyish bob made in her appearance. Thick, black hair fell in gentle waves, concealing most of the uneven gaps she had made cutting it. The short length made her eyes look larger in her round face and even she wouldn't recognize this person peering back at her. Corey smiled approvingly.

Andy turned out to be a good provider. That evening they dined on fish caught from the lake and cooked on sticks over an open fire. With a full stomach, Corey lay back and watched the wispy blue smoke float lazily into the air from the dying fire. Her house seemed thousands of miles away, along with her worries. Her thoughts shifted to Andy and she watched as he dropped more wood onto the fire. When he had finished and sat down again, she asked, "Where is your home, Andy?"

"Wherever I happen to be."

"No, I mean where did you come from, where's your family?"

"Ain't got none. Ma died back in Minnesota in seventy-two 'n Pa followed durin' th' terrible sickness eight years later," Andy answered pensively.

"What…er…your mother…" Corey asked, uncomfortable discussing death, yet she felt a strong need to know how Andy's mother had died.

Andy poked at the fire, drew a deep breath, and began his story, with descriptions so vivid Corey lived every detail.

CHAPTER 5

Midsummer 1869 brought two reasons to celebrate for Jed and Elise Curruthers. Their small Minnesota farm was going to yield a good crop that year, barring unforeseen disasters, and Elise discovered she was with child. Twenty-four years of marriage had produced no children and hope had faded with their youth.

Jed watched his wife as she sat in her favorite chair in front of the rock fireplace stitching a small gown. He felt tears building in his eyes, prompted by the pride that filled his soul. The years of hard work etched so vividly on her face had melted away and her thin body was filling out again. The warm glow from the kerosene lamp cast a magical radiance upon the scene. Jed had the feeling he was getting a premature glimpse of an angel. He was the happiest man alive.

The following months were not so kind to Elise, however. She was in the twilight of her childbearing years and her body had lost most of the youthful strength required for the complex changes she was experiencing.

After weeks of fighting a terrible cold brought on by the early winter, a lingering, racking cough had robbed her of what little strength she had left. She was forced to take to her bed, and Jed watched with concern while his wife grew weaker. Finally, he could take no more.

"Elise, I'm going to the settlement in the morning to get some medicine for you. I'll fix you a bed by the fire before I leave and bring blankets for you. As the fire dies, put a blanket over you, and each time you feel cold, put on another one. I'll try to be back before dark. It shouldn't get too cold for you before then, if you do as I ask. There'll be food by your bed and I want you to eat. Promise me, Elise."

"Jed, I'm afraid for you. What if you get stuck in the snow and freeze to death? Please don't go. I'll be all right if I stay in bed for a while."

"I'll be fine, Elise, and you're going to need some help. I just can't stand by and watch you get weaker. I feel so helpless. Get some sleep and, before you know it, I'll be back. We have to think of our child, too. You're going to need your strength when our son or daughter gets here."

"Our son—that sounds so beautiful." She closed her eyes and drifted into a peaceful sleep.

Jed left before sunrise, and as near as he could figure, it was now close to noon. The lower half of his body was beginning to grow numb from his cold wet clothes. Several times he sank to his waist in the snow and his two pair of pants and long woolen underwear were soaked through. There was no sign of the settlement in the distance and he was deeply troubled by the amount of time it was taking. Each step became more difficult as cold and fatigue overcame him. Again he sank into the snow. Try as he would, he couldn't pull free and he laid his head on his arm, weeping desperately.

Suddenly, the sound of barking dogs reached his ears. He lay very still, thinking perhaps it was his imagination. Once again he heard the sound, this time accompanied by a human voice calling, "Hullo, hullo over there. Are you in trouble?"

Slowly Jed raised his head and saw the two young men approaching with their dogs. At first he was unable to answer. "Are you all right, mister? For a minute there we thought you were dead."

Jed looked at the young man who had spoken and laughed feebly, "For a minute I thought so, too, but I guess our maker had second thoughts. For whatever miracle brought you out this way, I'm thankful."

"It's no miracle. My brother and I were out hunting turkey for our Thanksgiving supper. Our house is just over that rise yonder. We'll help you there and you can get dried out."

"I thank you for your invitation, but I must get on my way," he said and explained his situation.

"You have several more miles to go and you won't make it in your condition. Come on over to the house and we'll see what we can do from there."

As the two boys led Jed across the yard, a stocky ruddy-faced man greeted him from the porch. He quickly ushered the trio into the warm house.

"Ingrid," the older man called to his wife, "some blankets, please." He indicated a chair in front of the fireplace as he introduced himself. "Lars Jensen, my wife, Ingrid, and you have met my two sons, Jon and Eric."

"Jed Curruthers. A pleasure to meet you, ma'am," Jed acknowledged each introduction with a nod.

Mr. Jensen took the blankets from his wife. "Mr. Curruthers, if you will step into the bedroom there and remove your wet clothes, we can hang them up to dry."

After Jed was warmly wrapped in blankets, his clothes drying before the fire, his hosts listened to his story.

"We'll send one of our sons to the settlement. The other will return with you. He'll help in whatever way he can. I'm sorry my wife can't go, but whenever the weather permits…"

"I couldn't take your family away at Thanksgiving," Jed replied. "I appreciate your offer more than you can know, but I can't let you do this." Jed had never asked for help before, nor felt the need to become involved with his neighbors since they had come to the farm the year before. He was finding it difficult to accept help, even now.

"How could we sit down and give thanks at dinner tonight after turning out a friend in trouble?" the elder Jensen questioned. "Ours would be a much greater thanks for having delivered help when it was so needed. Could you deny us this?"

What a loss Jed felt over that year spent without friends. Now he realized even more how empty his life had been in the confines of his self-imposed exile.

The moon broke through the clouds overhead, bathing the snow-covered countryside in a silver iridescent glow as the two weary men made their way to the cabin. They could see its dark shape ahead and fear filled Jed when he looked at the chimney and saw no smoke rising from it. Summoning a final burst of energy, he covered the short distance in a matter of seconds. He rushed to his wife's side while Jon Jensen built another fire. Much to his relief, Elise was sleeping peacefully beneath a mound of blankets, and Jed nodded at Jon to let him know she was safe.

The next day dragged endlessly as Jed wore a steady path to the window, watching for the younger Jensen boy. When the last rays of the sun were barely visible, he began to worry. If something had happened to Eric, he'd never forgive himself for allowing him to make the trip into the settlement through all the snow.

Suddenly, the coffee boiled over, causing the fire to hiss and sputter. As Jed lifted the pot from the fireplace, he heard the familiar sound of barking dogs. Quickly he ran to the window and saw the boy jump from a horse-drawn sleigh and come across the yard, accompanied by an older man carrying a black bag. He took two more cups from the shelf, poured the hot bubbling liquid into them and went to the door to greet the weary travelers.

After Dr. Holloway examined Elise, he called Jed aside, "Mr. Curruthers, your wife is very weak. Only sheer determination kept her from losing this baby, but even that can last just so long," he explained carefully. "I'm going to leave this tonic with you; it will help build her strength. She must remain in bed at all costs, probably until the child comes. You wife is a very strong-willed person and I believe she has a good chance, but it will depend upon how well my orders are carried out."

Days passed into months, and Elise became steadily stronger under the watchful eye of the doctor and Jed's constant supervision. Mrs. Jensen visited as the weather allowed and helped as she could. The companionship of another woman seemed to ease Elise's anguish over her confinement. The approaching spring planting season coincided with the expected birth, so Ingrid agreed to stay with Elise while Jed was in the fields.

The snow was gone and as Jed looked out across the land, words from a lullaby his mother used to sing, echoed through his mind:

> Come, little flowers, come from the snow
> Raise up your heads, it is time to grow
> Put on your mamelets of beautiful gold
> Springtime is coming and winter is old.

Springtime was coming. Jed could feel it in the air. The harsh cold that usually rode the wind had now softened. He could sense the awakening in his spirit that all life must feel as it emerges from the sleep of the long winter. How fitting it was that his child would begin life at this magical time of the year.

Jed closed the door quietly behind him and went to walk his land. Although the trees were still barren, he could just detect the velvet nubs forming on their branches. Soon they would burst forth as leaves, shaping canopies of brilliant greens. He looked across the fields and envisioned tall green shoots of corn reaching out of the earth and peace filled him.

As planting time arrived, Elise's time drew near. Since the fields were some distance from the cabin, a signal was arranged. Ingrid would fire one shot into the air if it was a girl, two if it was a boy.

Jed had been working since the first hint of daylight. His back ached and beads of perspiration formed on his brow in the warm noonday sun. As he straightened to pull his handkerchief from his pocket, two shots rang out across the valley.

"A son! I have a son!" he yelled. Dropping the hoe, he raced toward the cabin.

Ingrid met Jed at the door. A smile spread across her face as she held the tiny bundle for him to see. He reached out to touch his son, but seeing his dirt-covered hands, dropped them to his side and contented himself with just looking at the sleeping baby. It was truly a miracle, this human formed so perfectly in miniature!

"Elise?" Jed asked.

"The doctor is with her now," Ingrid spoke softly, "She's fine—a little weak and tired, but fine."

"I've given her a draught to help her sleep. She needs rest and quiet now," the doctor advised, coming through the doorway. "If you want to see your wife, you can go in, but don't stay too long."

Jed tiptoed into the room and stood beside his sleeping wife. Her face was pale and her hair, wet with perspiration, formed ringlets about her face. The corners of her mouth were upturned with the faintest sign of a smile. He bent over and kissed her on the forehead.

"You did good, my brave angel, you did good."

🍁 🍁 🍁

"What happened then, Andy?" Corey asked anxiously, bringing Andy back from the other time.

"Well, Ma never wuz a strong'un after th' sickness 'n then th' birthin'. She took pneumony when I wuz jest two 'n we lost her. Never knew her 'ceptin' whut Pa told me an' I rekin I listened to thet story over 'n over til Pa died eight years later," Andy related, looking deep into the fire, lost within its depths. He shook his head briskly as if to loosen the past's hold on him and changed the subject. "Time to hit th' sack, kid, we gotta long haul ahead of us in th' mornin'."

"But what did you do after your pa died? You must have only been—" she made a quick mental calculation—"ten, same age as I am now," Corey prodded Andy. She was reluctant to have the story left unfinished.

"Twelve," Andy corrected. "I overheard th' neighbors tryin' to work out whut wuz to be done with me, seeing as how times wuz rough tryin' to keep their own goin'. Well, I jest hit out on my own, I wuz a big feller fer my age 'n I could always find work to keep me goin'. Rode th' rails from town to town. Been ridin' 'em ever since."

"Didn't you ever get married? Or at least have a girl somewhere?"

Andy fished into his pocket and brought out the stump of an old cigar. Bending over, he pulled a stick from the fire and lit it. "Naw, never did." His tone had softened and he lay back on the ground, gazing at the stars overhead. Then, realizing Corey was watching him curiously, he straightened up, fussing and fuming. "Nosy kid, anyways. Didn't your folks ever tell you to mind your own business? Ain't polite to go meddlin' whar you ain't got no place."

Andy sputtered and poked at the fire, but he hadn't fooled Corey. She knew there was more to the story than he was telling, and one day, when they talked again, she would get it out of him.

The pain had dulled through the years for Andy, but he still felt a twinge as he thought of Angelique. Rolling over with his back to Corey, he tried to block the memory. He would not think of her—not now.

CHAPTER 6

Lizzie James paced the floor, wondering what to do. Corey had been gone two days and no word of the child. She had assumed Corey would be back, pleading for forgiveness and vowing never to leave again, especially after being alone with no food and no place to go. Lizzie wasn't worried about the child, but about what the townspeople would say if they found out.

"Wouldn't that old snit of a gossip, Grace Canfield, have a field day with that tidbit?" Well, Lizzie would just have to come up with a story explaining the child's absence.

"That ungrateful child! She really caused a mess. You just wait until I find her," Lizzie fumed aloud as she went into the kitchen to prepare dinner.

"I thought you said she was with the housekeeper in Oklahoma," George said, lowering the newspaper he was reading.

"Yes, yes, I did tell you that," she lied. "It's just...well, I don't know where the housekeeper is. I don't want people to start talking and whispering about why she left. You know how they can be. I mean, I did get a little carried away when I punished her."

"But, Lizzie, people will know she's gone eventually. What are you going to say when they start asking questions? Maybe we should get in touch with the police out there and have them send her back here. They can locate Mrs. McPhearson. Although, it might do her and you good to have this little vacation," George assured his wife.

"Don't start up with the police again, George. I told you before she is just punishing me. Kids are that way." Lizzie stood before the stove, her mind searching for a story. "That's a good idea, though, I will just tell them she went to her mother's relatives to visit for the rest of the summer. That will give her time to come back."

"Her mother didn't have any living relatives."

"I know that, stupid, but no one else does. When that child came to live with us, I didn't discuss any of the legalities with anyone, did you?" She glared at George.

George could only shrug his shoulders in defeat as he tried to return his attention to the newspaper in front of him. There was no end to her sharp tongue. In a way, he envied Corey her escape. Nevertheless, he was going to have to do something about getting her back home. He was her legal guardian now.

The more Lizzie thought about the story of Corey visiting back East, the better she liked it, and the next morning she went into town to start the tale. As luck would have it, the first person she met was Grace. Lizzie smiled smugly; she wouldn't need to go any further.

"Well, Gracie, so nice to see you. You really must come to tea again soon. I so enjoyed the last time," Lizzie cooed.

"Likewise, dear Lizzie, but it really is your turn to come to my place," Grace answered. "By the way, where is that darling niece of yours? I was just saying to Helen Burroughs over at the post office a moment ago that I haven't seen the child for days."

I just bet you did, Lizzie thought, and then replied sweetly, "Oh, didn't I tell you? Corey went to visit some of her mother's people back East. She might even start school out there. I haven't really decided yet."

"How nice," Grace said, patting Lizzie's hand. "Well, dear, I really must run. We will get together real soon."

Lizzie watched the little old woman swagger down the street before she breathed a sigh of relief. Had she been imagining it or did Grace Canfield look a bit disappointed with her explanation of Corey's absence? The old busybody was probably hoping for a juicy story, Lizzie fumed silently as she headed for the market, especially since Grace had been at the house when Corey left before.

Corey awakened with a start, her body still trembling from the nightmare. First she had been locked in the cellar and the dark forms of meat hanging from the ceiling were so vivid she could almost reach out and touch them.

Then she was in a box with dirt being thrown on top, shutting out any air. Her breath was coming in gasps, and it took her a few seconds to awaken enough to realize she had been dreaming. Relieved that Andy was not around to see her terrified and disoriented, she went down to the lake to wash her face and to wash away the remnants of the nightmare.

"Hullo in camp!" Andy called, returning with a bunch of fish for their breakfast, Muffin trotting happily at his heels.

"Fish for breakfast?" Corey asked in dismay.

"Seems we wuz outta bacon 'n eggs, kid," Andy muttered. "You can always go without nuthin' to eat."

"I'm sorry, Andy, I should be thankful to you instead of complaining."

"You got that right. Thar'll be days you'll be wishin' we had these here fish. Now help me git a fire goin'."

"Andy, I sure appreciate you helping Muffin and me. I don't know what we would have done without you."

"Weren't nuthin'," puffed Andy. "Soon's I git you on your way good, we'll hafta be partin' ways, though. Can't make no time with th' likes of you two taggin' along."

Corey lowered her eyes to keep Andy from seeing the disappointment. She had become attached to the hobo in their short time together and had assumed he felt the same way about her. There had been no talk of leaving each other in the past three days. What would she do when he left? Where would she go? She would certainly not go back to Aunt Lizzie; she'd rather die first. Corey shook her head to clear such thoughts.

After breakfast Andy made sure the fire was out before they continued on their journey, the silence still hanging heavily between the two. Corey filled Andy's bottle with water and took one last look at this beautiful spot. Above them the wind had picked up and swept through the treetops. The pine trees made a sighing sound as they bent and swayed under its force. It was a sad sound and Corey's mood reflected that sadness, with the thought of Andy's leaving still worrying her.

They walked most of the day, leaving the green countryside behind and entering the barren land of the desert. Toward evening they caught another train, preferring to be traveling while they slept. Andy still had not said much and it was just as well with Corey. She did not feel inclined toward conversation, anyway. Again she was faced with not being wanted and it hurt her deeply. As she lay back with her hands cupped behind her head listening to the sounds of the wheels clicking along the rails, she vowed to cause no further trouble for Andy while she was with him.

It seemed Corey had just dozed off when Andy shook her. He told her they had to get off the train while it was stopped to take on water. "Th' linemen be checkin' the cars on these stops," he whispered. Even now, she could hear voices from down the track and they were getting closer.

The night was exceptionally dark with no moon to light their way as they followed the tracks. The stars looked like so many jewels scattered upon a blanket of black velvet. As Corey gazed at the twinkling lights, one seemed to come to life and shoot across the sky.

"A-h-h!" she exclaimed.

"Whut's thet?"

"Did you see the falling star?"

"Nope, seen a lot in my time, though. 'Specially out here in th' desert."

"Where do you suppose they go when they fall, Andy?"

"Most o' them burn up out thar in space, but onct in a while one'll hit th' ground. Them whut makes it, makes holes big enough for a town to fit in. I seen one onct, here in th' desert, it wuz."

Corey was so engrossed in what Andy had said she did not realize they were entering a tunnel until Andy reached for her.

"You'd best hold to my hand till we git through here, kid. It's a long tunnel 'n apt to be darker'n pitch."

She took a deep breath, telling herself there was nothing to fear. After all, Andy and Muffin were with her. Still, she could feel the darkness closing in on her and beads of perspiration broke out on her forehead.

They had walked halfway through the tunnel when a roaring sound reached their ears and the railroad ties beneath their feet began to tremble. Corey's heart jumped into her throat as she realized what it meant. She became even more terrified when she stepped off the tracks and saw how narrow the tunnel was at this point—three feet at most.

"Corey, listen to me very close. We're gonna hafta press ourselfs agin th' side o' th' mountain like we wuz part of it. Keep your face flat agin th' rock with your eyes shet tight. Whut ever you do, keep still 'n don't breathe lessen you hafta. You'll be fine if'n you do whut I say," commanded Andy, for the first time calling her by her name.

"What about Muffin? He'll be crushed!" she cried.

"I'll hold him twixt us. Now do whut I say," shouting the last instruction above the roar.

With his left arm, Andy scooped the dog up quickly and placed him between Corey and himself. Then, with his arm wrapped around her shoulders, he pressed her against the wall of the tunnel.

Corey felt the train coming closer and its loud roar made her ears ring. The air was getting hotter from the steam engine and it was becoming increasingly difficult to breathe. Soon the train was whipping past, spraying them with cinders. The suction, as the train passed, tugged at their clothes almost tearing them off their backs. Andy pressed Corey and Muffin even closer against the hard cold rock wall.

It seemed an eternity before the last car passed them and Corey could feel the vibration several minutes after the train had gone. Her head was still filled with the roaring sound when she felt the pressure of Andy's arm lift as he moved it from her shoulders. His hand grasped her wrists, forcing her to sit down. At first no one said a word as they sat on the rail and summoned the strength to carry them out of the tunnel.

It was Andy who finally spoke. "C'mon, kid, we'd best git outta here," and he lifted her gently to her feet.

Corey walked stiffly at first. Then, seeing the gray light at the end of the tunnel growing closer, she started running. Once outside, Andy began laughing. Corey could not believe what she was hearing. They had barely escaped with their lives and Andy was laughing! Had he lost his senses?

Seeing the look on Corey's face, Andy pointed a finger at her and again laughed uproariously. "You should see your face, kid. It's black as the ace o' spades. You look like you been scramblin' 'round in th' coal bin."

"Yours isn't so clean either, I want you to know, and you don't see me laughing, do you? How can you possibly find anything funny after we just barely missed being crushed to death?" she scolded.

"Aw, c'mon, kid, don't be sore. We came out in one piece, praise be, ain't no sense ponderin' on it. Be thankful you're alive, laugh 'n enjoy it. Ain't ever'day you git a second chanct at life," he consoled.

Corey brushed vigorously at her clothes to get some of the soot off. Right now she would give almost anything for a bath.

"Is there a creek or any kind of water around where I could wash some of this dirt off?"

"Not here in th' desert. Ain't a drop till you git up in them mountains. They be a full day's walk away, mebbe two. Can't spare none o' ours neither."

"Well, let's get started then," she answered with a sigh.

The sun was barely over the horizon and Corey could already feel the heat. It was truly going to be hot, she thought as she looked out across the desert landscape for some sign of trees to give them a bit of shade. There were none to be seen, only clumps of bushes and the tall cactus pointing their thick green arms silently skyward.

Other bushes had long tentacles like an octopus and groves of cactus with paddle-shaped arms and prickly thorns dotted the landscape. It seemed everything out here had those sharp-looking needles on them. Seeing a bird land on a tall cactus, Corey asked Andy why it didn't get stuck.

"I guess their feet is made special so's they don't git hurt. See them holes in thet tall saguaro?" he asked, pointing to the tall cactus with the thick arms. "Well, thet be where th' birds go to git outta th' heat. Keeps a even temperature all year 'round inside thar. Ain't nature smart to plan all thet out for th' critters? And see thet li'l tree? Thet be a palo verde. She's called the mother tree, cuz she draws up th' water outta th' ground fer the baby cactus till it gits big 'nough to make it on its own.

"C'mere and see. I betcha they be a li'l baby cactus growin' by her side."

When they reached the tree, a small, round cactus was pushing through the ground, covered with prickly thorns. "See," Andy said, "ain't th' desert grand? Everything has its purpose, jest like people."

"You are so smart, Andy. Where do you learn all these things?"

"I rekin I traveled most o' this here beautiful country o' our'n four…mebbe five times over. I learnt something ever' time, but I wouldn't say I was smart, not by a long shot. Ain't had no book learnin' or schoolin' like yerself," Andy answered wistfully. "Well, are ya hungry?" he asked changing the subject.

"You bet, I feel as though I could eat a horse."

"'Fraid we're fresh outta them," he laughed, "but I'll see if I can find us something else. Gather up some bresh for a fire whilst I fix a trap out yonder. Mebbe we can have us some rabbit for breakfast. Careful where you walk, though. Thar's snakes out thar. They won't hurt you lessen you come up on 'em sudden like."

"That's all I need now…to tangle with a snake," Corey moaned.

"I thought thet's whut you liked, snakes 'n lizards 'n th' like. It's been along time sinct I was a boy myself, but I reccollect as how I useta catch them things." He grinned at her, and before Corey could answer, Andy was looking for a place to set a trap.

Corey watched Andy disappear into the bush. It was getting harder to continue deceiving this man. Yet, she was afraid if he found out she was a girl he would leave her behind for sure. On the other hand, he was sure to find out eventually. Then he would really be angry with her for deceiving him. Well, she would just have to take the chance and tell him. That would at least solve one of her problems.

After their late breakfast, Andy pulled the remains of his cigar from his pocket, lit it, puffed heavily, and leaned back on one elbow in the shade of a mesquite tree. Now was the time, Corey knew, to have her talk with him while he was in a good mood.

"Andy…" Corey began hesitantly.

"Hm-m?" Andy answered dreamily, enjoying his smoke to its fullest.

"I have something to tell you. I hope it won't make a difference…between you and me, I mean."

"What's thet?" Andy replied, still only half listening.

"I'm a…I'm really a girl," Corey stammered, shutting her eyes tightly against the anticipated storm. When there was no response, she repeated her statement and, in her anxiety, it came out louder than she realized.

"I heard you, kid. Durn it, you don't hafta yell. I ain't deaf, you know."

"But you don't seem surprised."

"Nope, figgered it out fer myself a while back. Just been waitin' fer you to tell me yerself."

"I don't understand. How did you know?"

"Ain't many li'l boys so all-fired anxious to take a bath th first sign of a li'l dirt, as I 'member. They be other things, too, but thet ain't important."

"Are you going to leave me now that you know I am a girl?" This was something she had to know and she might as well get it out of the way right now, no matter how badly she hated to bring it up.

"Makes no never mind, boy or girl. I told you afore, don't need no snotty nose kid hangin' on my shirttail. And when I git to th' proper place, thet be it," he muttered, stroking his whiskers and trying to look stern.

Corey smiled to herself. With all that blustery nonsense, he did not for one minute convince her he would really leave. There had been too many opportunities before, yet here they were, still together. She was beginning to see right through this rough front Andy had been putting up for her benefit and she realized perhaps, he was beginning to like her, too.

Andy continued the charade, puffing on his old cigar and muttering loud enough for her to hear how kids weren't much use till they had growed up. Then he cast a sidelong glance to see if Corey was taking it all in. When he saw she was paying no attention, he removed the battered knapsack from his back and took out a blanket, in much the same shape, and spread it under the tree.

"Rekin we'd best wait out th' heat whilst we got us some shade. Bet you could use some shet-eye, huh?"

🍁 🍁 🍁

Andy, Corey, and Muffin walked all night and well into the next morning, following the railroad tracks, until the heat forced them to stop again. Still they had not reached the mountains, and Corey was beginning to wonder if they ever would. She was hot, thirsty, and so very tired of this endless heat.

"We'll be outta th' desert afore you know it, Corey girl. Traveled the best part of it on th' train," Andy soothed, noticing her frustration.

Corey could not answer for fear she would begin to cry, and she was determined not to show any more weakness to her friend. How she longed to be back at the lake with the tall green trees and cool water. She thought of the sounds of the wind whispering through the pine trees and the water slapping against the bank. Clinging to that memory, savoring every detail, she was able to take her mind off the infernal heat.

Andy watched the child's quiet suffering. He had fully intended to drop her off at the first "sally," (the hoboes' term for the Salvation Army), knowing they would find a proper place for her. But thinking of the Salvation Army caused his gray eyes to narrow because it represented charity to him and a haven for winos, certainly not a place for a little girl. And Andy wanted no part of charity, not as long as he was able to work for his needs. Of course, he had only seen a small number of those the sallies helped. For that reason, and some he was not even sure of, he had purposely avoided the towns that offered a sally.

He squinted against the blinding sun toward the mountains. They were almost there; perhaps then things would improve, at least until he came up with a better idea concerning what to do with Corey. Right now they would rest.

After an all-night walk, they reached the foot of the mountains at daybreak. Clasping their hands together, Corey and Andy danced in a circle and shouted jubilantly at having beaten the desert. Sitting down to rest briefly before starting the long incline, Corey took off her shoes to shake the sand from them. It felt good to have her shoes off and she stretched out on the blanket, wriggling her toes luxuriously.

Andy took the bottle of water from his shoulder and offered it to Corey while he surveyed the mountain for the path they would take. She poured some water in her hand for Muffin and took a small amount herself, making sure to leave some for Andy.

"We'd best git a move on, so's we can git a fair distance afore we lose our light," Andy called to Corey. "Don't wanna walk off'n no cliff in the dark."

Slowly Corey pulled her shoes on, wishing she were out of the rocky terrain so she could walk barefoot. As her left foot pressed into the second shoe, her big toe erupted in pain like the sting of a hundred bees. Her screams, piercing the silence, echoed from the boulders above them. In seconds Andy was at her side. Pulling the shoe from her foot, he shook it and a small yellow scorpion, its tail raised to strike again, fell onto the sand. Instantly, Andy ground it to pieces with the heel of Corey's shoe. He had to keep calm and think what to do, but seeing the emptiness around them, panic surged through his body. There was something he had heard about drawing out the poison, but he could not remember what it was.

"Damn it all!" he yelled, hitting his forehead with the palm of his hand as if to beat out the buried information. "Gotta think a minute...Tobacco! Thet was it!" Chewing tobacco made a good poultice, but where was he going to get chewing tobacco out here? He thought of the stump of the old cigar in his shirt pocket; it was tobacco, and perhaps if he chewed a piece of it.

Andy fished the cigar butt from his pocket, bit off a piece, and chewed until it was a wet lump; then he placed it on the wound. As he tied the handkerchief to Corey's foot, he spoke calmly to the girl, "We gotta try to git up this here hill 'n find us some shelter long enough for this stuff to work. Mebbe thar's a cave on up a ways." He did not want to tell her she was going to be very ill. It wouldn't do to get her scared right now.

"That stuff you put on burns terrribly, Andy," Corey cried.

"I know, girl, but it'll draw out some o' th' soreness. Can't have you gittin' sick on ole Andy, now can I? Can you stand up for a minute 'n let me git a hold o' you?"

"But, Andy, you can't carry me up the mountain. I'm too heavy."

"Now, don't gimme no sass, jest do liken I say. You let me worry 'bout ever'thing. Ole Andy'll take care o' you."

They had gone a short distance up the mountain when, although Andy was in good condition for his fifty-two years, the steep incline began to take its toll. Finding shelter before nightfall would mean leaving Corey, and then coming back for her when he found a likely place. The pine trees dotting the hillside were more abundant ahead. There would be shade for her, and with the dog around, she would be safe for a while.

"Listen, Corey girl, I'm gonna put you down whilst I find us a place to bed down. I want you to stay put till I git back. D'ya hear whut I'm a-sayin' to you?"

"Yes, Andy, I'll do as you say. Only don't take too long, please."

"I won't be gone any longer'n I hafta. 'Sides, Muffin'll be here with you." He checked Corey to make sure she was comfortable. Her cheeks were beginning to flush and her eyes looked glassy. *First signs of th' fever comin' on. Gotta hurry and find a place,* Andy thought.

Corey did well for a time, until her fever got worse and the water ran out. In her delirium she thought Andy had finally left her behind.

"Must find Andy...tell him I won't cause any more trouble if he will just let me stay with him...But he's in that dark pit...afraid to go down there...Aunt Lizzie is saying something to me...can't understand her...Gotta get away, but my foot hurts so bad...What's wrong with it? Oh yes, I remember, that ugly bug stung me. What did Andy say it was...a scorpion, that was it...Please, Andy, come back. Gotta find you..."

Managing to struggle to her feet, Corey held to the tree until she was steady. The pain and dizziness made walking difficult. After a few falls, she started wandering aimlessly after Andy.

Andy had been gone longer than he planned, and now he couldn't get back fast enough. It shouldn't be too much farther until he could see Corey, and then the uneasy feeling would go away. There was his knapsack hanging from the tree where he had left it. He couldn't see Corey yet, but she would be lying down and it was still too far to see that clearly.

When he was closer and still didn't see her, panic seized him. He began running and calling out to her, but neither Corey nor the dog was anywhere to be seen. He knew she couldn't have gone far, but in which direction? He had not seen her on his way back and, looking farther down the mountain, there was still no sign of her. The only thing to do was zigzag back up and hope to find her as soon as possible.

Andy covered quite a bit of ground, but he was wasting precious time. He stood for a minute to catch his breath and looked out across the desert floor. There was lightning in the distance and a black curtain of rain was moving quickly in his direction. Andy began walking faster, knowing these summer storms could be treacherous. The fading light added to his frustration, and he was beginning to lose hope when he heard a noise. The sound of a barking dog was coming from the rise above him, and he began running toward it, hoping with all his heart it was Muffin, yet afraid of what might be causing the commotion.

When he reached the area, a man on horseback was trying to calm Muffin enough to reach the child lying on the ground.

"It's okay, Muffin, thar now, settle down. It's me, ole Andy," he called as he eased closer. "Back 'way, feller, 'n let me git this here dog settled down," he said to the stranger, who immediately did as he was told.

Muffin quieted down when he saw Andy but still kept a watchful eye on the stranger, growling occasionally to let the man know he was still watching.

"Is he alive?" the man asked.

"Yeah, you got any water on you?"

The man tossed the canteen to Andy, setting the dog to barking again.

"Hush up, Muffin! Th' man be tryin' to help us," Andy scolded.

Corey, burning up with fever, was mumbling incoherently, although Andy thought he heard her calling his name occasionally.

"If your dog will let me get down, I have a handkerchief you could wet and wash his face," the man offered. "Might help bring the fever down."

"Be okay. Just move kinda slow and easy."

"What's wrong with the child?" he asked, handing the cloth to Andy.

"Scorpion stung he…er…him on th' foot. Made a poultice for it, but th' fever's got him," Andy explained, thinking it best to let the man continue thinking Corey was a boy to save all the questions it might arouse. He figured the less the man knew about their business, the better for all concerned.

"I've got a lean-to just over yonder. That's where I was headed when I ran across the boy, here. You are welcome to bed him down there to ride the fever out."

"I'd be rightly obliged to you 'n willin' to work for our keep," Andy accepted, then offered his hand to the man. "Th' name's Andy 'n this here be Corey. I don't believe I got your's."

"Gus Thatcher. Pleased to meet you, Andy," Gus acknowledged, taking Andy's hand firmly. "Now, we got that out of the way. If you'll help me get the child on my horse, we can get some cover before it really starts raining." He held out his hand as if to catch the large drops that had started to fall.

When Gus had said his lean-to was 'over yonder', Andy assumed it was just up the hill, but they had traveled the better part of an hour before reaching it. By then it was dark and the drizzle had turned into a downpour that reverberated upon the tin roof of the cabin. While Gus lit the kerosene lamp, Andy removed Corey's wet clothes and put her to bed on an old cot in the corner of the room.

Gus took his rain-soaked hat from his head. His white hair, starting to grow thin on top, was equally soaked and clung to his head. Drops of water embedded in his white beard made it glisten in the light of the lamp. Winglike fluffy eyebrows perched atop his brown eyes gave his face a quizzical expression.

"Would you like some coffee, Andy? It won't take a minute to brew a fresh pot," Gus asked.

"Yeah, I could use some. Better make it good 'n strong to carry me through th' night. 'Pears to me it's gonna be a long 'un."

Andy's gaze shifted from the rock fireplace where Gus prepared the coffee to the rest of the cabin. Clothes hung from nails on the clapboard walls along one side, and hastily thrown-up shelves held canned goods. Cooking utensils hung above an old kitchen table against the other side. The front boasted a door made from slats of wood and framed by two windows. Bare earth, worn slick with constant sweeping, formed the floor.

"I'll wet a cloth for the child's forehead. Seem's that's generally what they do for a fever. We can spell each other looking after him during the night."

"Much obliged, Gus. B'lieve I can handle things okay, though. You've done more'n enough for us."

"Well, it's up to you. Right now I think I'll rustle us up something to eat."

The night proved long and trying for Andy as he listened to some of the fears and abuse Corey had suffered at the hands of her aunt. At times she cried out at having been locked in the cellar, and other times she begged not to be hit again. Taking her small hand in his, Andy held it tenderly while he wiped her face with the cool, wet cloth. He could not understand how one human being could be so cruel to another, especially a child…and kinfolk at that. There was no way he would allow Corey to go back to that, even if it meant taking care of her himself. Though he knew nothing about caring for a child, there couldn't be that much involved. Still, he had to give it more thought; he had to be certain to do the right thing.

CHAPTER 7

Andy awoke with a start, momentarily unsure where he was or what had awakened him. Daylight was beginning to creep into the cabin and he could barely make out Corey's form sleeping on the cot in front of him. Her breathing was the slow, deep rhythmic sound of a restful sleep. He reached out his hand, felt her face, and found it to be only slightly warm. *Good,* he thought, *fever musta broke during th night.* Striking a wooden match with his thumbnail, he stood between the flame and Corey and checked her foot.

To his relief, most of the swelling had gone down. Andy felt as though a weight had been removed from his shoulders. Corey was a healthychild, but you never knew how a person might react to the sting of a poisonous scorpion. Andy stretched generously to relieve the cramps in his body from sleeping in the chair most of the night and headed toward the door in search of Gus.

"Andy…Andy, where are you?" Corey called sleepily.

He stopped and turned around, "I'm here, kid. How do you feel?"

"Okay, a little hungry maybe," she answered. "Oh, Andy, I had this terrible dream that you had gone off and left me. I couldn't find you anywhere and Aunt Lizzie was after me with the strap. It was just terrible." Then looking around her, she asked, "Where are we, Andy?"

"We be at Mr. Gus Thatcher's place. He's th' one whut found you when you wandered off yesterday. How come you didn't stay put like'n I told you? Scairt th' pants right off'n me when I got back 'n you was gone," Andy scolded.

"I'm sorry, Andy. I don't remember leaving. I guess it was the dream that made me do it." Almost in the same breath she asked, "How's Muffin?"

"Onery as ever. Been at your side most o' th time, but I suppose Gus let 'im out to do his business. Now, I'll git you something to eat and you can git some more rest." Before Andy turned to leave, he added softly, "Mr. Thatcher b'lieves you're a boy and we'd best keep it that way."

Andy stood on the front porch and breathed deeply to fill his lungs with the clean mountain air. Everything smelled so fresh after the rain. A soft breeze murmured through the tall pine trees, breaking the silence of the early morning and Andy stood drinking in the beauty and tranquility of this place until he felt heady with it.

"Good morning, Andy, thought you might be up by now. How's the boy?" Gus asked, rounding the corner of the cabin carrying several eggs and a small can half full of goat's milk.

"Doin' right well. Fever's broke and he's hungry. Jest fixin' to see what I could drum up for him to eat."

"You don't have to look any farther. If you'll take these things inside, I'll go down to the smokehouse and get a slab of bacon to go with them."

"Rightly obliged, but you don't hafta go to no extry trouble on our account."

"No trouble," Gus grinned, already halfway to the outbuilding. It really was no trouble for Gus. He was delighted to have the company, since he seldom saw people up this way. He whistled a non-descript tune as he took a small slab of bacon from its hook and headed back to the cabin. It looked like it was going to be a beautiful day, he thought, glancing upward and the clear blue sky.

Breakfast was a combined effort; Gus cooked the bacon and eggs while Andy put on a pot of coffee and Corey set the table.

"Right homey place you got here, Gus," Andy said, gingerly sopping his plate with a piece of biscuit. "Must keep you purty busy, huh?"

"That it does, and sometimes it gets ahead of me," Gus sighed, "But I like it up here. After my wife died five years ago, I moved up here so I wouldn't be a burden to my children. Lord knows, they had enough just taking care of their own families. They raised all kinds of billy heck, saying I was too old to be off by myself like this—sixty-three isn't that old—and besides, it has been good for me. I think they see it, too. Once a month I make a trip to the village about four miles from here, to get supplies and send them a letter to let them know I'm still breathing." Gus pushed back his chair and began clearing the table.

"Rekin it's time I started earning my keep," Andy groaned as he stood up, stretching more kinks out of his body.

❧   ❧   ❧

A week slipped by quickly as Andy helped Gus with the work that had to be done around the place. Corey took over the job of feeding the animals and she had become very attached to them, especially the goat, Nanette. Nanette followed Corey everywhere, much to the displeasure of Muffin whose nose was considerably out of joint at having to share his mistress.

Most of the work had been done and Corey could tell their visit was coming to an end. Andy was getting restless and his mind seemed to be in other places. Gus sensed it, too, and was already beginning to feel the emptiness hovering about him. He was going to miss the evenings when they sat on the porch as they were now.

Gus and Andy talked of the "good old days" before the smelly, noisy automobiles invaded the cities, before Prohibition had unleashed the gangsters and killings, before the Commie witch-hunts. Back in January, several of the federal legislators had been arrested on suspicion of being Socialists and the scare of Communists invading the country had panicked everyone. America had become a nation of violence and scandals, both men agreed, shaking their heads as Corey listened intently to their tales. But, as the darkness enveloped them, a quiet expectancy hung in the air.

"I figger Cory'n me'll move on in the' mornin', Gus," Andy broke the silence first. "I'll be nigh onto a week sinct we moved in on you. Afore you know it, we'll be outstayin' our welcome."

Gus answered, his voice unusually husky, "I've enjoyed every minute of it, too, Andy. You know that you and Corey are welcome to stay as long as you like." He had expected it, but he had hoped it wouldn't be this soon.

Corey, seated next to Gus, felt the sadness in the old man. As he struck a match and touched it to the bowl of his pipe, she saw the tears forming in his eyes. She reached up and put her arms around his neck and kissed him on the cheek. "I'll write to you, Gus, every chance I get, and you can read it to Nanette because I'll write something special for her."

"I'd like that, child, very much." For a few moments he watched the trail of blue smoke that rose from his pipe, then he asked Andy, "Where will you go from here?"

"Don't know right offhand. Figger we'll go on up to Flagstaff 'n see can we catch a train headin' for the Nor'west er mebbe Californy."

Once again the silence settled over them, broken occasionally as Gus puffed noisily on his pipe. No one made an attempt to go to bed, even though it was time. It was as though if they prolonged the evening, the morning would be that much farther away.

Finally Gus made the first move, standing up, and stretching as he said, "We'd best turn in. You're going to need a good night's rest for the trip tomorrow. I'll pack some provisions to take with you." And he quickly went inside the cabin, leaving Andy and Corey to their pallets on the front porch.

The next morning Corey was up before anyone else. There was barely enough light for her to see, but she wanted to have some time with Nanette before they left. She was going to miss this place. It had been like home to her and she would miss Gus and Nanette most of all. But then, she had places to go and new places to see with Andy. This excited her. As she stood looking at the cabin with its chimney sending smoke curling into the air and at the corral with its new pieces of split rails Gus and Andy had replaced, a warm soft nose nuzzled her hand. Corey bent down, putting her cheek against the stiff hair on Nanette's face.

"You are going to be a good girl after I'm gone, aren't you? And don't go wandering off and getting lost, you hear?" she whispered, scratching the bridge of the goat's nose.

"Corey," Gus called. "Better wash up; breakfast will be ready soon."

Breakfast over, the provisions packed, Corey said good-bye to the animals, and now it was time to bid farewell to their new friend. Gus stood before them, his beard neatly trimmed and hair freshly combed. He looked older than his sixty-three years and his brown eyes shone much too brightly. He shuffled his weight awkwardly from one foot to the other. No one spoke for a minute, and then all three started to talk at the same time and laughed uneasily.

"I'm gonna hold you to that promise, Corey, to write and let me know how you two are doing," Gus spoke, "And if you are ever out this way again, I hope you will come by and see me…"

"You betcha we will, Gus, 'n take care o' yourself," Andy said. "I wish you wuz comin' with us."

"If I didn't have so many things depending on me, I would be tempted." There was a suspicious sniffle from Gus and he took a handkerchief from his back pocket and blew his nose into it. "You two had better get along before I really start blubbering. Always did hate good-byes." He bent down and gave Corey a hug before shaking Andy's hand firmly and bade them both a safe journey.

As long as she could, Corey kept looking back at Gus waving to them from the front porch. She could see Nanette pulling at her tether, trying to follow Corey as she had become accustomed to doing. Then they rounded a bend and the cabin was gone. It was late at night when Corey and Andy reached Flagstaff. They had had no trouble hopping a slow train and Corey immediately found a spot in the corner of the boxcar and curled up on the floor. Muffin circled a few times and lay down at her feet with a heavy grunt. It had been a long day and the two were already asleep as the train reached full speed.

The next afternoon they left the train just outside Oxnard, California. Andy was going to find a job at one of the orange groves until they could earn enough money to replenish their supplies and get farther along their way. Where, Corey did not really know or care. Andy had promised to take her to see the ocean before he started work and she could hardly wait.

Corey smelled the ocean before she finally saw it…an odor of fish combined with something else she couldn't identify. And then there it was, stretching as far as her eyes could see. Water. This water was moving, not like the ripples in the lake, but in huge waves curling over and breaking into foam that washed onto the shore and then back out again, leaving the sand smooth and wet.

She removed her shoes to wade in the foam, but the sand was so hot she had to run on her heels until she could reach the sand that had been cooled by the surf. The waves swirled around her feet, tugging at them as they went back out again.

After Corey had splashed about in the water for a half-hour, the three wandered down the coastline where the sand gave way to the rocky cliffs. As they walked, Corey collected seashells until she could carry no more. Andy selected a spot against the cliffs and pulled the tattered blanket from his knapsack. He spread it upon the ground and Muffin immediately established one corner as his own, watching Corey's every move as she sorted through the shells trying to determine which ones she would have room to keep. She knew they would soon have to find a place to camp for the night. Already the air was developing a chill although the sun had not yet dropped below the horizon.

"Rekin we'd best head on over to th' orange groves, Corey girl. Gotta find us a place to bed down for th' night. I wanna be knockin' on doors come first light," Andy advised as he picked up the blanket, shaking the sand from it before replacing it in the knapsack.

They traveled until they reached a country store and Andy made some inquiries about work. One of the customers overheard him and said he thought Courtney Farms was looking for help. If they wanted, he could give them a ride over into the valley where the orange groves were located.

An hour's drive brought them to Courtney Farms, which at night, looked quite impressive. They thanked the man for the ride and checked out the area. There was a culvert nearby that would give them shelter, and an irrigation ditch where they could get water to make themselves presentable.

Luck was with Andy the next morning. Clive Courtney, having fired one of the workers for stealing not two days before, was indeed looking for help. He was a short, stocky man with sandy brown hair that stood at all angles on his head. Half a cigar was clamped firmly at the corner of the straight line slashed across his face, forming his mouth.

"Along with your wages, I'll provide you and your...er, grandson, is it, with a place to stay. There are linens and cooking utensils, but you have to provide your own food. I'll take you to your bungalow, and when you get settled, you can start work," recited Mr. Courtney all in one breath as he started across the yard, motioning for Andy to follow.

"This here feller don't waste no time, do he?" Andy grinned as he whispered to Corey.

When they reached the bungalows, the scene looked worse than a shantytown. Cardboard replaced missing windows and covered holes in the roof. Flaking bits of grayish-white residue was all that was left of the paint on the clapboard siding. Sagging porches, the wood rotting from neglect, had gaping holes in their floors. Behind the row of six bungalows, amid weeds and piles of rubble that served as a garbage dump, were the outhouses.

Corey and Andy followed Mr. Courtney inside their assigned bungalow. There was only one room with a lumpy bed on one side and a wood-burning cookstove on the other. In the center was a table, covered with cracked, stained oilcloth, beside which stood two rather wobbly chairs. Two orange crates hung from the wall served as a cabinet for three cracked plates, two jelly jars for glasses, and two handleless cups. An old handmade table standing beneath the crates supported a washbasin.

Andy shrugged his shoulders at Corey but made no comment in the presence of his new employer. He could hardly start a job with complaints; besides, he had been in much worse places.

Muffin was making his own inspection of the place, sniffing every inch of the bare wooden floors. When he got near the bed, a mouse ran out from under it and out the open door with Muffin in pursuit.

"Come back here, Muffin," Corey yelled, but he had already disappeared behind the bungalow. "Oh well, I guess he'll come back when he gets tired of chasing that thing," she sighed.

Andy's eyes were on the disappearing figure of Mr. Courtney while he muttered, "Rekin I best git to work afore th' boss starts foamin' at th' mouth. Boy, he sure ain't gonna let grass grow under his feet, is he?" He chuckled as he picked up the sack left for him to use. "See you 'bout suppertime."

Corey wandered outside searching for something to pass the time until Andy would return. A small group of six or eight children had gathered in front of the bungalow next door, while a frail-looking old woman sat on the porch watching her young charges. Every now and then her head would nod as she fought back sleep in the warm sunshine. Corey ambled in her direction, thinking she could offer to watch the children and allow the old woman to take a nap.

"Hello, my name is Corey and my…er…grandfather and I just arrived this morning," Corey stammered. "I was wondering…maybe you would like for me to watch the children for a while. I'm sure you must have things to do."

"What? Oh yes, dear, what were you saying? I'm sorry, but it's a little hard for me to hear."

Corey cleared her throat and repeated the offer in a louder voice.

"Why that's very kind of you, but I really couldn't. You see, they've been put in my trust, and it just wouldn't do for me to turn them over to a stranger, you understand. But you're welcome to sit a spell and visit if you like." She patted a place on the step beside her.

The woman's gnarled hands, covered with brown spots, fussed with a few wispy strands of white hair that had escaped the little knot in back of her head. Her thin hair in front exposed a pink scalp above her wrinkled face and was covered with the same brown spots. Her eyes, a washed-out blue, watered from the bright sun and she dabbed at them occasionally with a handkerchief.

"I'm Missus Langley and I live here with my granddaughter, her husband, and three children. That's them over there," she smiled proudly, pointing in the direction where two little girls and a boy sat in a small circle. "You live in the place Mr. Crabtree had. He was a queer fellow. Caught him stealing from the boss's larder and bounced him, they did."

"What's a larder, Missus Langley?"

"Oh, you young people," she giggled. "That's where Mr. Courtney kept his food supplies. It's a big pantry at the back of his house. Yeah, Mr. Crabtree thought everyone was in bed and he sneaked right up to the house and was rummaging through the supplies, stuffing food in the front of his shirt. Mr. Courtney caught him red-handed." Then, giving a little shiver, she added, "I really didn't trust him; he was a sneaky sort."

"How do you mean, sneaky? What did he do?"

"Wild look in his eyes, too," she continued, not hearing Corey's question. "Had this strange thing with fire and he was always striking matches and watching them burn. I got onto him once about it, the children you know, and can you guess what he did? Flipped a lighted one at me. I thought my dress was going to catch fire. He laughed, a real strange laugh, and clapped his hands." She shook her head slowly while smoothing out the apron across her lap.

Corey wanted to hear more about Mr. Crabtree, but one of the children called to Mrs. Langley.

"It's been nice talking to you, child. I have to go and tend to little Harry now. You come back and visit with me again real soon."

Corey watched as the woman limped out to the children, holding her long gray dress to keep it from dragging in the dirt. Yes, she thought, she would visit Mrs. Langley again soon.

That evening when Andy returned from the orange groves, Corey had cooked a pot of beans for their supper along with the last piece of salt pork and stale bread. While they ate, she told Andy about Mrs. Langley and her story of Mr. Crabtree.

"'Pears to me we was lucky to have missed the feller. Kinda makes a body feel a mite troubled thet he be still runnin' 'round loose, though. Shoulda called th' law on him 'stead of lettin' him git away."

"You don't suppose he is still running around here, do you, Andy?"

"Naw, prob'ly ain't stopped runnin' sinct he got caught. Ain't likely he'd stay 'round and take a chanct on goin' to th' hoosegow."

"You're probably right, but just the same I'm going to prop a chair against the door when we go to bed."

Living conditions were very poor around the bungalows to say the least. Too many people were living in one little shack and the food was scarce. The wages were not enough to allow a large family to eat well and save enough money for the move to the next job, so many children worked right alongside their parents.

A lot of people did not practice cleanliness, whether it was a lack of soap or some other reason, so roaches and mice ran rampant in the bungalows. Colds and sickness visited upon the young and the very old as the cool, damp night air seeped through the cracks and holes. It was not a happy time for Corey, but she helped as much as she could, hoping the time would pass quickly and they could soon leave.

Two weeks had passed and Andy assured her there wasn't much time left here. Corey felt uneasy too. Muffin had been growling a lot at night, and Corey had been hearing unusual noises when everyone was in bed. The few times she had gone to the window, she had seen nothing. When she told Andy, he said it was just the mice running about and to stop worrying.

Corey had made a new friend, and when she began worrying at night she would think of him. Mr. Barker, or the "bottle man" as the others called him, had been collecting old, unusual bottles for fifteen years and carried them with him as he moved from job to job. They removed him from his drab life and were all that he owned of any value.

"They are my claim to fame, Corey. Everyone knows about my bottles and I am somewhat a celebrity around here. I had my picture taken for the newspapers four years back," he had told Corey one day when he invited her to see his collection. His eyes shone as he told her the story of each bottle and how he had found it. She enjoyed hearing his tales, and her visits to Mr. Barker's became a daily ritual. Soon her visits would end, though. Mr. Barker would be going back to work. He had injured his back carrying the crates of oranges and lifting them onto the truck to be taken to the big house for storage. Now, his back was almost healed.

One morning Corey was awakened by the sounds of children fighting. Strange, she thought, usually the children didn't give Mrs. Langley so much trouble. Judging from the amount of light in the room, she realized she had slept later than usual. She dressed quickly and hurried outside.

Mrs. Langley was nowhere to be seen, and Corey finally got the children quieted down enough to ask where she was.

"Nana is in bed," Pamela, Mrs. Langley's great-granddaughter, answered. "She doesn't feel good today."

"You should be ashamed of yourselves. Don't you think it makes her feel worse with all this racket? Now you play nice while I go check on her," Corey scolded.

Corey knocked softly at the door then went inside. She walked to the bed, taking Mrs. Langley's hand in hers. It was hot and dry, her breath raspy.

"Who's that?" the old woman whispered.

"It's me, Corey, Mrs. Langley. What's wrong?" Corey asked loudly.

"It's just a little cold, dear. Are the children all right?"

"They're fine. Don't you worry about them," Corey soothed. "Can I get you anything?"

"What?"

"Can I get you anything?" Corey repeated.

"No, dear, I don't want anything. I'll be fine. Will you look after the children while I rest a few more minutes?"

"Yes, ma'am," Corey answered, pulling the blanket up around Mrs. Langley's chin. It wasn't like her to stay in bed, even with a cold, and Corey was very concerned about her friend. Perhaps she should find her granddaughter and have her get some medicine.

It took Corey a while to find Sarah Jane, but when she told her about Mrs. Langley, Corey was not prepared for the answer.

"I just can't take off everytime one of us has the sniffles, Corey. I can't afford to miss any work. She'll be fine, believe me. We've all had colds and, as you can see, we got over them," Sarah Jane said, exasperated at having been bothered. She glanced furtively around to see if Mr. Courtney was watching.

"But she is old, Sarah Jane, and her breathing sounds really bad."

"Corey, I don't want to sound like I don't care about my grandmother because I do, but if I miss any work she could die of starvation! We just barely make enough to feed everyone as it is. Please, I have work to do."

The rest of the day Corey divided her time between the children and Mrs. Langley. She recruited the help of the eldest child, seven-year-old Susie Collins, to help organize games and keep the children occupied. By the end of the day, Corey was exhausted but still could not sleep. She could hear her friend coughing most of the night.

Then there were those noises again. Muffin heard them, too, and paced the floor growling. Several times she thought she had seen a shadow go past the window, but dismissed it as her imagination. *Doggone mice anyway,* she thought, and finally drifted into a fitful sleep.

"There's some oatmeal on the fire thet you kin take your sick friend, Corey. Gotta go to work now."

"Is it morning already?" she groaned, trying to focus her eyes. "It seems I just got to sleep."

"Been hearin' those noises again? I told you not to fret. It's jest them mouses tryin' to dig up some grub."

"I know, Andy, and I'll probably get used to them just when we start to leave," she laughed.

"I best git goin' afore I'm late."

Mrs. Langley wasn't any better, in fact, she seemed much worse. Corey offered her hot cereal, but she wouldn't eat much. She wiped the old woman's face with a wet cloth and placed it on her forehead. While Mrs. Langley napped, Corey straightened the room as best she could and went to sit on the porch and watch the children play.

A hot, dry wind was blowing and the dust whipped around, getting into everybody's eyes. Soon the games stopped and some of the children began to cry. Quickly, Corey herded them into her place, where they would stay for the rest of the day.

When it came time for the children to go home, Corey dropped across the bed, not even raising her head when Andy came through the door, fighting the wind to close it.

"Are you asleep, Corey girl?" he whispered.

"No, but I feel like I could sleep for the next week. I don't even think those pesky mice can keep me awake tonight," Corey yawned.

"Kinda tuckered out myself. Whut say we jest open up thet can o' li'l weenies fer supper?"

"Sounds good to me, if I can stay awake that long."

As she had predicted, Corey had no trouble getting to sleep, but some time during the night she was awakened by the noises again. This time it was different. At first she couldn't tell what the sound was. It sounded like strange laughing, or maybe the wind whipping around the building. Angry at having been awakened, she pounded on the pillow trying to get comfortable enough to go back to sleep. By then a red glow at the window caught her attention and she called to Andy.

"Andy, wake up! There's something glowing outside," she yelled, running across the room to Andy's bed and shaking him. She ran back to the window, "Oh my gosh, it's on fire, Andy! Andy, it's on fire!"

"Whut? Whut's on fire?" Andy mumbled, but Corey was already out the door, across the yard, and pounding on Mrs. Langley's door.

"Wake up, oh please, your house is on fire! Sarah Jane! Mrs. Langley!" Corey screamed.

Andy had come up behind her now and kicked the door open, while everyone inside was scrambling around trying to grab some of their meager possessions.

"Andy, get Mrs. Langley out of here and I'll help them get some of their things."

"You'll do nothin' o' th' kind. You git yerself outta here, now!" he shouted, "Everybody git out! This whole place'll be gone afore you know it! There ain't time to mess with nothin'."

The rest of the people were running out into the yard, carrying what they could grab. They all stood huddled together, watching as the flames fanned by the wind leaped from one bungalow to another. Children as well as adults cried or wandered around in a daze. The roar was almost deafening and then there was the sound of small, muffled explosions.

"My bottles, oh my God, that was my bottles," Mr. Barker cried and sank to the ground when his legs would no longer hold him.

Corey bent down and picked up Muffin, thankful he was with her. As she straightened, she caught sight of a strange man dancing around and clapping his hands behind the remains of their cabin. She could barely make out his shape through the flames and smoke, but he was there all right. Mr. Crabtree! It had to be him. Corey had to find Andy and tell him before the man got away. Quickly she searched through the people until she spotted Andy talking to Mr. Courtney.

"Andy...Mr. Courtney, that fellow...Mr. Crabtree...is here. He's over behind the fire acting really strange."

"Where, Corey?" Mr. Courtney asked and followed her to the spot where she had last seen him, but he was gone. Several of the men had joined them when they heard what Corey had said. "Some of you fellows come with me," Mr. Courtney called, "We'll catch this guy before he does any more damage. I should have had him locked up when I had the chance."

They had not been gone long when they returned with a fighting, spitting Mr. Crabtree. "Somebody get a rope," one of the men yelled.

"Are you going to hang him?" Corey asked, horrified.

"No, Corey, we'll just tie him up until the police get here," Mr. Courtney answered, "you run up to my house and tell Emma...Mrs. Courtney...to call them."

"I burned the old witch for telling on me," Mr. Crabtree chanted. The flames cast an orange glow over him, reflecting in his strange little eyes. Corey shivered, knowing it would be a long time before she would be able to shake that picture from her mind. She hurried away from him, toward the big house.

Corey was only halfway to the house when she heard sirens and saw Mrs. Courtney running toward her. "What happened, dear? How did it start?" she asked breathlessly.

"Mr. Crabtree set fire to Mrs. Langley's place and *woosh*, the whole place went! I was just on my way to get you. Mr. Courtney wants you to call the police."

"They are already here. I went to the door to see if I could see Mr. Courtney…he was out checking on everything before he went to bed…when I saw the flames and called the fire department immediately. Of course, the police generally show up, too," she looked over at the people gathered in a group and asked, "Was anyone hurt?"

"I don't know. Everything happened so quick and then we caught Mr. Crabtree. I haven't even seen Mrs. Langley since Andy took her out of the house. She's very ill, you know."

At that moment the firemen began dousing the remaining flames and a police car pulled up to the group holding Mr. Crabtree. A lone figure left the crowd and headed toward Corey and Mrs. Courtney. Corey knew by his walk it was Andy.

"Andy," she called, "we're over here."

"Howdy, Miz Courtney," Andy greeted as he approached. He seemed nervous and kept glancing back where all the commotion was.

"Hello, Mr. Curruthers. What a terrible thing to have happened. Did everyone get out?"

"Yes'm, jest barely, thanks to Corey, here." He turned to the girl, "Corey, the cops will wanna talk to you 'bout thet ole coot what started the fire." They walked toward where their neighbors had gathered and Andy tugged at the back of Corey's shirt, motioning for her to hold back a minute. "Miz Courtney, your mister is right over there if'n you wanna see him."

"Why yes, Mr. Curruthers, thank you," she answered and started for her husband.

"What's wrong, Andy?"

"This here could get a mite sticky if'n you don't watch yourself, bein' a run'way, if'n you know what I mean. Best give my name as your own, 'n remember, you've been a feller sinct you left."

Corey hadn't thought about that, with all that had been going on, and she began to get scared. What if she slipped and said the wrong thing?

"You best let me do th' talkin' and jest answer the questions they be askin'." And, as he spoke, he took her hand, squeezing it gently.

Andy did most of the talking as he said he would, with Corey verifying what he said. Only once did her fear cause her to falter, but that was to be expected from the trauma she had been through. After all, the police said, he was only a child and it was quite understandable. Corey breathed a sigh of relief as the policeman put his pen in his pocket and closed the notebook. It was almost over!

"Well, young man, you will most probably be a celebrity before this thing is over. Saving all those people's lives like that will certainly make the newspapers," the policeman grinned as he started for his car.

"Oh, Andy," Corey groaned, "what are we going to do now?"

"Don't fret, thet be why I told you to use my name. Ain't none o' your folks goin' to see this anyway. It's gonna be jest fine."

"Have you seen Mrs. Langley lately? With everything going on, I haven't been able to check on her."

"Naw, Corey, I ain't, been busy myself. Her family be with her, though."

"Well, I'm going to see if I can find her. Some man said we are all going to the schoolhouse for the rest of the night and I want to see if she shouldn't have a doctor look at her." Before Andy could tell her it was up to her family now and some folks didn't like meddling strangers, Corey was gone.

Corey searched everywhere, but Mrs. Langley was not to be found and even Sarah Jane had disappeared. A group of children stood near the spot Andy had put the old woman. Perhaps they would know what had happened to her.

"Yeah, some men took her up to the big house a while ago," a boy answered Corey's question.

"Would you do me a favor?" Corey asked, "If you see my fr…er…grandfather, would you tell him I went to the Courtney house? Thanks."

Corey arrived at the house as a man carrying a black satchel climbed the steps. Sarah Jane's three children had been sitting on the porch swing and, upon seeing the doctor arrive, started to follow him into the house only to be turned away by their mother. They couldn't understand why everyone else could go in where their great-grandmother was while they had to stay outside. Corey joined the group at the door and looked at Sarah Jane, a question in her eyes. She gravely shook her head as she shut the door and took the doctor to Mrs. Langley.

Outside, Mr. Courtney paced the length of the porch, puffing heavily on the cigar that seemed a permanent fixture in his mouth. Occasionally he stopped, leaned on the railing, and peered into the darkness as though it sheltered a bad dream that would disappear as soon as the dark curtain lifted.

Only a few more days of work left, a week at the most, before his crop would be harvested, but how could he keep his help working if they had no place to live? What about next year? He would have to build more bungalows if he hoped to have a crew working for him then. This year would be a complete wash-out, thanks to an old crazy man he should have had locked up. He refused to consider the fact that the old buildings were already dilapidated, which allowed them to burn so quickly. Nor did he admit that he did not pay his workers enough so they wouldn't go hungry, forcing one man to resort to stealing food, deranged though he might have been.

As she watched Mr. Courtney pacing up and down the porch puffing heavily on that cigar, Corey blamed Mr. Courtney for all that had happened. It was partly his fault, too, that her friend was so ill. Resentment filled her and she had to look away to keep from screaming at him.

The door opened and the doctor stepped out. Sarah Jane followed, her face void of expression, as she walked slowly down the steps and into the darkness. Her children silently arose from the swing where they had kept their own vigil and followed their mother. Corey looked from the doctor to Mrs. Courtney, who had just stepped out onto the porch, for confirmation of what she already knew. As a guilt-stricken Mrs. Courtney reached out a hand for comfort, Corey, too, fled into the solitude of the darkness.

"Jest let her be," Andy said as he reached the edge of the porch. He did not realize he had let it slip Corey was a girl, and apparently no one else picked it up either. The tragedy of the evening had left everyone unable to think clearly, or even function well. "A body needs room at a time like this. Corey'll be back when sh...er...he's ready." This time he caught himself.

Andy went back to the remains of their bungalow, thinking it would be there Corey came looking for him. The wind had settled and the calm night air hung heavy with the odor of burned wood and musty, wet cloth. The cool dampness seemed to seep through Andy and he crossed his arms, squeezing them close to his body to fight back the chill.

Soon it would be daylight and Andy felt it best if he and Corey moved on. They had enough money to buy the supplies they needed for a while. The rest of their needs would come from the land as it had in the past. There was really nothing to keep them here. In fact, Andy had been ready to move on for some time.

Although Corey would not talk about Mrs. Langley's death when she returned, Andy knew when she was ready she would get it all out. She had been relieved when Andy told her of his decision to leave and had agreed to go with him to the Courtney house for the pay they had coming. As a result, they were at the big house when an entourage of newspaper reporters and photographers drove into the yard.

"Here's the kid that woke everyone up and helped catch the firebug!" one of the men shouted as the cameras clicked all around Corey.

"Hey, kid, how does it feel to be a hero?" Another asked. "C'mon, give us a smile."

"Leave the kid alone," Andy growled just before he was shoved out of the way.

"Who are you, anyway?" A man asked.

"Ain't none o' your business. Jest leave th' kid be. It's been a bad night for all of us, and you're not makin' things better with all th' fuss," Andy answered, pushing Corey behind him.

A photographer slipped into position to take another picture, but Andy reached out and snatched the camera from the man's hand. He glared at the others, daring them to try the same trick until they put their cameras down.

"Now, Mr. Courtney, if'n you'll jest give us our money we'll be on our way," Andy said, still watching the reporters.

"Sure, Andy, but I'd like for you to stay until we get all the oranges picked. I'm gonna be a day behind as it is, not to mention shorthanded, too."

Andy stared at the man, unable to believe what he had heard. He shook his head and refrained from letting him have it. He just wanted to get away from here.

"'Fraid I can't do thet, Mr. Courtney. Jest give us our due, thet be all we ask."

CHAPTER 8

Lizzie James threw the letter on the table angrily and muttered, "Darn little fool, even gone she causes trouble. Just when I thought I was done with her, now this."

"What's the problem, Lizzie?" George sighed.

"If you'd keep your nose out of the paper long enough you'd know what was going on around here. Is that all you can do, read the paper?"

It's the only way I can keep my sanity around here, George thought, but aloud he asked a second time, "What's wrong?"

"It's a letter from your brother's lawyer. It seems they've sold Henry's house and business and the money is going to be put in a trust of some kind for Corey. He wants you and the child to go over to Oklahoma next month when it will be finalized so he can set things up. What are we going to do now?"

"Anything can happen in a month. Perhaps Corey will be back by then." He was saying it but didn't believe the child would return. Why should she? She couldn't possibly be anymore unhappy with Mrs. McPhearson than she had been with them, and he escaped once more into the silence of the newspaper.

Lizzie started toward him shaking her finger, when a picture on the back page caught her attention. There was something strangely familiar about the boy in the picture. Snatching the paper from George's hand. she read the first paragraph:

> Corey Curruthers, ten year-old grandson
> of Andrew Curruthers, saved workers from
> a fiery death and helped capture an arsonist.
> Young Corey alerted workers at the Courtney

Farms outside Moors, California, yesterday
as their living quarters were burning around
them....

Lizzie's gaze went back to the child and her eyes narrowed. Her prodigal niece was staring back at her from the picture. She would recognize those eyes anywhere. How clever Corey was to disguise herself as a boy, she thought, and who was that old bum standing with her? Andrew Curruthers. *Well, Mr. Curruthers, you are going to be sorry you ever set eyes on my niece,* she smiled to herself.

"George," Lizzie almost sang his name. "We have found the kidnapper of our poor little niece."

"For God's sake, Lizzie, what are you talking about?"

"Our little Corey never made it to her kinfolk; she was kidnapped. See for yourself. They are both right here in this picture," she simpered, shoving the newspaper under his nose. "We have just solved our problem, or rather Mr. Curruthers has solved it for us. I must go to the authorities right away and report this terrible deed."

"You told me she was back in Oklahoma," George accused. "All this time I thought she was with Mrs. McPhearson."

"Well, I couldn't let you go to the authorities just yet. I figured she *was* back at her house in Oklahoma and we'd hear from the maid any day now."

"I should never have listened to you. She could have been killed and it would be my fault for not doing anything. You've really gone too far this time."

"What are you going to do?" Lizzie asked, a touch of panic in her voice, and then more calmly, "She had money, George. I really thought she had taken a bus back to Oklahoma. I was going to send a letter off today to that Mrs.—what's her name."

"You can't just walk in and say Corey has been kidnapped. What are you going to tell them when they ask why you haven't reported this before? And why didn't Corey tell the police when all this was going on?" he pointed to the picture. "She had the perfect opportunity when the newspeople were interviewing her." George tugged at his chin angrily. He was just as much at fault by accepting his wife's explanation. He hated confrontations with her and always took the easy way. He had no guts, he knew this, Lizzie knew this. *Now,* he thought, *look where it's gotten me.*

"Don't be silly! Look at her poor, frightened little face," Lizzie mocked. "Who knows what terrible things he threatened her with, should she tell?"

"She doesn't look frightened to me and that fellow looks very protective of her. He doesn't look scared like he has done something wrong and is about to be caught," George observed, looking at his niece and then at Andy. "Lizzie, couldn't we just go to this farm and find out before getting that poor fellow involved? I mean, do you know what they do to kidnappers? What if you're wrong and he just took up with her?"

"Use your head, George. What do you think she would do if she saw us? She would run away again and we wouldn't be any better off. Besides, this bum has probably done worse things he hasn't been punished for. Who's going to care about him, anyway?"

"Well, I am leaving on the train first thing in the morning for California and bringing Corey home. You do what you have to," George stated firmly.

The next morning Lizzie took great care in dressing for her visit to the police station—dark somber clothes to denote grief and, of course, a handkerchief for the tears. *One must shed tears to be believable,* she mused. An approving glance in the mirror and she was off.

"Mrs. James, if you will just start at the beginning," Deputy Clark suggested. "I know this is very difficult for you, but I can't make any sense out of what you have told me."

"Of course, Deputy, I'm sorry. It's just that…it's so awful for me to think what terrible things this man must have put my poor Corey through." Lizzie was careful to insert the tears and anguish at the right places, proud of her performance.

"You see, Corey wasn't recovering from her parent's death very well. We were strangers to her and she longed for familiar surroundings. She was quite attached to the housekeeper and couldn't understand why she wasn't allowed to stay with her." At least this part was the truth; she didn't have to lie too much. "When she left the note saying she was going back to be with Mrs. McPhearson, the housekeeper, we thought it might do her good. Well, she had taken the money from my purse…I assumed to buy a bus ticket…and since we did not know where the housekeeper was living…well, we had to wait until we got word from her that Corey had arrived," Lizzie stopped and sniffed into her handkerchief while she studied the young detective to determine if he believed her story.

"When we heard nothing, we were preparing to get in touch with the attorney in Oklahoma and have him check around out there. It was about that time we got the post card saying she was fine and not to worry." That lie was a nice touch, she thought.

"And did you confirm the fact Corey was indeed with the housekeeper, Mrs. James?"

"I had no reason to think otherwise and we were so relieved to hear she had arrived safely, besides, there was no return address on the post card."

"You heard nothing from this Mrs. McPhearson in the month and a half the child was gone? Nothing to say how she was doing or when she would return?"

"No," Lizzie answered simply.

"You have no ransom note or correspondence from the man in the picture with your niece?"

"I told you, this was the first I knew of Corey being taken when I saw the newspaper item." Lizzie raised her voice. "Why all the questions? Do you think I had something to do with my own niece's kidnapping?"

"I'm sorry, Mrs. James. Please forgive all the questions, but I have to get it clear why so much time has passed since the disappearance of your niece and you are just now reporting it to me. I know you are distraught, but there are procedures we must follow and kidnapping is a serious offense," apologized the deputy. Then, picking up the phone, he said to Lizzie, "I'll notify the authorities in Moors and have them pick up this man."

"You can also inform them I will be there to pick up my niece and make sure they prosecute this horrible man as soon as I can get a train out of here."

Lizzie was pleased with her performance and smiled smugly as she left the police station. She had to go to the bank where George worked and tell him she was going with him to California.

"That fool," she muttered, "It's a good thing he wasn't with me. He would have had a nervous breakdown when that officer asked all those questions."

George could tell by the expression on Lizzie's face when she entered the bank that she had accomplished her mission. How did he put up with the conniving woman? he wondered, but he knew before the question was finished. Fear. Fear of being alone, fear of having to make decisions and surviving on his own. Even worse was the fear of standing up to his wife. All these years it had been easier to go along and not dwell on what she did. But he was going to put his foot down from now on when it came to his niece, he vowed silently.

As Lizzie recounted the story to her husband, he cringed at the thought of the poor man whose only deed had been to help Corey and for that he was going to pay dearly. He didn't believe the man was a threat to his niece.

It was four o'clock and Lizzie had just finished packing when a knock sounded. Annoyed at the interruption, she peeked out the small window in the front door. Grace Canfield stood on the front porch fussing with the straw hat perched on her head.

The last person Lizzie wanted to see at this moment was Grace. The deputy had suggested keeping the case quiet until word came from California that Mr. Curruthers had been taken into custody, as a precautionary measure. Should she let anything slip, this old busybody would have it all over town within the hour.

"Well, hello, dear Gracie!" Lizzie cooed as she opened the door. "It seems you have caught me at the most inopportune moment. You won't be offended if I don't ask you in, will you, dear? We are leaving for California tonight and I have a lot to do."

"Aren't you the lucky one, Lizzie? Whatever are you going to do in California?" Grace prodded.

"It's going to be a vacation of sorts. It's been so lonely since Corey left and George insisted we take this trip."

"You should have said something earlier about your trip and I could have arranged to go with you and George wouldn't have to take off work. Wouldn't that be fun? I could probably still go…"

"I appreciate your offer, dear Grace, but I wouldn't impose on you like that. Besides, George is going with me. Now, if you will excuse me, I really have to get back to work or I'll never have things ready in time." She hurriedly shut the door in Grace's face.

Grace stood for a minute, not really sure what had happened, then haughtily pulled her hat down on her head against the wind as she left the porch. She turned once more to look at the house and, shaking her head, started down the walk to her car.

Leaning against the closed door, Lizzie held her breath as she listened to Grace leave. That was close! Of all the times for that fool to appear at her door…A dreadful thought occurred to her, what if Grace had seen her at the police station earlier? She was always in town and not much escaped her attention. What a bother that woman was!

Lizzie hurriedly bathed, dressed in her traveling suit, and began checking to make sure she had everything they would need. George came in while she was transferring the suitcases to the front room and, giving a curt nod, went back to their room.

Suddenly there was another knock at the door. Much to Lizzie's relief it was Deputy Clark this time.

"Howdy, ma'am. I brought you the name of the person in charge of your case in California. Inspector Thurgood Jones will be meeting the train and will make the arrangements for your hotel room, if you don't mind, that is. I will be calling him back tonight to let him know when you and your husband will arrive. He wants to know if you have a preference where you would like to stay."

"Very good. I'll leave it to the discretion of the good inspector as to what hotel would be best. Tell him we will arrive in Moors at seven on Thursday evening. Isn't that right, George?" she called to her husband. "Seven o'clock on Thursday?"

George stumbled from the bedroom where he had changed from his business suit. He pulled the tickets from his pocket. "Yes, dear, you are correct." Seeing the deputy, he avoided the man's eyes. "Excuse me, I must get the rest of the baggage," he mumbled, turning back down the hallway and making a hasty departure.

"Deputy Clark, Grace Canfield was here a while ago and I don't know if she suspects anything or not, but I would appreciate it if you wouldn't say anything about where we will be staying, should she ask. I'm afraid she might have seen me leaving your office and tie my trip with the visit—"

"You can rest easy. I have no plans to discuss anything with her or anyone else," the deputy interrupted. "As I told you earlier, we must take all precautions to keep this as quiet as possible until arrests have been made. We don't know that Mr. Curruthers doesn't have someone watching here...you have a safe trip," he touched the brim of his hat and turned to leave.

🍁 🍁 🍁

Grace Canfield strolled casually along the aisles in Henderson's Drugstore, picking up an item and pretending to examine it, all the while her attention focused on the police station across the street. Lizzie had been there earlier and was now suddenly taking a trip to California. Grace Canfield was going to find out what was going on. Soon it would be suppertime and she knew one of the officers would come to the drugstore for a sandwich at the soda fountain. She would seize the opportunity to strike up a casual conversation and somehow bring Lizzie into the discussion.

Minutes later Deputy Clark eased onto the stool, teasing the young man behind the counter about a pretty young girl who had just left. They laughed, sharing a few words before the young man moved down the counter to prepare a sandwich. When he moved, Jerry Clark caught sight of Grace in the long mirror behind the soda fountain. Watching as she moved toward him a heavy sigh escaped his lips. He had hoped to have a peaceful supper and, for a few minutes, forget about the pressures of his job.

"Aren't you Josephine Clark's son, Jerry?" Grace tittered.

"Yes, Mrs. Canfield, I am," the deputy grimaced.

"How is your dear mother? I haven't seen her in weeks."

"She is fine," he answered, trying to keep the conversation brief. "I'll tell her you asked about her."

"Oh yes, please, and it was so nice seeing you," she gushed and turned to leave. "By the way, did I see Lizzie James coming from your office this morning?"

Jerry Clark was spared further comment as another deputy burst through the front door and rushed to the counter.

"I need to speak to you right away," he said and, looking at Grace, added, "in private."

"Why yes, I was just leaving," Grace sputtered and moved away from the men, trying to keep within listening distance, her curiosity greatly aroused.

"Inspector Jones just called from California and said that he went to the farm to pick up the suspect and he was too late. The man and the child had already left and no one seemed to know where they had gone."

Jerry looked at the clock on the wall...six-thirty, forty-five minutes before the train left. There would be no sense in them making the trip now. He could send his partner to inform her of the news, but that would leave him with the widow Canfield. Instead, he elected to skip his sandwich and do the job himself. He had suddenly lost his appetite anyway.

The train station in Naples was very small and it was easy to see in a glance that the Mr. and Mrs. James had not arrived. He decided it would be easier to wait for them, rather to find them en route.

Heads turned and quick glances darted around the room at the sight of the uniformed officer. Suspiciously, some of the people drew their belongings closer as if threatened by the possibility a criminal was loose in their midst. Children stared while their parents silently reprimanded them with a quick look.

Jerry winked at the children, knowing their startled curiosity stemmed from their parents' threats of calling a police officer should they disobey. Hadn't his own parents done the same when he was growing up? If only people...but his thoughts were interrupted when the door opened and Lizzie came in, followed by her husband struggling with three large suitcases.

It would be difficult for Jerry to talk with them in a room full of people who were already suspicious. He halted their approach with a frown and silently motioned for George to meet him outside.

"So, what happens now?" George asked once they were out of the station.

"Of course they will circulate the newspaper picture throughout the state as discreetly as possible. I can assure you, Mr. James, they will not leave a stone unturned until they locate your niece. Until they catch this man or get a strong lead on him, it would be best if you and your wife stay here. We will, of course, keep you informed of the progress."

"Yes, I agree, and I appreciate your concern," George answered, worried about what Lizzie's reaction might be.

"Would you like for me to explain to your wife, Mr. James?" the deputy asked, noting the George's look of concern as he lowered his head.

"No, that won't be necessary, young man. I'll tell her. Good night and thank you again," George sighed.

Lizzie was only mildly annoyed when told the news. The fact they had escaped posed no real problem, since it was now on record that Corey had been kidnapped and that was all she needed for the lawyer. Whether they were caught made no difference to her, she really didn't want Corey back.

Grace Canfield watched the whole scene from her car across the street. She had driven to the train station in hopes of finding out just what was going on. Now, she would have to give them time to get home and then she would pay her friend a visit. Something was definitely going on and it involved the police.

Lizzie unpacked her clothes and walked into the kitchen to put the kettle on for tea when she heard a rapping on the front door. Annoyed, she hesitated answering, but when the rapping continued, she thought perhaps it might be the deputy with more news.

"Why Lizzie, dear, I thought you would be on your way to California by now and then I saw the light in your window."

"We have postponed my trip for a few days." When Grace made no attempt to leave, Lizzie asked, "Was there something else?"

"Why, no, that was all. It is quite late to be calling, isn't it? Perhaps tomorrow I could drop by for tea and we could chat."

"Another time, Grace. I'm going to be busy for the next few days. Now, if you'll excuse me, I have something on the stove."

"Yes, of course, good night, Lizzie."

"That old biddie. Who does she think she is fooling?" Lizzie muttered as she closed the door. "Probably thought she could weasel her way in and find out what was going on."

Tommy Rice lay on the floor going through the newspaper to find a suitable item for his class assignment on current events. It was his first assignment of the new school year. His eye caught the picture of Corey, but at first he didn't recognize her. He read the story, thinking how great it would be to have his picture in the newspaper or, even better, to have been a hero. He looked closer at the picture to see what a real hero looks like, if there was anything different about this boy that would set him apart from all the others. There was something familiar about the face, he thought, and looked at the name again. Same first name as his friend's…and she did ask for scissors to cut her hair. It was Corey! Where was she? California, the paper said.

"Hooray, she made it!" Tommy shouted, happy that his friend was safe and far away from her aunt. But, he thought, what if she had seen the picture and recognized Corey, too? No, she probably took no notice at all, if she even looked at the paper. Still…

"What's happened?" Mrs. Rice called from the kitchen.

"Nothing, Mom. I just found something I needed," he answered, turning the newspaper over quickly in case his mother came in to see. What if they were to recognize Corey and start asking questions? He would have to tell them the whole story? He shuddered to think of the trouble he would be in. "Has Dad finished with the paper?"

"I believe so, son, why?"

"I have to cut something out for my homework. You don't think he'll mind, do you?"

"I'm sure he won't, especially when it's schoolwork. Besides, he'll be working quite late tonight and I don't think he'll feel much like reading the paper when he gets home," Mrs. Rice answered, coming in from the kitchen. "Are you almost finished? It's getting late and you have school tomorrow."

"Just a few more minutes."

Tommy took the picture to his room and pulled out the box that held his private possessions. There was a hair ribbon he had taken from Jennifer Culver when he thought she was the only girl in the world for him, a dried flower given to him by his favorite teacher on her wedding day, and a lock of Corey's hair. He would add this to his collection and some day he would ask Corey all about her adventures. Then, he wondered if she would ever come back.

CHAPTER 9

Corey and Andy counted their money a second time. Andy had found several more jobs in the month or so since leaving the orange groves. For once they were going to have a real breakfast and see how the other half lived.

"Are you ready, my lady?" Andy grinned, straightening his disheveled clothes mockingly and offering Corey his arm.

"Yes, my good man," Corey giggled as she continued the charade and entered the small diner with Andy.

There were several groups of people seated around the diner, and as Corey and Andy approached the counter and sat down on the stool, a silence fell over the room. When Corey turned to see what was wrong, she saw that a group of men and women at the table nearest them had stopped eating and was staring in their direction. The women began whispering and pointing, while a burly, red-faced man began speaking to the waitress loudly enough for Corey to hear.

"Well, Sarah, looks like you let just anything in here now. Are you trying to run the decent folk away?" His fellow companions nodded in agreement, while he looked very pleased with himself.

Other patrons took up the conversation until the waitress finally came over and asked Corey and Andy if they would mind going elsewhere with their business. Andy bowed to the waitress, paused long enough to look openly into the eyes of their persecutors, and led Corey outside. Corey was in tears and he bent over her, using his handkerchief to wipe her eyes.

"Oh, Andy, those people are so mean. I hate them!"

"Naw, Corey girl, you should feel sorry fer them."

"Sorry for them?" she sputtered. "Why should I feel sorry for them?"

"'Cuz, Corey, they be people who jedge a feller's worth by th' wrong measurin' stick. They got their fine houses and clothes and all th' things you're suppost to have. If'n you don't foller their rules, then they look down their noses at you. But if'n the truth be known, I betcha a lot o' them are miserable. Prob'ly tied to a job they hate and hocked up to thar whilst they make believe everything is fine and dandy. I believe, in every feller's bein' is th' urge to break free from all the ties thet be forced on him, but fer some reason or th' other he can't.

"You see, Corey, I be whut I be'cuz I wanna and some people get a lil scairt 'cuz deep down thet's whut they'd like to be…free."

Corey thought about this for a minute and said, "I still don't understand, Andy. Why are they so mean?"

"Some fellers bury it so deep they don't understand it themselves; others jest be bitter," he smiled down at Corey. "You know, girl, ain't no feller any better'n th' other. He may have more belongings, or more money, but it don't make him any better." Andy was recalling a conversation with his father so many years ago, and while he related it to Corey, his mind drifted back.

🍁 🍁 🍁

Jed Curruthers led his ten-year-old son, Andy, across the fields and up the little knoll that had become his favorite spot overlooking the countryside.

"Listen, son, can you hear the music?"

"What music, Pa? I don't hear anything."

"Stand quiet and listen. Hear the wind singing through the trees, the birds whistling from the meadow, and, if you listen really close, you can hear the brook laughing as it runs across the rocks and spills down the hill. That's the music I'm talking about…the music of life. No matter how big or important you may feel when you get older, I hope you will always take time to stop and listen to that music."

"I don't understand. Those are just everyday sounds you hear all th' time."

"True, they are everyday sounds, but we don't always hear them because we take them for granted. It's the same with people. They are always there, but we take them for granted. That is what saddens my heart, for I am as guilty as the rest." He sighed and shook his head. "Listen to the frog. His song is not as beautiful as the bird's and he is truly an ugly creature to you and me, but in his own way he contributes to that music of life. What I am really trying to say, son, is that no matter how insignificant and small a man may seem, he has that right to contribute and he is just as important."

Jed took his son's hand in his and the two stood quietly, watching as the sun slipped gently beyond the horizon. The sounds of the evening intensified, etching the moment forever in young Andy's mind…

🍁   🍁   🍁

Once again the hobo could smell the woods and grass and hear all the sounds his father had been talking about. How much better the world would be if more people thought the same, for Andy had used the words wisely, enjoying life and all its inhabitants to their fullest.

"Well, kid," Andy finally spoke, breaking the mood. "What say we head on out? We can always find something for breakfast later on."

October was beginning, and everywhere Corey looked, the countryside was ablaze in brilliant shades of red, orange, and yellow as the leaves announced the arrival of fall. Corey could sense the air changing, too, not so much in its coolness, but because it made her feel more alive. The animals felt it as well. Horses pranced across the pasture, broke into a full gallop, and raced back to the fence to paw at the ground and snort in angry protest at their confinement.

Andy was also thinking about the changes taking place, but for a different reason. Winter would be upon them soon and he would have to decide about Corey. In fact, he had been doing a lot of thinking about the child lately and the kind of life they had been living. It wasn't good for a child, especially a girl, to be wandering around the country, exposed to the weather or countless other situations that would be forced on them. She definitely could not return to her people, yet she needed a home and guidance, something he had not been able to give her.

He had had no schooling and the company Andy kept had done nothing in the way of educating him. Every time he opened his mouth, he was painfully aware of this. He was hoping his friends could help him with an idea when he met with them at their camp in Oregon, the annual get-together before winter. It was to this camp they had been traveling the past two weeks. He could not bring himself to tell Corey the real reason for going there, only that she would be meeting his friends.

In his mind, Andy could smell the chicory coffee boiling over the open fire long before he saw the camp. Knowing how strong and bitter it would be, his mouth still watered for a steaming cup of that brew. Days had passed since his last cup, and anything that bore a resemblance to coffee sounded good right now.

🍁   🍁   🍁

"Hullo, Lord Mayor," he called to the old man leaning over the campfire.

"Hullo yerself, Andy," he answered. Then, seeing Corey and Muffin following at Andy's heels, he said, "Wot's that ye be bringing with yerself?"

"This here's Corey and Muffin. Say hullo to Timothy O'Reilly, Corey; his friends call him Lord Mayor."

Corey was intrigued with the old man and could not take her eyes from him. He was short and stocky with unruly gray hair. Bushy eyebrows arched above twinkling blue eyes that seemed to echo laughter from somewhere within. When he spoke, it was almost musical and with an accent Corey had never heard before. His clothes were worn and rumpled, but they were clean and, unlike Andy, his face was clean-shaven, except for a bushy mustache, which he wore with an air of grandeur.

"'Twas me sainted father who was Lord Mayor," he laughed, "And I got stuck with the nickname when me cronies heard about it." He poured a cup of coffee, offered it to Andy, and turned to Corey. "Tell me how it is ye've come to be with me friend here?"

Corey glanced with uncertainty at Andy, not sure how she should answer the question.

"It be awright, Corey girl. Lord Mayor's a friend," Andy reassured her and proceeded to tell her story.

Lord Mayor shook his head when Andy finished. "Your aunt must be touched by th' devil himself, treating a child like yourself that way. But don't ye worry none, little Corey, ye be with friends now," he soothed, pulling a pipe from his pocket and tapping it on the fallen tree where he was sitting.

The two men began talking about what had taken place since they last met, asking about some of their mutual friends on the hobo circuit. Corey took advantage of this time to explore the woods around the camp that would be their home for the next few days.

Leaves were beginning to fall and Corey merrily waded through them with merriment. She loved the smell of the leaves and the woods at this time of the year, and she began to think about home. She remembered her father raking leaves into piles while she jumped into them, covering herself. He would make a game of looking for her while she giggled uncontrollably, giving away her location.

Corey could almost smell the aroma of burning leaves that filled the air in her neighborhood. She thought of the holidays that would be coming: Halloween, Thanksgiving, with all its spicy delights, and Christmas…Christmas with all the decorations and the excitement of shopping. She had not thought of these times so fondly at Aunt Lizzie's house because she did not feel included in the celebrations…what few celebrations there had been.

Corey took out the brooch with the picture of her mother, father, and herself, and for the first time in months, she felt the agony of their death. She pressed the picture to her cheek and lay upon the carpet of pine needles, crying herself to sleep. Her emotions were drained and their early rising that morning had taken its toll.

Concerned when Corey did not immediately return to camp, Andy began looking for her. He followed the direction she had taken for a short distance, and then cupped his hands over his mouth to call her name, when he spotted her. He eased closer and stood looking at the sleeping girl in the early evening light.

Dirty smudges under her eyes bespoke the fact she had been crying. Picking up the brooch from her open hand, he knew the reason. *Poor li'l soul,* he thought, replacing the trinket very gently. *Got a lot o' hurt still.* Tenderly, he smoothed the damp hair from her face, his hand lingered lovingly against her cheek.

"Hi, Andy," she said groggily. "I must have fallen asleep. Have you been here long?"

"Naw, just this minute got here. Got a mite worried when you was gone so long and come looking fer you." He looked toward the sky as she quickly slipped the brooch into her pocket. "Gonna be eatin' soon. Wanna come with me to thet crick over yonder and wash up a bit?"

Another man had joined Lord Mayor when Andy and Corey arrived back at the camp and they were deep in discussion. They grew silent when they saw the two approach.

"Hullo thar, Curly," Andy greeted the new arrival.

"Hullo, Andy," the man returned the greeting, his eyes darting to the girl following him. "See you have a traveling companion there."

Andy had not missed anything, but he kept it to himself. "Yup, this here's Corey. Corey, thet's Curly," He grinned as they both looked at the man's bald head.

"How do you do, Corey?" Then he asked Andy, "Could I talk to you in private?"

"You can talk in front of Corey; she's okay." When Andy saw that Curly was adamant, he followed Curly to a large tree about ten yards away.

Curly leaned against the tree and spoke in a low voice. "I was at a store yesterday and the police stopped me. Showed me a picture of you and the kid and wanted to know who that man was." He watched Andy for a minute before continuing, "I told him I didn't know."

"Did they say anything else? Why did they want to know 'bout me?"

"I didn't ask, just like I ain't gonna ask now. Ain't none o' my business, but I thought you might like to know."

"Where was you when he had this here picture?"

"I was in Seattle on my way here. Don't know if they was asking anyplace else 'cause I hopped a freight just outside town and beat it here."

"Thanks, Curly," Andy murmured, wondering how the police would have a copy of a news item that had taken place in another state. If it had made the papers all over, maybe Corey's aunt had seen it and gone to the police. They would have to be more careful now, at least until he could come up with something. It would be easy enough to hide in the Oregon wilderness, but he could not stay here indefinitely. He would have to find a safe place for Corey as soon as possible. In fact, he was beginning to get an idea, one he would have to work out a little better…

By noon the next day two more of Andy's friends arrived. They, too, had been stopped by the police with the same question. Until now Andy had said nothing to Corey, not wanting to alarm her, but he felt it was time to let her know. At the same time, he would let his friends know what was going on.

"But why would Aunt Lizzie do this?" Corey asked when Andy told her. "She doesn't want me around; she said as much many times."

"You don't know what's happened sinct you left, Corey girl. Could be lots o' reasons. One thing I can't figger out, though, is why the cops was askin' 'bout me instead of you. I ain't never done nothing thet would interest them in me," Andy said, scratching his head slowly. "Don't look too good, if'n you ask me."

"Well, you can count on our help, whatever it is we can do," Curly offered as the others nodded in agreement. "And the 'boes out there that knows you won't squeal on you either, but what are you going to do?"

"'Preciate it, boys. I think I got me an idee, but th' less you fellers know, the best it'll be fer you. 'Sides, I got me some figgering to do."

Corey sat watching her friend with great remorse. It was her fault Andy was in this mess. Somehow she would get him out of it, even if it meant leaving him. If she were out of his life, the police would no longer look for him.

After dinner the men sat around the fire talking while Corey studied the new arrivals, Injun and Pete. Injun, a big man over six feet tall, had an olive complexion, high cheekbones, and dark hair, denoting his lineage and justifying his nickname. He was a pleasant, quiet man who spoke only when he had something important to contribute to the conversation.

A strange, silent man with a wild look to his green eyes, Pete did not join on the conversation. He sat apart sipping a "pink lady," a drink made from straining sterno through a handkerchief, removing the paraffin and leaving a strong alcoholic beverage. A painfully thin man, the hard lines etched upon his face made him look older than his thirty-five years. His grimy fingers trembled as he tossed the remainder of his drink into the back of his throat.

Corey shuddered at the sight of the man and turned her back to him. She would wait for the men to go to sleep, and then she and Muffin would leave. Corey listened for a while until the drone of the men's voices lulled her unwittingly to sleep. Sometime later she was startled from her sleep by someone stroking her head. She bolted upright with a sharp cry. His hand halted in mid-air, Pete stared back at her with a pathetic look on his face. Corey knew she would never forget it or the expression in his eyes, reflected in the firelight, for the rest of her life.

Corey's cry had awakened the others and while Injun led Pete away from Corey, Andy squatted down beside her.

"Thar, thar, Corey girl, ole Pete won't hurt you none. I know he scairt you," Andy soothed, "but he don't mean you no harm, truly he don't."

Trembling violently, Corey pressed against Andy's chest. "Wh—what was he doing? What did he want?" she stammered.

"I guess th' best way to explain is to tell you somethin' about him. You see, his wife and lil girl run off one day when he was at work. Jest up and left without so much as a how-dee-do, and it near drove him crazy. Fer years he searched ever'where fer them and finally wound up ridin' th' rails. I guess he still hopes one day he'll find them. Mebbe, drunk as he was, he thought you wuz his lil girl, or mebbe he was jus rememberin'. He's a tortured soul, Corey girl, and I hope you don't think too unkindly of him. Jest try to think on th' reason he did whut he did."

Corey lay back down while the men returned to their beds on the ground. This time she would keep awake; she had wasted precious minutes, maybe hours. She had no idea what time it was and could only hope that the men would fall asleep soon and she would be able to get a good distance from camp before morning.

It seemed a long time before the men were snoring loudly. Slowly, Corey raised her head so she could see the dark figures lying around the glowing embers in the firepit. Good, she thought, they were all asleep. Quietly, she eased herself off the ground, picked up Muffin, and tiptoed away. When she had reached the edge of the clearing, she put the dog down and breathed a sigh of relief. Surprisingly, the first step had been easy enough. Now she had to put some miles between herself and the camp before daybreak.

Already the sky was beginning to lighten in the distance and she began walking at a fast pace, careful not to trip in the darkness. Suddenly a huge arm seized her, suspending her in midair.

"Where are you going?" a voice growled the question. "You could get hurt wandering around in the dark."

"Injun, is that you? Put me down, Injun."

"Where were you going?"

Corey had not heard him following her through the bushes and now surmised there might be another reason for his nickname.

"What's going on here?" Lord Mayor asked as Corey was carried back into camp.

"Caught Corey leaving," Injun replied.

"Corey, where wuz you going?" Andy asked anxiously.

"Oh, Andy, it's all my fault the police are looking for you," Corey cried.

"Friends stick together when they is trouble afoot. You oughten to know thet by now. Whut made you git th' fool notion o' runnin' out like thet?"

"I thought if I left, you wouldn't be in trouble anymore."

"Then they would prob'ly think I went and done you in. Did you ever think on thet? Now, no more o' your foolishness 'bout leavin' ole Andy, you promise?"

Corey nodded.

"Good. Let's get some sleep whilst we can, it'll be a long day and we're gonna need all the rest we can git."

Andy did not fall asleep; instead he packed their belongings and prepared for their departure after breakfast. He also had time to work out their dilemma, at least the part about Corey. He had ruled out the possibility of taking her back to Gus; he was too far away and they would take a big chance on getting caught. No, he would go to Angelique…

❦   ❦   ❦

Ah, Angel, funny how she kept drifting in and out of his life. He smiled, thinking about the first time they met. She was eighteen, a mere slip of a girl, and the prettiest one he had ever seen. Blond hair billowed to her tiny waist, and her bluish-white eyes sparkled mischievously that afternoon as she addressed him.

"Mr. Curruthers," she had said, strongly emphasizing his name, "What does it take to get you to notice a girl, anyway? I've done everything but fall at your feet and not once have you even acknowledged my presence."

Angelique's father owned the mill where Andy worked, and no way had he intended to put himself, or his job, in jeopardy by trifling with the daughter. He knew his place and was determined to keep it. Only after she had gone to her father and he to Andy, did their relationship grow until that fateful night.

❦   ❦   ❦

"I think I'll be gettin' on, too," Curly broke into his reverie. "Gonna go down to Florida for th' winter. If I don't see you for a while, take good care of yourself and stay away from the law," he grinned.

Andy put his arm around Curly's shoulder. "You take good care o' yourself, too, my friend. Mebbe I'll git down thet way myself, later on." Andy was genuinely fond of Curly, almost as much as he was of Lord Mayor and Injun. They had been through some healthy scrapes together, ones that provided happy memories, and he always looked forward to seeing him. It was time to be moving on, though, and he released the man, moving over to Corey.

"You'd best git up now and git your things ready. We gotta git to thet bridge to catch the next train. Rise 'n shine."

"Maybe I'll see you then," Curly said, "I'm gonna catch the next train outta town. Gotta go there and get me some tobacca first. You need anything from town, Andy?"

"Naw, Curly, thanks, but I rekin we got everything."

Injun and Lord Mayor were going as far as the bridge with Andy and Corey, then planned to head south to California. Pete had left before everybody got up, perhaps to avoid any confrontations from the incident the night before.

Muffin ran ahead of the group, stopping every now and then to investigate a bush or chase a rabbit flushed from the undergrowth as they walked along the trail. It was a pleasant hike. The air was cool with an edge of crispness, and everywhere was the odor of fall. They could see the clearing ahead where there was a gorge twenty to thirty feet deep and maybe half a mile across. A river, slender as a ribbon, ran through it and under the long bridge that supported the train track.

They would walk along the edge of the gorge until they reached the end of the bridge. Then as the train passed slowly by, they would board it from the safety of the trees. Now, as they walked, a sharp train whistle filled the air and the train moved across the bridge. It was too late. Even as they ran, there was no way they could catch the train. While they stood watching, a small figure frantically waved his arms from the door of a boxcar. Andy and his friends whistled and waved back.

"Well, Curly made it," Lord Mayor laughed. "Guess you two will have to be after catching the next…"

His words hung in the air as they watched in horror at what happened. They could see large trees uprooted and falling before the sound reached their ears. The engine had jumped the track and fallen on its side, taking two more cars that had just crossed the bridge with it. Their gaze shot back to the car in which Curly had been riding, but he was no longer there. They scrambled down the cliff, losing their footing and sliding, one behind the other, by the seat of their pants.

When they reached the base of the bridge, Injun headed toward the front of the train to see if he could help the engineer, while Andy and Lord mayor climbed the piling to find Curly.

"Corey, girl, you wait down here for us," Andy yelled as he started up and looked down to see if she had heard him. It was then he saw Curly lying in the shallow water a short distance from them. He yelled for Lord Mayor and practically flew to the still form.

"Oh, Curly, me boy!" Lord Mayor moaned as he came up behind Andy. "Saints preserve us, he's not breathin', Andy!" Frantically, they worked on their friend, trying to restore some sign of life.

"Ain't no use, Lord Mayor, he's gone," Andy sighed. He stood up and turned to stop Corey before she got to them, tears streaming down his face.

Injun returned with much the same news; the engineer and fireman had been killed. A bad section of track beyond the bridge seemed to have been the cause of the wreck. Evidently the engineer had not seen it soon enough, although the reason wasn't clear to Injun.

"Andy," cautioned Injun, "you and Corey go. Those fellows in the caboose will come soon and there'll be questions…and authorities."

"I suppose you're right, but—"

"Go on, Andy," Lord Mayor ordered. "Injun's right. We can be after handling things here."

Andy didn't want to leave his friends, but what they said made sense. He would probably do more harm than good the way the situation was now.

CHAPTER 10

Five years had passed since Andy had last seen Angelique, shortly after her husband's death. He had come across the newspaper, left behind in the hobo jungle, and, seeing the picture of Angelique with her husband, had persuaded one of the men to read the story to him. Two days later he was at the sawmill. He had spent the month after that running the mill and helping her in whatever way he could. There had been no time to dwell on their past, she was in mourning and he was too busy working.

Now, standing at the edge of the woods and gazing across the sweeping lawn in the direction of the massive house, Andy was filled with memories of that night. How many years ago, thirty-five, thirty-six, since he'd last stood on these grounds and made the final decision? His mind lifted the veil guarding the past and he looked upon the scene as if it were only yesterday…

Twenty-year old Andy stood quietly, unobserved in the shadows, watching the people in their fine clothes as they danced or strolled casually among the small groups, laughing and sharing a few words with their friends. The warm summer night hung heavy with the scent of roses and other flowers from the massive well-tended gardens behind him. The still air seemed to press down upon him at times, causing him to draw long, deep breaths.

Doors were thrown open in search of an elusive breeze, and the music drifted down from the house, wrapping itself around Andy until he could feel its rhythm in every part of his being.

While Andy watched Angelique, he was hearing her father's words from their earlier conversation. "How long do you think Angelique will be happy away from her friends and the only way of life she knows? Oh, for a while she will be amused in this new adventure, but when it is no longer an adventure and she becomes bored. And she will get bored, my friend—what then?"

Andy looked at Angelique in her beautiful gown, her face aglow with happiness. He tried to picture her removed from these luxuries, placed in the drab surroundings he would be able to provide. He knew then her father had been right. This was the life Angel knew and enjoyed; he could not take that from her, nor would he accept the handout of money and position her father offered him to stay.

"Well, hello, Andy," Josh Harper greeted, "What are you doing out here? Aren't you going to join the party? Angelique has been waiting for you."

"Hullo, Mr. Harper. No, I think I'll pass. Ain't dressed to go in thar. I did wanna have a word with you, though."

The older man noticed the expression on Andy's face. He knew the young man had reached a decision, one that would cause his daughter pain. He would not be able to protect her as he had done in the past. Nor could his money intervene in her behalf. He knew whatever he could say would not change this strong-willed, independent man and he didn't want to try. This was the quality his daughter loved, and he had respected in Andy from the beginning.

When she had come to him and persuaded him to talk to Andy about dating her, Mr. Harper had assumed it was a fascination that would soon wear out. Andy was handsome, somewhat of a gypsy, and this had attracted Angelique, but he was also illiterate and penniless and had absolutely nothing in common with his daughter. How could he have known their relationship would go much deeper?

"I can't stay, sir," Andy continued. "I'm leavin' tonight and I'd like you to tell Angel…er, Angelique thet something come up and I had to leave sudden like." Again he took a deep breath as though it was hard for him to breathe the heavy air. "I can't be whut I ain't, anymore'n she can. I see thet now."

"Aren't you going to see her before you leave?"

"Naw, it's best I jest leave. She won't understand right now. It took me a while to see it. 'Sides, I don't wanna ruin her party. She's useta me not comin' to these things, so she won't think much on me not being here tonight." Andy glanced once more in Angelique's direction.

"Where will you go, Andy?"

"I'll hit the rails agin like'n I did before I come here. S'long, Mr. Harper, and thanks again fer everything," Andy ended the conversation. He had made his decision and was eager to get moving before he changed his mind again.

🍁 🍁 🍁

"Andy, I am talking to you. Andy!" Corey scolded, breaking into his reverie.
"Whut's thet, kid?"
"I said, is this where she lives, your Angel? She must be very rich."
"Yep, this here be her house. Come on and let's see if she's home."
Andy pointed to the bench situated just out of sight of the front door. "You sit here 'til I have a chanct to talk to her first."
Andy nervously scuffed his foot on the tile floor of the entry as he waited for the butler to summon Angelique. When she finally appeared in the doorway, his breath caught in his throat. Angelique stood but a minute, squinting against the sun, before recognition brightened her face. She grabbed Andy and crushed him in a generous hug. When she separated from him, tears brimmed in her eyes.
"Well, come in, old friend. We have much to catch up on."
Angelique Harper Martin retained the beauty she had possessed in her youth. It was more polished and refined with age and her figure was fuller, but she still had the quick, lighthearted step Andrew Curruthers had admired so many years ago.
At a time when all the young debutantes in her peer group were so careful to walk and act in the manner they believed was proper and ladylike, Angelique couldn't be bothered. Instead she went by her own rules. She had been strong willed and defiant and that trait was still evident in the way she carried herself as she led Andy through the rambling house toward the garden in the back. As they neared the french doors, the sounds of feminine voices stopped Andy.
"Well, Angel, somethin' new's been added. You never used to hold with them hen parties. Mebbe I'd best come back when you ain't got company."
"Still don't. Those old biddies think me an incompetent old fool until they need something from me, then they start with the invitations and visiting like I was their most dear friend," Angelique laughed with a tinkling note of mischief. "I play their silly games until I tire of it, only because I get so lonely in this big mausoleum. As for your leaving, I won't hear of it. Maybe we can start a delicious scandal. Are you game, Andy?"

Andy could only chuckle and shake his head. "That's my Angel," he muttered, then in a more serious tone, he said, "Angel, I think I'd best come back later, when you're alone. You see, I got me somewhat of a problem and th' less people I see, th' better."

"What kind of a problem, Andy?"

Andy nodded in the direction of the door separating them from the ladies.

"Don't pay any attention to them," she instructed, leading him into another room and closing the door behind them. "Now, tell me all about it."

Andy told Angelique everything from the time he first met Corey until their arrival at her home while she listened intently.

"Where is the child now?"

"Sittin' on thet fancy bench o' yours out front."

"Go get her while I get rid of my guests. There is a side door around the corner from where she is sitting. Use that and you can avoid the ladies as they leave."

After her guests left, Angelique telephoned a private detective she had used successfully on several occasions, assuring him it was of the utmost importance he come as soon as possible. To help Andy, she must first find out what the trouble was. Jack Humboldt was the way.

Ten minutes later the detective was being ushered into the library where Angelique, Andy, and Corey were waiting. He was a slender man of average height and build, in his midthirties. His black hair and pencil-thin mustache of the same color stood out boldly against his wan complexion. Upon entering the room, his gaze swept the room almost unnoticeably, making a mental note of its contents and occupants.

"I can tell you right now why the cops want your friend here," the detective said, after hearing their story. "They think he kidnapped the kid. Their picture made the front page of the newspaper this afternoon, along with the headlines of the alleged kidnapping."

"Whut's thet?" Andy choked on his words, bolting upright in his chair. "I didn't kidnap Corey! Who says I did?"

Humboldt shrugged and continued, "According to the newspaper, Corey was on her way to visit a housekeeper of the family when she was kidnapped. The kid's aunt said she didn't have any idea what had happened until the picture appeared in the newspaper after the fire in California. Corey, I'd like you to tell me your side of the story...everything you can possibly remember that might help me."

Andy sat stunned, watching the detective as Corey told her story. How could this be? What kind of woman could tell a lie like this when she knew exactly why the child had left? Well, it would easily be straightened out when he and Corey told their story. But, what if she pulled this off to save her own hide? What would happen to him? It was her word against that of a hobo's, perhaps they wouldn't even listen to Corey.

He studied the detective's face to see if this was as serious as he imagined, but the man gave no indication of what he was thinking. He held a notepad and occasionally scribbled something, or scratched his mustache with his pen. Only once was there a glimmer in his brown eyes, but it quickly disappeared. Everything about the man was under control from the top of his raven black hair to the tips of his well-polished shoes.

When Corey had finished confirming Andy's story, Humboldt glanced at Angelique. "Mrs. Martin, I would appreciate it if you would keep the kid and your friend out of sight until I've had time to do some probing of my own. You probably won't hear from me for a few days, perhaps a week, but don't do anything until you do."

Then, turning to Andy, he said, "I don't want either of you taking off until I get this straightened out, otherwise you'll be putting your friend, Mrs. Martin here, in a more serious position than you already have. That is to say, you've made her an accessory to this. The only reason I don't suggest you turn yourself in this minute is because I think I can find out more if you remain here for now. Besides, it sure won't hurt to have more to go on before you meet the cops. Maybe, with a little luck, we can straighten out this mess before it comes to that." He closed his notepad and left.

"You can rest assured, Andy, that whatever the problem is he will find out. He's good, darn good," Angelique soothed. "Now, eat some lunch while I go make the sleeping arrangements. I fear some of the rooms will need airing since they have been closed off for a while. Just help yourselves to the sandwiches Harvey brought in. I'll return shortly."

Corey all but inhaled the first sandwich. It had been hours since they had eaten, and she hadn't realized how hungry she was until she took the first bite. Even Andy had recovered from the shock enough to eat, having taken Angel at her word that the detective would straighten out this mess.

Andy and Angelique were deep in conversation about the past as Corey slipped out the front door with Muffin. She was curious about the rest of the place she would be calling home. A cobblestone drive circled a fountain in front of the house then continued back in the direction of the front gate. Corey followed a similar drive, which angled off to the side of the house and led to garages, beyond which lay the woods separating Angelique's house from that of the neighbor's.

Looking straight ahead, she could see the cottage where the caretakers lived. In the other direction, across the vast sloping lawn and past the gardens, was a large pond dotted with lily pads. It was a bigger pond than the one she and Tommy used to fish in back home and she wondered if there might be fish in this one, too. Quickly she ran to the water's edge, peering intently beneath the surface and much to her delight, caught a glimpse of movement.

As she sat watching, her thoughts turned to Tommy, and she wondered what he would be doing now. How she wished she could write and tell him of her adventures since the night he had helped her. She was curious to know how he had explained the missing pants to his mother or even if she had discovered them missing. In her musings Corey lost track of all time until the wind came up, blowing across the pond and causing her to shiver. Andy would be worried about her by now. She smiled a slow easy smile at the thought. It was nice to know there was someone who worried about her once again, especially after the year she had spent with Aunt Lizzie.

Andy was still in the library with Angelique when Corey walked in. The fireplace was lit and the warmth of the room made Corey tingle after the cold outside.

"Why, Corey dear, you will catch your death getting chilled like that. Don't you have a wrap with you?" Angelique fussed.

"No, ma'am, I didn't bring one with me. It was still summer when I left," Corey answered. "Boy, this fireplace feels good," she sighed, toasting herself as she turned slowly before the fire.

"I'll get Harvey, my butler, to bring some hot chocolate and draw a warm bath for you. I don't suppose you have nightclothes with you, either?"

No, ma'am, these are all the clothes I have. I usually just sleep in them, too."

"Well, I shall go borrow something from Mrs. McHenry, our caretaker's wife. She has a granddaughter about your size, and she keeps some of the child's things at her house. Then tomorrow I'll do some shopping for you." Angelique left the room to give instructions to her butler.

"Whatcha been up to, Corey girl? Find something special out there?" Andy asked, puffing dreamily on a cigar.

"Me and Muffin found a pond out back with fish in it. Do you think we could go fishing in the morning, Andy?"

"Mebbe, we'll see if'n Angel has a pole. Ain'tcha had enough fishin' by now?" Andy laughed.

The butler knocked on the door and entered with the hot chocolate, having anticipated the need for it before Angelique requested it. "The young madam's bath is drawn. Whenever she is ready, I will show her the way," he announced to anyone who might be listening.

Harvey was a tall man, with gray fringes of hair bordering his bald head. He stood very erect, his solemn face and gray eyes devoid of expression, a manner he deemed fitting his position. Harvey took great pride in his job and the household in which he worked.

"I'll go now and take the chocolate with me, if that's all right?"

"As you wish, Miss Corey. Allow me to carry your drink."

Corey grinned and made a pompous gesture, mocking the departing butler, then she bent down and whispered in Andy's ear, "By the way, I like your Angelique." She turned and followed Harvey up the winding staircase, leaving Andy chuckling to himself.

Corey had all but forgotten how soothing a hot bath felt. She slid down into the soapy water until her chin touched the surface and the steam tickled her nose. Every inch of her body responded to the warmth, relaxing little by little until drowsiness overcame her.

Angelique knocked softly on the door. "Your clothes are laid out on the bed for you, Corey. When you have dressed, pull the bell cord beside the bed and Harvey will bring you supper."

"Thank you, ma'am, but…" she had started to object at eating dinner alone, she had wanted to see Andy again before she went to bed, but she decided against it. Perhaps Angelique wanted to be alone with Andy, and Corey knew it wasn't her place to object to her wishes. "I'll be finished soon," she answered.

"Take your time, dear. I'm going downstairs and be back later to see how you're doing."

Corey shrugged off the feeling of being left out and stepped from the tub, wrapping herself in a large, fluffy towel. The room had been warmed by the steam from her bath and a small gas heater, but it still felt cool and Corey snuggled into the towel while she drank the rest of her chocolate.

Someone had built a fire in Corey's room, providing a soothing glow. In the soft light she could see that the covers had been turned back on a big canopy bed. Everything was perfect and she felt like a princess as she pulled the bellcord to summon her supper. Now, she crawled between the sheets, sinking deep into the feather mattress and promptly fell asleep before her supper arrived.

The steady rhythm of rain hitting the window awakened Corey the next morning. She had looked forward to having Andy to herself again while they fished in the pond, but with the rain her hopes diminished. Maybe he would explore the house with her since they would be confined inside. She dressed hurriedly so that she could present him with the idea before he became occupied with something else.

"They are in the morning room having coffee, miss," Harvey told Corey when she came down the stairs, "Would you like your breakfast now?"

"In a minute, I have to ask Andy something first."

"Very well, miss, I will show you the way."

Corey approached the door and, hearing Angelique talking to Andy, she hesitated.

"I don't know about this, Andy…the child remains too much of…"

Corey didn't wait to hear the rest, instead she started back in the direction from which she'd come.

"I'm sorry. Maybe I'll go and have breakfast," Corey whispered to the butler as he followed her down the hall.

Corey picked at her food. The empty feeling inside her was not hunger but rejection. Aunt LIzzie's words were ringing in her ears: "You are an outsider…nobody wants you…" But there was something else, too…jealousy. For the past two and a half months, she had had Andy all to herself and now there was someone else in his life. It was as though he had forgotten all about her. He hadn't even come to say good night when she went to bed. Maybe she had been too quick to tell Andy she liked Angelique.

"Hullo, Corey girl, thought you was goin' to sleep th' day away," Andy greeted, coming through the double doors into the dining room. Angelique was at his side.

"Good morning, Andy…ma'am," Corey answered stiffly, then noticing the coat and umbrella Angelique carried, her hopes rose again. "Are you going out, Mrs. Martin?"

"Yes, dear, I thought I would take Andy down to the mill for a while. Maybe I can talk him into staying and helping out with the place." She smiled at Andy and patted him on the cheek.

Corey looked from Angelique to Andy and said, "But, I thought maybe Andy could show me around the house this morning, since we couldn't go fishing."

"Well, I'm sure Harvey would be more than happy to give you a guided tour and he can fill you in on all the secret places. Wouldn't you enjoy that much better?"

Corey hesitated, hoping Andy would volunteer to stay with her. When he made no attempt, she bowed her head and mumbled, "Yes, ma'am, that would be nice."

"Very well, enjoy yourself and we will see you later." Angelique smiled down at her and patted her head.

"Don't you go gettin' lost in this here big house, Corey," Andy laughed and followed Angelique out of the room.

"Would there be anything else, Miss Corey?" Harvey asked, returning from the kitchen.

"No, sir, I think I'll just go back to the room for a while."

❦   ❦   ❦

A week had passed since Corey and Andy arrived at Angelique's. She had seen very little of Andy because he had been going to the mill every day, assured that with his new clothes and grooming he would not be recognized from the picture in the paper. Today, however, he had promised Corey he would take time off and do anything she wanted. She had taken great care not to oversleep, having instructed Harvey to make sure she was up at seven. Now, she quickly dressed in her old jeans and shirt she had worn in their travels. It would be like old times again.

"Come on, Muffin, before Andy changes his mind," she called to her dog and bounded down the stairs to the morning room. As Corey reached for the doorknob, something in the conversation made her pause.

"…and he said Lizzie James would drop the kidnapping charge if her niece was returned right away.."

Corey's hand flew to her mouth, stifling the scream tearing at her throat. Return to her aunt? The cruelty she had suffered before would seem like a picnic compared to what awaited her when she went back! If she went back. She didn't wait to hear more of the conversation but turned and fled.

Andy had Angelique now and might think nothing of returning Corey to her aunt. Hadn't he wanted to be rid of her before? Tears burned her eyes as she ran down the drive, not sure where she would go, nor did she care at this point.

"I won't send Corey back to thet ol' crone!" Andy ranted, slamming his fist against the table. "Ain't there something thet feller of yours can do?"

"I don't know. He did say he had uncovered some indiscretions, but wouldn't go into detail over the phone. He said he would be leaving there tonight or tomorrow and would get in touch when he returns. In the meantime I'll contact my attorney and see what he can come up with."

"But whut 'bout Corey?"

"You don't think we are going to give her back without a fight, do you? Trust me, Andy," Angelique reassured. "Now, you go to her while I get on with my business."

Andy knocked softly at Corey's door. Hearing no response, he called her name as he opened the door. No Corey. He went back downstairs to see if she was at the breakfast table.

"Have you seen Corey?" He asked of Harvey, when he found the dining room empty.

"No, sir, she has not come down to breakfast yet. Perhaps Madam…"

"I jest come from there. If'n you see her, tell her I'm lookin' for her." He ran back to Angelique, hoping Corey may have joined her after he left.

"She ain't in her room and Harvey says she ain't even ate this mornin' yet," Andy informed Angelique, taking no notice she was on the phone.

Angelique held up her hand to silence him as she spoke into the receiver, "Yes, David, this afternoon will be fine…anytime, I will be here all day. Yes, good-bye," And she replaced the phone on the hook. "Now, what were you saying?"

Andy told Angelique once again he had been unable to find Corey and added, "Did this here feller tell Corey's aunt whar she was? You don't rekin she sent the law after Corey this mornin', do you, Angel?"

"No one could've gotten past Harvey without me knowing it," Angelique laughed, and seeing that Andy was very concerned, she added, "Just calm down and think. Maybe she had something to do this morning. Did she say anything last night?"

Andy scratched his head trying to remember, and then slapped his hand against his thigh, "I was supposed to take her somewheres today. It plumb slipped my mind, whut with th' phone call 'n all," he groaned.

"Then all we have to do is wait and she'll come back shortly. She wouldn't have gone far since you had plans."

"Mebbe I'll jest walk down to th' overseer's place and see if'n she's there. Let me know if'n she comes back, Angel."

"Why, yessir, I did see the child," Mrs. McHenry said to Andy. "She ran by here about twenty minutes ago like she was being chased by the devil himself. I called out to her, but she just kept on going. I didn't think anything about it. You know how kids are."

"Which way did she go?"

"Out the front gate toward the country, her and the little dog. Is there something wrong?"

"I dunno, ma'am...thank you kindly," and he stood for a moment wondering why Corey had left the property when they had planned to spend the day together, and in a hurry yet.

"Half an hour or so...hm-m-m," Angel pondered the timing when Andy told her what had happened, "Well, Harvey hasn't seen her this morning, so he wouldn't know anything..." Angel went over everything that had transpired this morning. The silence was long and deafening for Andy and he began to pace back and forth. "Wait a minute, that was about the time I got the phone call regarding her aunt. You don't suppose she heard what we were discussing and got scared?"

"But we wasn't gonna send her back! She woulda heard that."

"Suppose she only heard part of it and didn't stick around to hear the rest. Oh, poor thing. It must have been terrible for her there," Angel cried.

"I gotta find her, Angel, and tell her not to worry," Andy called over his shoulder, running out the door. "I think I know whar she might be headin'."

Corey had been happy at Gus's and Andy was sure that would be where she was headed, but she didn't know anything about which way to go except that a train would take her there. She could ride the rails for a long time before getting the right connection, if she ever did, and a little girl alone...he shuddered to think what could happen to her.

"Where will you begin, Andy?" Angel asked, following behind him.

"First off, I'll git word out on th' 'bo grapevine to keep a eye peeled for her. I got me lots o' friends out thar. Then I'm gonna ketch th' first train outta here headed towards Flagstaff. Tell you whut, Angel, there's feller's address by th' name o' Gus Thatcher in Corey's belongings. if'n there's any word, you can reach me there."

CHAPTER 11

Corey watched the men's feet under the train until they had disappeared toward the engine. They had finished taking on water from the tower and were preparing to leave. Quickly she pushed Muffin through the open doorway and hopped in beside him. How simple it had been, but then Andy had taught her well. A lump formed in her throat when she thought of Andy and wondered if he had discovered her missing.

She would not think of him now, it was too painful. Corey would only concentrate on getting to Gus and seeing Nanette again. She smiled. Dear little Nanette, she had wanted to follow them so badly when they left. Once again she could see the cabin in the mountains with Gus standing on the porch waving to them and Nanette pulling at her tether. From now on she would put her trust solely in animals; they returned love and devotion without asking much in return, or betraying that trust.

The train was building up speed and Corey lay on her stomach, her heels in the air, watching the countryside pass before her. It would be late in the afternoon when she left this train and perhaps had a long walk before she got another. How clever she had been to get the yardman engaged in conversation and find out which way the train was heading. When she made the new connection, she would do the same again, but now she must rest for the trek ahead of her.

The sun was dipping low on the horizon when the train stopped at Rockland, Idaho, and Corey decided it was time to get off. The yardman had said it would not be stopping again until it was farther east than she wanted to go. She jumped out of the boxcar on the side away from the activity and headed out toward the woods beyond the tiny community. Her stomach was rumbling from hunger. If she was in luck, she would find a hobo camp in the woods and perhaps share their supper.

Once at the horizon, the sun dropped rapidly and darkness closed in, bringing with it a cold November breeze. Corey had run out without so much as a coat and now the cold seeped through the light clothing she wore. She thought about building a fire and forgetting about finding supper when she heard voices and smelled the aroma of food cooking. Andy had been right about finding a hobo camp near town and railroad tracks.

"Hullo in camp," she called as she approached the fire.

Two dirty, bedraggled old men sat hunched before the fire. One stood as Corey came nearer. "Who's thet?" he called.

"My name is Corey," she answered, "I smelled your food back there and thought, if you had plenty, you might be willing to share a bit with me. I've been riding the rails most of the day and I sure am hungry," she continued, proudly using the 'lingo of the 'boes', as Andy called it.

"Well, looky here, Carl. What d'ya suppose it is? It talks real growed up like, but it ain't much bigger'n a minute," and he cackled loudly, causing a shiver to run up Corey's spine.

"M—maybe you know my friend, Andy?" she asked shakily. "He's a 'bo like yourselves."

Again the cackle went into the air, only this time it was joined by that of the other man. "A 'bo, is he? And whar might this friend o' your'n be?" he chuckled, looking into the darkness behind her.

These men scared Corey. They were not like the others she had met, but then, she had been with Andy. That, of course, had made a difference.

"He's back there a ways," she lied, hoping they would leave her alone long enough for her to escape. Muffin sensed something, too, and began baring his teeth, and growling. Corey had never heard him do this before and became even more frightened.

Muffin made a sudden lunge at one of the men's trouser leg and the man gave him a swift kick. The dog went flying through the air. Corey started to run after him but was jerked off her feet when the man grabbed her. The unexpected action caught them both off balance and they tumbled to the ground. Her head struck something, and pinpoints of light danced before her eyes. For a moment, she lay stunned listening to the voices fading in and out. She blinked desperately trying to see if Muffin was unharmed, but she could not see or hear the little dog. Perhaps if she were still, the old men would think they had killed her and run away. She closed her eyes, all the while straining to hear what they were doing.

A hand grasped her by the arm, pulling her to a sitting position. "Playin' possum, ere you? It won't wash, kid. Now let's see whut you got in them pockets," he growled. "Then we'll wait fer yore friend, that is, if'n he really is back thar. Or mebbe you wuz lyin'."

Corey turned her empty pockets inside out, relieved she hadn't taken the time to bring anything with her. What if they became angry when there was nothing to take, though? Suddenly, one of the men let out a screech filled with surprise and terror. He had been standing in the shadow watching his friend but now hung suspended, feet flailing about wildly, from the hands of what seemed a giant to Corey. She could not see the big man clearly until he stepped closer to the fire and a gasp escaped her throat as she recognized Injun. Then she began to laugh, almost hysterically, both from the relief that flowed through her body and at the sight of this terrible man hanging in midair.

"Injun, oh Injun! I'm so glad it's you!" Corey exclaimed.

Injun grinned slow and easy as he set the man down, keeping a firm grip on his shirt, "Me and Lord Mayor heard your party and decided it was a mite rough. You don't mind that I broke it up?"

Ignoring his attempt at humor, Corey demanded," Have you been out there all this time?"

"Nope, just got here when the action started," answered Lord Mayor, stepping from the darkness and carrying Muffin under one arm.

"Oh, Muffin, I thought those men had killed you," she cried, taking the dog from Lord Mayor and burying her face in his fur, she wept.

"Well, friend, looks like your buddy left you to face the music alone," Injun spoke to the man in a quiet, almost deadly tone. "What should we do with you? Any ideas, Lord Mayor?"

"Please, please," the old man begged. "It warn't me. I didn't lay a finger on th' kid. It wuz Roy's idea! Please jest let me go 'n I promise ye'll never see this old face o' mine again."

"If we thought that yella-livered friend of yours would be after coming back for you, we'd keep you here. We don't have any patience with a mealy-mouthed tramp like yourself," Lord Mayor growled. "Now, you best start running and don't be stopping 'til you're in the next county, 'cause the next time we see you, we won't be so generous."

Demonstrating his agreement, Injun gave the tramp a shove that sent him sprawling. The tramp scrambled to his feet, stumbling once or twice, then broke into a run.

When things had calmed down, Corey turned to Injun and said, "Boy, they sure were right about your nickname. "I didn't hear you come up."

"We heard the commotion back a ways and since those tramps were pretty busy, we had surprise in our favor. What in God's name were you doing out here by yourself, anyway? Where's Andy?"

"What about you and Lord Mayor? I thought y'all would be up north in the lumber camps, and how did you get Muffin?" Corey evaded the question.

"Headin' for Florida, we were, Corey me girl," Answered Lord Mayor, "Hurt me wrist 'n couldn't do any work, so's we figgered we might as well head for th' warm country. That be when we saw you gettin' off that train and headin' out across the field. We followed you and found your little friend with th' wind knocked out of him just over yonder," he nodded in the direction they had come from. "Now, me girl, tell us your story."

Hesitantly, Corey explained her situation. How she had come upon the men and thought they might share their camp.

"Those men were tramps and there is a difference, Corey. They don't do a lick of work, just beg for handouts. They have no pride and be selfish besides. A 'bo works for whatever he needs and is always willing to share. I ain't saying they're all bad. Just like your 'boes, some are good and some are bad, but you got more bad tramps than 'boes," Injun lectured.

"Now, this here business of Andy turning you over to your aunt…you should know him better by now. Don't you think he would have gotten rid of you back when all the trouble started if he didn't care for you?"

"But he has Angelique…"

"And you don't think he has room for two people in his life," Injun interrupted. "You've got a lot to learn about your friend, Andy, little one," and he shook his head slowly. "Poor old fellow, he's probably worried sick about you. Not much we can do right now, though. Best you get some rest and come first light we'll make tracks back to Angelique's."

Lord Mayor nodded in agreement and added, "I'll be after keepin' me eye on things, just in case those hooligans decide to be coming back."

🍁　　🍁　　🍁

The way back seemed much slower for Corey. She was anxious to let Andy know she was sorry for thinking badly of him. She wouldn't even blame him if he did decide to wash his hands of her after all the trouble she had caused. From now on she would talk things over with Andy before she made hasty judgments.

They had reached a narrow trail that would take them to the railroad tracks and Injun dropped behind Corey and Lord Mayor. Muffin trotted along behind, keeping on the trail. Suddenly, his ears stood up and he began growling at something or someone behind them.

"I hear 'em, fella," Injun whispered to the dog. "Mayor, you and Corey walk slow and easy. I'll see if our friends are back." He disappeared into the brush. A few minutes later Injun burst through the bushes, dragging a struggling hobo. Corey breathed a sigh of relief that it was not the tramps.

"Be after offering the man a seat, Injun. Where's your manners, lad?" Lord Mayor chuckled, dusting a log with his handkerchief in a mocking manner. "Now, me bucko, what is it we can be doing for you?"

The hobo sat on the log gasping for his breath to return, his eyes darting from Lord Mayor to Injun. "It's th…" his voice cracked and he swallowed hard before he began again. "There's word out ta watch fer a lil girl…" again he swallowed. "She run away from a feller 'bo afore he got a chanct to explain something to her. I seen this here girl with th' two of you Thought mebbe she'd fallen into bad comp'ny." He looked questioningly at his captors.

"Where didya hear this?" Injun asked.

"It come down the 'bo grapevine. Said she wuz prob'ly headin' fer Arizony. That's all I wanted. Honest, fellas," the man pleaded.

What the man said made sense and Injun apologized. He related his confrontation with the tramps and that Corey was among friends, now. They sent the hobo on his way with instructions to pass the word Corey had been found.

🍁　　🍁　　🍁

The sight of Injun standing in the darkness was an overpowering one for Angelique and a gasp escaped her when she opened the door.

"It's okay, ma'am. We just brought Corey back. Is Andy here?" Injun asked.

"Forgive me," she apologized, "it's just that it is so dark and…boy, you are a big one," she laughed. "Please come in."

"We really should be movin' on." Injun blinked as he stepped into the brightly lit foyer. "We'll just have a word with Andy, if you don't mind."

"Oh, I'm sorry, Andy's gone. When he discovered Corey missing, he left right away."

"Did he say where he was going?" Corey asked.

"A Mr. Gus Thatcher's place, I believe. Yes, that was it."

"Lord Mayor, Injun, will you take me there?" Corey asked anxiously.

"Oh no you don't, young lady." Angelique protested. "You are going to stay put. We will notify Andy that you are here." Then, turning to the men, she asked, "Won't you let me fix you something to eat and perhaps a snack to take along?"

Injun opened his mouth in protest but was silenced by a quick jab from Lord Mayor's elbow. Injun cast a scornful glance at his partner before nodding.

After the men left, Angelique took Corey into the library. "Corey, dear, I know that you probably resent me a great deal—" she raised her hand to silence Corey's protest—"and you probably feel that everyone you love is being taken away from you, but that is not the case with Andy. He loves you very much, perhaps more than you can know right now. Because of that, you are very special to me. Won't you give me a chance to prove it, dear?" Angelique had become quite attached to Corey and it was never more evident than during her brief disappearance.

"I guess so," Corey answered awkwardly, picking at a loose thread on her pants to avoid Angelique's eyes.

"Good," Angelique nodded and got up from her chair, "It's late and you must be completely worn out from your trip. Why don't I take you up and get you settled in bed?"

Corey took the hand Angelique offered, feeling the pressure as Angelique squeezed it. Together they climbed the stairs, each reflecting on the events of the past two days.

"Ang…er, Mrs. Martin, when Andy left a long time ago…" Corey started as she climbed into bed.

"Another time, dear. It is way past your bedtime," Angelique interrupted. "One day I will tell you all about it, but right now you get some sleep." She tucked the covers firmly about Corey and, bending over to place a kiss on her forehead, added, "By the way, it's quite all right to call me Angelique, if you like."

Angelique turned at the doorway, taking one last look at the child before she turned the lights out. She knew there was something she must do tonight. She walked to the far end of the hallway and stood before the door, her fingers caressing the key in her pocket. Fighting back the urge to leave without entering, she quickly removed the key and inserted it into the lock.

"Are you sure you want to go in there, Miss Angelique?" Harvey asked, appearing from a door across the hall.

His sudden presence startled her and for a moment she braced herself against the doorframe until the weakness in her knees subsided. "It's been a year, Harvey, and I think it's time to put it in the past where it belongs."

"Would you like for me to stay with you?" he asked softly.

"No, thank you. This is something I have to do for myself," she murmured and, seeing his reluctance to leave, said, "I'll be fine, Harvey. If I need you I'll ring."

"Very well, madam. I'll be in the kitchen," he answered, slipping back to a more formal manner.

Poor dear, she thought, *he still tries to protect me as he did when I was a girl.* She shrugged her shoulders as she turned the key slowly, only to have it stick halfway. She jiggled it and turned it again, this time with success. She flinched as the lock clicked and the door eased open.

The cool dampness hung like a curtain just inside and echoes from the past seemed to mingle with it. Taking a deep breath, she reached for the light switch beside the door. The room exploded in a brilliance of yellow, the light reflecting the sunny color of the furnishings. Her eyes swept over the dressing table with its flouncy eyelet skirt that held a vanity set made for little hands. A rocking chair sat idly in a corner, a doll perched against the arm as though making room for someone beside it.

Finally, Angelique's eyes came to rest on the bed. This was where her granddaughter had lain, coughing the last breath from her frail body. Tears filled her eyes and she no longer fought them back. *Have to get it out*, her mind repeated, *have to face it and be done with the grief.* After the tears were spent, she lay upon the bed and a young girl's voice rang clearly in her mind.

"Gran'ma, I'm gonna be eight tomorrow and Mommy said I could have a big girl's bed..."

Angelique closed her eyes and once again little Carrie was with her, dancing excitedly about the room, her long blond curls bouncing with every move. A week later Carrie had developed the whooping cough that took her life. Soon after that Caroline and John, Angelique's daughter and son-in-law, left for Europe, unable to live in the house with its memories.

Now Angelique was going to remember the good times, thankful she had Carrie, if only for a short time. A restful feeling ebbed within her and she said aloud, "Good, it is done. Good-bye, my darling." Peacefully she turned off the light, closed the door behind her, and returned to the library below.

Harvey was waiting with a glass of brandy when she came down the stairs. "I thought this might help, Miss Angelique."

"What would I have done without you all these years, Harvey? How long has it been now?"

"Forty years, madam," he answered with pride.

"That long. Where does the time go?" she sighed heavily. "I have a letter to write before I go to bed. Why don't you retire for the night? I don't think I'll need anything else."

CHAPTER 12

Jack Humboldt shifted uneasily on the hard bench, allowing him full view of the door. He hated these small-town police stations, but even worse he hated waiting for this conniving old biddie, Lizzie James. He should have had this business wrapped up and been on the train back to Oregon two days ago. If he hadn't put the pressure on her this morning, there was no telling how much longer he would have to spend in this one-horse town. Without her signature on the release forms, it would be his word against hers that she was dropping the kidnapping charges against Mrs. Martin's friend.

Where the devil is she? he muttered. The agreement had been they would meet at the police station at seven-thirty. He pulled the watch from his pocket…eight fifteen. Then his attention shifted back to the young police officer who had just answered the phone. Something in the conversation struck a nerve.

"Where did you say he was picked up?" Deputy Clark was asking. He glanced covertly at the detective then turned his back. "Yes, I will notify Mrs. James."

The detective didn't wait for the rest. He left the station with such speed it was as though he had disappeared into thin air. There was no point in trying to find out any information from the officer, because the whole department had been very closed-mouthed where he was concerned. His first step would be to call Mrs. Martin and inform her of the news. Then he would deal with Mrs. James.

"I thought you said she had dropped the charges," Angelique almost screamed into the phone. "How could you let this happen?"

"The old...er...Mrs. James kept putting off signing the papers, Mrs. Martin. I finally gave her an ultimatum this morning, and we were supposed to meet at the station an hour ago. That's how I happened to find out about the arrest. Besides, I thought he was staying put like I told him."

"Never mind, Mr. Humboldt, we don't have time to explain that right now. I want you to go back to your hotel. As soon as I hang up, I'll call my attorney and have him contact someone there. Give me a phone number where you can be reached."

Humboldt hung up the phone and gave himself a mental thrashing. In all his ten years working in this business, he had never slipped up like this. Every move he made was usually cool and calculated, leaving no room for error. He really believed he had scared Lizzie James with the threats of false accusations, liable and child abuse. It was probably this cornpone town...*No, Humboldt my boy, you are losing your touch. Put the blame where it belongs.*

🍁 🍁 🍁

"Mr. Humboldt," a woman's voice called, followed by pounding on his door. "There's a telephone call for you."

"Hm-mm. yeah, I'm coming," he groaned, as he groped in the dark for his trousers.

Mrs. Stevens stood in the hall, smudges of flour on her forehead and more on the apron tied around her rotund waist.

"What time is it, anyway?" he asked, aware of the darkness outside.

"Five-thirty and I have to get back to my cooking. I hope my breakfast isn't ruined while I've been standing here yelling my lungs out for you."

"Just put it on my bill, Mrs. Stevens. Now where can I take my call?"

"Down the hall yonder and to the left," she called over her shoulder, waddling back to the kitchen,

"Humboldt? Kerry Foster here," announced the voice at the other end. "Just got into town a few minutes ago. Been driving most of the night. Want you to meet me at the diner in fifteen minutes, and you can fill me in on all this mess over breakfast."

My kinda fella, the detective mused. *Doesn't waste words.* "Fifteen minutes it is," confirmed Humboldt and replaced the receiver on its hook. He ran a hand over his chin, feeling the growth of stubble; he wouldn't have time to shave.

Minutes later, Humboldt walked briskly toward the diner, pulling up the collar of his coat against the cold wind. It was an ungodly hour to be up, much less out walking, but he would have done anything to get this over with and return home. He could see the warm, inviting lights from the diner's windows just ahead and he quickened his pace. Wouldn't do to keep Foster waiting. As it was, he was ten minutes late and from the sounds of this man he was accustomed to punctuality.

There were very few people inside and it was easy to pick out the attorney. Foster sat at the far end of the room facing the door. He was a big man with unruly hair and a matching walrus mustache. Leafing through some papers, Foster glanced up when Humboldt entered the room. Deciding this was the man he was waiting for, he nodded.

"Have some coffee, Humboldt. Didn't think about you being without a car. Could have picked you up." Foster's voice boomed over the silence in the room. He signaled the waitress with an empty cup and continued, this time lowering his voice. "Order some breakfast, had mine already. Doctor put me on soft foods—stomach problems, you know. Didn't think runny, boiled eggs would be too appetizing for you this early in the morning. Sure isn't for me, anyway."

"No, thank you, I don't usually eat breakfast. The coffee will be fine," Humboldt answered, handing the menu back to the waitress.

Foster poured the hot tea from the pot sitting in front of him. "Now, tell me what kind of trouble we've got here.

Humboldt told the attorney Corey's story and, turning his notes over, he finished with what he had learned since his arrival. "This woman's very shrewd and I think the whole thing has been to cover her tracks. Here's the clincher; she has spent most of the money left for the child's care, at least the part she could get her hands on. There has been a property settlement, and I think she wants this girl back so she can get her hands on that, too."

"With all the information it should be easy enough to get her to drop the charges against Mr. Curruthers," the attorney began.

"She first agreed to it, but she has been dragging her feet. I think you are the edge we need."

"What about the—" he leafed through his papers—"child's uncle? What sort of fella is he?"

"Very controlled by his wife. She says jump and he doesn't even ask how high, he's so afraid of her. He keeps to himself so much it's difficult to find out anything about him, except those who know him seem to like him." Humboldt stopped speaking until the waitress poured more coffee and left. He cringed as he thought of this little man, so dominated by his wife that he had lost his identity. Humboldt had little or no tolerance for anyone who allowed himself to become a puppet.

"I think the next step is to pay these people a visit," Foster was saying. "Then we'll get Mr. Curruthers released." He took a cigar from his pocket, looked at it longingly, and started to put it away. Instead he shrugged and put it in his mouth. Striking a match, he touched it to the end of the cigar and puffed greedily. Then he leaned back and continued, "After we have arranged for the release of Mr. Curruthers, Mrs. Martin will be meeting him here for the next step to be taken in the interest of this little girl. In the meantime, I would like to have a copy of all your information that might be of help to us."

Humboldt drew out his watch and announced, "If we want to speak to Mr. and Mrs. James together, we'd best get over there before he leaves for work. As far as the information you require, I have made a copy for Mrs. Martin, which I am sure she would want you to have."

George James watched the two men coming up the walk and a frown etched tiny lines in his forehead. He recognized the detective right away, but the man with him was not familiar; furthermore, he did not care to meet him. George could guess why they were here and he swore beneath his breath. He thought, *If only...*, but wishing wouldn't accomplish a thing. He should have put his foot down a long time ago. The deed had been done by his wife and now, someway, somehow it had to be undone for everyone concerned.

"Good morning, Mr. Humboldt," George greeted, nodding to the attorney as he held the door open for them to enter. "Lizzie, we have company," he called to his wife.

Lizzie came in from the kitchen and stopped short when she saw the men. She had expected the detective, but not quite this early. She made no attempt to speak to either of them as she strode across the room and sat down in the rocking chair.

Mr. Foster introduced himself. "I have been retained by Mrs. Martin on the behalf of your niece and her friend, Mr. Andrew Curruthers. You know he is being held on kidnapping charges with which you have falsely accused him. It is my understanding that you were to drop those charges but as of yet have failed to sign the necessary release forms. Now, Mrs. James...Mr. James, unless these forms are signed immediately and my client is released, I have been instructed to bring charges against both of you for—" he referred to his notes—"child abuse, misappropriation of your niece's inheritance, false accusations against Mr. Curruthers...Shall I continue?"

"That won't be necessary, Mr. Foster." It was George who spoke and he avoided the stunned look on his wife's face. "We will go to the station as soon as I can inform my employer I will be late. Please convey my apologies to Mrs. Martin and Mr. Curruthers for allowing this thing to involve them. I can promise you my wife will cause no further problems."

"But…but…" Lizzie sputtered.

"Shut up, Lizzie!" George commanded.

"Your husband is wise, Mrs. James. Had this affair gone to court, he would likely lose his job and, more than likely, both of you would have lost your standing in the community, even if you didn't go to prison," Humboldt informed.

"Then we can expect you and your wife at the police station within the hour?" Foster asked.

George nodded and walked the two men to the front door. When they had left, he directed a warning look at his wife and ordered her to get ready.

Lizzie stomped down the hall to their bedroom. All was not lost. At least there was money coming from the sale of the house and the business, even if it did mean putting up with that brat again. Perhaps, after it was all over, she would get lucky and Corey would run away again. This time she would not have to fight to get her back, there would be no reason. She could put up with the brat until the money came through.

🍁   🍁   🍁

Angelique squeezed Corey's hand reassuringly as they stepped off the train in Naples. It had not been easy for the child to return and the only reason she had agreed was to see Andy again. There was also Angelique's word she would not have to stay with her aunt.

It was Corey who saw Andy first. She pulled her hand from Angelique's and ran to him, holding him tightly as tears streamed down her face. All her worries left when she saw for herself he was fine.

"How's my lil'est hobo doin'? Whar's thet dog o' yours? Didn't he come with you?" Andy asked, fighting back his own emotions.

"He's staying with Harvey 'til we get back. Oh, Andy, we missed you so…" and she buried her face in his neck, sobbing uncontrollably.

"Now, now, it's gonna be okay. Don't go messin' up thet purty lil face on my 'count. Here, wipe your nose," he smiled, offering her the handkerchief he had taken when they first met. They both looked at the handkerchief and began laughing, remembering the first time he said that to her.

On the way to the boarding house where they would be staying, Corey told Andy about the tramps she had met in the woods. He laughed heartily and slapped his knee when told how Lord Mayor and Injun had come to her rescue.

"Betcha them fellers ain't stopped runnin' yet," he laughed again. "Hafta do something special fer Injun and Lord Mayor next time I see them. Goin' to Floridy, was they?" He asked, staring out the window at the taxi, and everyone fell silent, afraid of what he might be thinking.

Corey looked out the window, too, thinking about the town. Outwardly it had not changed, but there was a difference. Perhaps it seemed smaller than she had remembered. It was not a bad town. In fact, if things had been different, she might have grown to love it. Although fall had stripped the velvety green from the rolling hills, there were still the pine trees for color and the air was filled with the earthy smells of fallen leaves that she loved.

There were some good memories here, too, the people who had become her friends and the special times she had shared with Tommy. She was eager to see him again, to tell him about her adventures and the places she had been since he had helped her get away. Maybe, after they got settled, she could go visit him and even take Andy to meet him. Now, she was beginning to feel excited about her return; she knew her aunt would not hurt her this time.

Corey's room, a duplicate of all the others, was sparsely furnished but clean. It had a brass bed, a chiffonier, and a ladder-back chair. The walls were covered with dull wallpaper, its design all but obliterated with age. A much-worn rug covered the middle of the floor, leaving a rich dark wood around the edge. A small cubbyhole covered by a drape served as the closet.

After Corey hung up the few clothes she had brought with her, she went to Angelique's room to ask permission to visit Tommy while Angelique had a meeting with the attorney and detective. The two men were already there when Corey knocked on the door and entered the room, causing an awkward silence.

"Of course, Corey, you may go. Will you need taxi fare?"

"No, ma'am, it's not that far and I would like to walk," Corey mumbled, embarrassed at having interrupted. She glanced at Andy sitting in the corner on the floor. She wanted to ask him along, but decided to wait until he wasn't busy.

"Be sure to be back for dinner at six, dear. Two hours will be enough time, won't it? Oh well, we have a couple of days here; at least you can see him again before we leave. Have a good time."

🍁 🍁 🍁

"Why, Corey dear, what a pleasant surprise," Mrs. Rice greeted when she opened the door. "I hardly recognized you. What have you done to yourself? You've cut your hair; that's it." Almost instantly Mrs. Rice bit her lip, thinking perhaps that had been part of Corey's ordeal at the hands of the kidnapper.

"Yes, ma'am, but it has grown back quite a bit," Corey answered, amused by the fact that, indirectly, Mrs. Rice had played a part in her hair cut. "Is Tommy here?"

"He was out back a few minutes ago. Let me call him for you."

"That's okay. I'll just go around there and find him. It was nice seeing you again, Mrs. Rice," Corey said politely as she turned from the door and started down the steps.

Tommy was feeding the chickens, and when he saw Corey, he threw the remaining grain on the ground, sending a whoop of surprise into the air.

"Corey!" Tommy exclaimed, "When did you get into town?"

"This afternoon. I just got my stuff unpacked and came right over." She grinned shyly at her friend. There was silence as Corey uneasily shifted from one foot to the other. Each was waiting for the other to speak.

Tommy scuffed at the dirt with the toe of his shoe and glanced around to see if everything was in order with the chickens.

"Well…hey, I have a picture of you in my room," he suddenly remembered the newspaper clipping. "Wait here while I go get it and you can tell me what happened."

"Sure," she answered as he ran for the house. There was something…why did she feel so uncomfortable with her friend? It had always been so easy before, their conversations coming free and unhampered. Why was it so difficult now?

Tommy returned with the picture, carefully unfolding it for her inspection. It was the first time she had seen it and, seeing the girl in the photograph, she felt detached as though looking at a stranger. So much had happened in that short time that it seemed an eternity ago.

"Tell me about it, Corey. What's it like to be a hero?" he coaxed. "Did you see the ocean? Tell me about the places you've been, starting with when you left my house that night. Oh, and how about this kidnapping thing?"

After Corey had answered all his questions, silence separated them again until she finally asked what he had been doing in her absence. He told her about the granddaddy frog he had caught that had won the frog-jumping contest, about the new place he had found to go crawdad fishing, and about his favorite teacher who had to quit to have her baby. Then silence again as they both stared into the distance, trying to think of more to say.

It wasn't going as she had expected at all and Corey longed to get back to the rooming house with Andy. She shifted her feet again and finally told Tommy she had to be going. He seemed relieved, too, and after a few mumbled words about his chores, they said their good-byes, with the promise they would see each other again before Corey left.

※   ※   ※

"Corey, dear, you are back so soon. I didn't think we would see you again until dinnertime," Angelique said with surprise and, seeing Corey's long face, asked, "What's wrong? Was he not there?"

"Oh, Angelique, it wasn't at all like I thought it would be. He's changed. Everything's changed," Corey cried.

Angelique put her arms around the young girl and soothingly replied, "But, Corey, perhaps it's you who have changed, not he. All the experiences you have been through these past months have forced you to grow up more rapidly. Don't be upset, dear," she consoled.

"Will we be going home soon, Angelique?" she sniffed. "I miss Muffin and there is nothing here for me anymore."

"Yes, dear, probably tomorrow, the day after at the latest. I had a good talk with Mr. Humboldt and Mr. Foster this afternoon, and we should be able to wrap this business up sooner than anticipated." Angelique smiled at Corey. "But you must see your young friend again. Give him another chance before we leave."

The next morning George and LIzzie James knocked on Angelique's door at precisely ten o'clock, the scheduled time of their appointment. Lizzie was annoyed and somewhat puzzled when the note had come for them to meet with Angelique. Perhaps she would be turning Corey over to them without a fight, but she was prepared should that not be the case.

"Good morning, Mr. and Mrs. James. Won't you come in?" Angelique greeted.

"Good morning, Mrs. Martin. I hope we haven't kept you waiting," returned George.

"No, as a matter of fact, you are right on time," and she directed them to a chair. "Now, Mr. James, I would like to speak to you about signing over the legal guardianship of Corey to me," Angelique began.

"Wait a minute," screeched Lizzie. "Did I hear you right? You want us to turn our niece over to you?"

"Hear me out," Angelique said, raising her hand to silence the woman. "I don't mean to adopt her. I realize you would want to keep the family name, but I want legal permission to rear Corey."

"Not on your life," interrupted Lizzie again. "We'll do nothing of the kind. I know what you're after. It's the money, isn't it? You want to get your hands on our money," she sneered, her eyes narrowing.

Angelique glared at Lizzie and when she spoke, her words were cold and steady, "I have more money than you could spend in the time you have left on Earth. It's the well-being of Corey with which I'm concerned and unless you have something important to say to me, keep your mouth shut."

A light flickered in Lizzie's greedy eyes at the mention of the money and the rest of Angelique's words were lost to her. An idea was forming in her mind and she spoke in her most cordial tone, "Well then, maybe we could make some sort of arrangement...I mean, if you take Corey...well, we will be losing out on the deal," she all but purred.

"What you are saying is that for a fee you will consider my request?" Angelique asked, not believing what the woman was implying.

Andy jumped from his chair, "I ain't never hit a woman afore, but they's a first time for everything. The very idee, sellin' your own kin..."

Angelique stepped in front of Andy, before he could get to Lizzie. "Andy, calm down. There's no need for violence, I'm sure we can settle this better if we remain calm."

"I ain't so sure o' thet, Angel. 'pears to me thet's all this here...woman... understands is violence, and money," he added and stormed at Lizzie. "Well, c'mon, I'll take you on. Whut's th' matter, ain't I th' right size?"

"That is enough, Andy. Maybe you had better wait in the other room."

"No, I ain't leavin' this here room," Andy barked and, seeing Angelique flinch at his harsh words, "Sorry, Angel. I ain't mad at you, it's jest that..."

"I know, old dear, I don't like the woman either, but she is of no importance right now. It's Mr. James that has to make the decision." Angelique and Andy turned to George, who sat in the corner watching the whole scene in silent horror. "Well, Mr. James, what about it? We love Corey very much and I think she loves us, too. I haven't heard your wife mention the word *love* once since we have been discussing this, or isn't it important in the rearing of a child?"

"Before I make a commitment one way or the other, I want to speak to my niece…alone," George answered softly.

"Of course. She's in the parlor just down the hall with my attorney. Go down there and tell him I would like to speak to him and you can be alone."

Once Mr. Foster had left the room, George turned to his niece. "Corey…I don't know where to begin," George stammered. "I truly regret that I was never close to your father and I hardly know you. Up until now I have allowed nothing but pain to come into your life and I'm sorry for that." He glanced around the room, avoiding her eyes, then chose a chair, and sat down. "Your friends think a lot of you, Corey, so much so they have asked me to let you live with them."

"What did you say to that, Uncle George?" Corey asked anxiously.

"I haven't told them anything yet. I wanted to talk with you before I gave them my answer. You see, Corey, I want to be sure I'm making the right decision this time. I've really messed our lives up by turning my back and trying to pretend relations were good between you and Lizzie. Well, that's only half true, really. I was afraid of your aunt and it was easier for me to close my eyes than face the conflict with her."

"And you're not afraid of her now?"

"I'm working on it, Corey, I'm working on it," he smiled wearily. "Tell me about your friends out there."

Corey talked for some time about Andy, about Angelique, her house, and Harvey, and, as her uncle watched the light dance in her eyes, he felt a twinge of envy that these strangers meant so much to her and he was so distant. If he had only reacted differently, perhaps he would have his niece's adoration instead of the hobo and his life would finally have some meaning. Was it too late? Would he gain favor with Corey if he signed those papers, letting her go with the people she loved? Or did he dare think he could keep her and Lizzie would mend her ways? *Yeah,* he smirked silently, *and the devil sells ice cream cones in hell.*

George knew what had to be done, what would be best for his niece. It was facing Lizzie that bothered him now. He sighed and turned to his niece, realizing she had stopped talking and was waiting for him.

"Corey, if I do this, I mean, if I give my permission for you to live with Mrs. Martin, would you...*er*...could you write to me from time to time?" He spoke with great difficulty, finally bowing his head and absently picking at his fingernails as he always did when retreating from a situation.

"I would like a second chance at being your uncle. If you were to write, well, through our correspondence perhaps we could get to know one another a little better...even see each other again sometime. Would you consider the possibility, Corey?" he asked hopefully.

"What about Aunt Lizzie?"

"I'll handle the old goat," he said without thinking.

Seeing the startled expression on her uncle's face when he realized what he had said, Corey began laughing. George joined in, grateful for the release of the tension that had dominated their reunion. He reached for Corey, who was now standing beside him, and gave her a joyful hug. He was caught up in the moment and allowed the invisible barrier that shielded his feelings to drop. The moment was passing, though, and he awkwardly released her.

"Yes, Uncle George, I'll write to you and I would like very much to see you again. Does this mean you are going to let me live with Angelique and Andy then?" Her voice rose in anticipation.

"Isn't that what you want?"

"Oh, yes...nothing against you, but..."

"I understand, Corey, and I think it will be best for you, to be where you are loved and wanted. I wish I could say it would be different if you stayed here, but we both know that is not possible." George stood up, bringing their discussion to a close. "Now, I must go back into the lion's den, so to speak, and face what awaits me there. Remember what I said about staying in touch," he reminded her as he walked across the room, suddenly an old man.

"How'd you get the goods on th' old bat?" Andy whispered to the detective as he watched Lizzie shifting uneasily in her chair. He was enjoying watching her squirm while her husband was with Corey.

"It was quite easy to find out about the money," explained Humboldt, "a copy of the will is on record, there in Oklahoma where Corey's family lived. Then I came here and talked to some people about Mrs. James, her relationship with the child, and various other points. In a town this size everybody knows everybody's business and there is always one or two people willing to discuss it with you.

"When I found out that bank clerks don't make a lot of money, I knew why Mrs. James was so adamant about having the child back. One visit to her house with all the new furnishings…well, it was obvious what she had been using to buy these things. Of course, the property settlement was what she really had her eye on, and as you know, that is why she was so determined to get her hands on Corey."

Humboldt drummed his fingers on the chair, emphasizing his discontent with this assignment. He disliked this cunning woman across from him for putting a nick in his otherwise efficient job. But for her delay, he would be on his way home.

The door opened and George entered the room with everyone's eyes on him. He gave a nod of silent approval to Angelique, not trusting his voice to speak without emotion getting the best of him.

Lizzie was out of her chair immediately. "Oh no you don't," she snarled, "I have some say in this, too."

George turned effortlessly to face his wife. "You sit down and shut up. You lost your say the first time you raised a hand to my niece. If I have any further trouble out of you, I will let these people have you locked up. It would almost be worth my going to jail, too." His tone had a deadly ring and he stood firmly, staring directly into her eyes; then he turned back to Angelique. "What now?"

"My attorney tells me the next step is to have this legally documented in court, but there should be no problem since both parties are in agreement." Angelique glanced at Lizzie who was now cowering in a corner unable to believe what had just transpired.

"Very well, if you do not need my services any further today, I shall go to work." Turning to Lizzie, he said, "Are you coming…dear?" The term of endearment he used mockingly.

Lizzie stood up, eyes downcast, and brusquely walked out of the door, giving George an opportunity to have a last word with Angelique.

"I would like to hear about my niece's progress if you don't mind, I am not totally without feelings for her no matter what you might think." He nodded to the men in the room and followed his wife down the hall. For a minute, he stood looking in the direction where he had left Corey and then strode silently from the boarding house, tears brimming in his eyes.

CHAPTER 13

A week had passed since their return to Oregon and life was almost back to normal; everything that is, except for Andy. He paced the floors with a vengeance, withdrawing from those he loved. Angelique watched sadly, for she knew what was coming. She thought of Corey, knowing she must prepare the child.

Angelique turned her face to the window so that Andy would not see the tears, and she let them flow freely. Best to get the weeping out of the way before she had the talk with Corey. Through her tears she could see the girl out by the pond and she watched her play. At least this time he would be leaving something behind to guarantee his return. She took the handkerchief tucked inside the sleeve of her blouse and dried her eyes. It was time to have her talk while Corey was still outside and they would not be disturbed.

Corey waved to Angelique as she came across the yard but dropped her hand to her side as Angelique came closer. Something was wrong, Angelique had been crying.

"Corey dear, may I speak with you a moment?"

"Yes, ma'am," Corey answered, putting the fishing pole upon the ground. Something in Angelique's voice and the expression on her face caused Corey grave concern. "What's wrong, Angelique?"

"Let's go sit on that bench over there," Angelique suggested, postponing her answer.

Corey directed a worried glance at the house. What had happened in there? Had she and Andy been fighting, and if so, why would she discuss it with her?

"As you have probably noticed, Corey, Andy has been…well, different lately," she paused to let Corey think about her observation, "I think he is ready to leave, but is afraid he will hurt us. Corey, we have to tell him it is all right and make him know we mean it." There, it was out, straight and to the point.

"I can't. I don't want him to go," Corey began crying. "He's got everything he needs right here. Why does he have to go?"

Angelique stared at the house and sighed, "He has everything but the freedom he wants and needs. He is like a fish out of water gasping for breath." She studied the face of the child before her. The next statement was made for her own assurance more than Corey's. "Sometimes you have to let the one you love go to keep him, Corey. Andy will die little by little if we keep him here. Love him enough to let him go. I did before and I can again." She saw the astonished look on Corey's face. "Yes, I knew he was leaving that time, long ago, probably before he even knew it himself. You see, when a woman loves a man as I loved Andy, she knows things without being told. It's hard to explain, but one day, Corey..." and she left the rest unspoken.

Corey was thinking about that terrible day she and Andy had been asked to leave the cafe because of those awful people. Andy's words came back to her as vividly as though he were speaking them now...

'I be whut I be 'cuz I want to, Corey, and some people git jealous, 'cuz deep down thet's whut they wanna be...free'.

Corey wanted Andy back, the Andy who bellowed out a laugh all the way from his toes. She wanted the mischievous twinkle back in his eyes. The only way to accomplish that was to do what Angelique had said. Perhaps in knowing he would be happy again, the pain she felt would not be as great...at least, she would keep reminding herself of that when he had gone. But the mere thought unleashed a torrent of tears. Corey left Angelique sitting on the bench and ran into the woods.

Angelique did not pursue Corey; she knew the child would be back with the worst part behind her. Strange how much alike she and Corey were. They sought the same solitude when troubled, and both were from hardy stock, being able to bounce back easily enough. At times Angelique could almost predict what Corey was thinking or what the child was going to do next, an awareness she had been unable to share with her own daughter.

Caroline had been her father's daughter, and their relationship had been so strong Angelique was unable to penetrate it. He had spoiled her irreparably; even to this day, Angelique could not get along with her daughter for any length of time.

An icy wind stirred Angelique from her musing. She pulled her coat more securely about her and stood up, preparing herself for Andy. Now she had to release him from the bond he felt holding him here. Tomorrow was Thanksgiving and she would convince him to stay for the holiday.

The kitchen was bustling with activity and filled with the aroma of pies and breads being baked for tomorrow. Mrs. Johnston, the cook, was giving orders to her newly hired helper and even Harvey had been recruited as Angelique came inside for a cup of tea before joining Andy. Wishing not to disturb anyone, she began filling the teapot when Harvey dropped what he was doing and came to her aid.

"I'll do that, madam," he offered, breathing a sigh of relief at the welcome interruption from what he considered 'women's work'. "Where do you wish this served?"

"In the library, Harvey, and if you see Mr. Curruthers, please ask him to join me there."

"Will the madam be requiring anything else?" He asked hopefully and turned his back against the cook's glare.

"No, that will be all, Harvey," she tossed over her shoulder as she left the kitchen.

Andy turned from the window when Angelique entered the room and asked, "Whut happened to rile Corey up?"

"I told her you would be leaving us."

"Whut made you say thet, Angel? I ain't said nuthin' 'bout leavin'." He turned slowly back to the window. "She takin' it purty hard?"

"She'll get over it; we both will. What we can't handle is your unhappiness, and we've decided the lesser of the two evils was letting you go. All I ask is that you stay through the holiday. Will you do that, Andy, for us?"

"How long've you knowed?" he sighed.

"I've suspected it since our return, but the real acceptance came today. I guess I wasn't ready to let you go before.'

"And 're you now?"

"Let's say I'm as ready as I will ever be, but that is neither here nor there. Will you wait until Thanksgiving is over?"

"Yeah," he sniffed the air and grinned, "I wouldn't miss all them goodies bein' cooked out yonder in th' kitchen." Then, on a more serous note, "I'd best go see if'n Corey's awright and mebbe have a lil chat whilst we're out thar. Oh, and Angel…thanks. Mebbe I picked th' right name fer you after all," he grinned, winked around the door at her, and left.

Muffin saw Andy before Corey did and trotted happily over to greet him. Andy squatted beside the dog, scratching him on the head, and giving Corey time to dry her eyes before he joined her. "Hey thar, fella, been keepin' our gal comp'ny, have you?" he murmured, watching Corey over the dog's head. What was he going to say to her? He had been up against a lot of tough situations, but this was by far one of the worst—except for the time he left Angelique. *Thar you go*, he thought, *wimen could sure make life hard fer a feller. Ain't' no use pondering on it, though, best jump right in with both feet.*

Andy went over to Corey and eased down beside her, propping his back against the tree. He picked up a pine needle and chewed silently on it, feeling the sharp yet sour bite on his tongue as it released its juices. Neither said a word for a few minutes until the cold crept over Andy, causing him to shiver.

"Downright nippy, ain't it?" He asked, wrapping his arm around her shoulder. "Wanna keep an old 'bo from freezin'?"

With that she threw her arms around him and buried her face in his shoulder. "I'm gonna miss you, Andy," she cried.

"Whoa, girl, it ain't like I wasn't gonna be back, you know. Why, this country ain't big enough to keep us apart fer very long at a time. Whut with all th' things Angel has planned fer you, you'll barely have time to miss me afore I'll be back agin."

"When will that be, Andy? When will you be coming back to see us?"

"Prob'ly when school's out, then you'll have time fer th' likes o' me," he answered, wiping the tears from her cheeks.

Corey sat a moment, a plan taking shape in her mind. "Could we take a trip together this summer? I mean, school will be out for a vacation then and maybe we could go see Gus and Nanette. Can we do that, Andy? Like old times?"

"You mean ride th' rails together agin? I dunno…Angel would prob'ly have a fit. She can be a downright ornery cuss when she wants to be," he laughed, but he knew Corey was serious and would not give up without an answer. "We'll talk about it. That's all I can promise right now, child. Now, whut's say we go up to th' house and see can we sneak something to eat outta th' kitchen?"

"Where do you think you will go from here, Andy?" Corey asked as they walked toward the house.

"Dunno, prob'ly find work somewheres till th' winter is over. Come th' first warm spell and I'll be movin' agin. Don't you worry yore purty lil head none, Andy's gonna be fine."

"I know, I just wanted to be able to picture the places you would be going and what you were doing. I'll just have to imagine all kinds of adventures for you."

"Prob'ly be better'n whut I be doin' anyways," he laughed and they walked into the warm kitchen to argue the cook out of something to eat.

Andy left the day following Thanksgiving amid tears and promises to return in the summer. The big house seemed to echo the silence and emptiness, and Corey was relieved to have her venture back to school to keep her mind occupied. It wasn't easy starting a new school again, especially since she began later than most of the students.

She kept to herself during the free periods, spending her noon hour in the classroom eating the lunch Cook had prepared and using the extra time to catch up on her studies. It was during one of these voluntary seclusions, two weeks after she entered school, that she heard the sound of weeping coming from the coatroom. Someone had entered the door leading in from the playground and, from the sound of it, was deeply troubled.

Corey tried to concentrate on the book in front of her, not wishing to intrude on the person's privacy, but to no avail. The sounds of the weeping grew stronger and Corey could no longer ignore the distress. She closed the book, quietly making her way through the maze of chairs, and knocked softly at the door.

"Are you okay?"" she called through the door.

"*Oui*...yes," a girl's voice answered, "please do not bother about me; it is not necessary."

Corey eased the door open and peered into the darkness but could not discern the girl from the shadows. "Sometimes it helps to talk to someone, but if you don't feel like it that's okay. Maybe later..." Corey offered and turned to leave.

"*Merci*...thank you," the girl sniffed and began crying once more.

Corey returned to her seat, opened her book to resume studying, but her curiosity got the better of her. She closed the book and listened more intently. The girl had concluded her crying with a very determined blow of her nose and presently appeared at the door. She was about the same height and build as Corey, with dark hair and deep blue eyes reddened by weeping. Like Corey she, too, was new at the school, having started a week later.

"Would you like a piece of my apple? Cook always fixes a big lunch for me and I never finish it."

"If you are sure you do not want it..." the girl answered slowly. "I leave my...uh...lunch outside. You are a new student, also?"

"Yeah, I started just before you did. I missed a lot of school and I've been trying to catch up," Corey said, indicating the book in front of her. "By the way, my name is Corey. What's yours?"

"Hello, Corey, my name is Francoise Bernard."

"Fran…er, do you mind if I just call you Francie? It's much easier for me."

"*Oui*…yes, but I would like it very much…Francie." she mused, "Yes, I like it very much."

"What are you studying? Perhaps I could help you. I have had much of what we are studying right now back in New York," Francie continued.

"Is that where you are from?"

Francie bowed her head and spoke in a barely audible voice, "No, I was born in France. My family moved to America two years ago when my father was sent here for his work. He is a geologist." Her voice was filled with apprehension and she turned her face away from Corey, fearing new torments.

"What's wrong, Francie? Are you unhappy because you had to leave your home? Is that why you were crying a while ago?"

"No, I was very…how do you say…excited about coming to America. It is the other children; they were calling me names. 'A…a snail-eating foreigner'," and once again tears brimmed her eyes.

"Oh, don't worry about them, they're probably just jealous," soothed Corey. "Besides, everyone has to come from somewhere, and I think it's great that you came all the way from France. Why, you have been on a ship and traveled across the ocean! I bet not many of them have even been outta this town. And you can speak two languages. I have trouble with one," Corey spoke with excitement filling her voice. How she would love to see all the places Francie had been.

"My friend, Andy, says everybody had to come from someplace else 'cept for the American Indians and that is what makes our country so great—so many different people with different ways. Why, I have a friend from Ireland and I love to hear him talk about his homeland. So don't let those dumb kids bother you, okay?"

Francie wiped her eyes with the back of her hand and smiled at Corey. "*Oui*…yes, I will not let them bother me. What they say is true. I am a foreigner and, in my country, we do eat snails," she answered in a matter-of-fact tone. Seeing Corey grimace, she added, "But they are considered a delicacy, *ma amie*. It is just the way those children were saying this that caused me unhappiness, but I will not listen the next time."

"What did you call me?"

"*Ma amie*...my friend. You will be my friend, will you not?"

"That is nice...*ma amie*," Corey repeated the words. "Yes, although I thought I already was your...*amie*," she laughed. "Now how about that help you talked about?"

❦   ❦   ❦

"*Bonjour,* Corey, *comment allez-vous*...how are you?" Francie's voice came excitedly over the phone.

"Francie! When did you get back?" Corey squealed. She had truly missed her friend the past two weeks. Francie had been in New York with her parents.

"*Tout a l'heure...excusez-moi,* I have been speaking nothing but French since last I saw you and I forget myself. We returned a little while ago. How was your holiday?"

"All right, but Andy did not get home for Christmas like I hoped he would and, with you gone, I kinda got bored. How was New York?"

"It was the same as I had left it and, like you, I too got bored, It is such a big city and everyone is in such a hurry to get somewhere they do not notice you. It is good to get back."

"Would your parents let you come over? I mean, since you just got home and all..."

"*Bien sur*...of course, I will come over soon. I have something exciting to tell you," Francie giggled into the phone.

"Please hurry, then, I'll be waiting by the front gate," Corey prompted.

Corey paced the floor to pass the fifteen minutes it would take for Francie to travel to her house. She wondered what the news was going to be. Were they going back to France? Is that why she was so happy? Before the trip to New York, there had been rumors Mr. Bernard would be finishing his work here soon, but would Francie be that happy about leaving? Maybe, in her excitement, she had not thought of leaving Corey.

Everything had been going so well. She loved living with Angelique, the school was working out better all the time, and her new friendship with Francie...

The anticipation finally got to Corey and she bundled herself up, called Muffin and headed down the driveway to the front gate. The powdery blanket of snow crunched beneath her feet as she walked and Muffin hopped uncertainly behind her, not really sure he liked the cold, wet stuff. The sun had finally come out, causing Corey to squint as she looked down the road to catch a glimpse of Francie, but there was no one around.

It seemed as though all sound had been muffled by the snow, leaving an almost deafening silence. Again Corey was faced with the thought her friend might be leaving and by the time she saw the car coming her stomach was churning with apprehension.

"*Bonjour, ma amie*, I am sorry it took so long, but I forgot we still had to remove some things from the automobile," Francie explained breathlessly. "O-o-o, *mon petite* Muffin. are you not cold?" she cooed to the little dog, bending down to scratch behind his ears.

"Francie, if you came to tell me you are moving back to France, I don't want to hear it. We'll just not talk about it until it happens, okay?" Corey blurted out, unable to wait for her friend to speak.

"Oh, *je suis desole*…I'm sorry, is that what you were thinking?" Francie asked. "It is quite the opposite, *ma amie*. My father has applied for a permanent position here in America. That is one reason we went to New York, and also to arrange passage for my mother and me back to France this summer. As soon as school is dismissed, we will be going back to get my brother and our possessions we had to leave behind. While we are gone, my father will find a house we can buy."

"You never told me you had a brother, Francie."

"No? He has been in—how do you say?—uh, academy for boys, but since we are going to stay here, my mother wants him here with us."

"And while you are in France I will be traveling with Andy! We will have so much to talk about when you return." Laughing happily and clasping hands, the two girls danced in a circle.

CHAPTER 14

"Good morning, birthday girl," Angelique greeted Corey happily, balancing the breakfast tray on one arm. "I thought I would have to drag you from the bed, but I see you are way ahead of me."

"Do you think Andy will be here today? He did promise to come when school was out and it's been a whole week now. He will remember this is my birthday, won't he?" Corey asked hopefully.

"I'm sure he will remember, dear, and if at all possible he wouldn't miss it for the world. Remember this, though, he might have a long distance to travel," and Angelique laughed. "The way he travels could take a while, too. But don't fill your pretty head with unhappy thoughts, because today is reserved only for happy ones.

"Now, Corey dear, one word of caution. The kitchen and dining rooms are off-limits for a while. We wouldn't want to upset Cook and Harvey's surprise." She winked and placed the tray on Corey's desk. "Eat your breakfast and I will see you later. I have a few chores to do myself."

"Angelique, if Andy comes will you let me know right away?"

"The very minute," she called over her shoulder on the way out the door.

The morning went slowly for Corey with no sign of Andy. She felt a sense of uneasiness, thinking Andy would not come. Had he just told her he would come back to make parting easier? She glanced at the clock and sighed…twelve-thirty, and the party was at two.

"Corey, there's a phone call for you," Angelique summoned from the library. "It's long distance, so hurry."

Corey's heart jumped to her throat. Andy wasn't going to make it! Would he also tell her their trip was off? Why did the ones she loved most always leave her, she cried under her breath as she forced herself toward the phone.

"Happy birthday, Corey!" Tommy's voice sang through the receiver.

"Tommy! Oh, thank you, Tommy!" Corey almost sobbed into the phone, relieved to hear his voice instead of Andy's.

"Are you having a party? What's it like out there? Are you coming back for the summer?" Tommy asked quickly, as his mother's voice prompted him to be quick with his conversation.

"Yes, later, and the weather is beautiful out here, just right for fishing. What's it like out there?"

"The same. Are you coming out this summer?" he repeated.

"I don't think so, Tommy, maybe another time. By the way, I got your letters and I sent one off to you the other day, you should be getting it soon…"

"Tommy, don't be much longer on that phone," Mrs. Rice's voice urged.

"I'll be looking for your letter, Corey, and happy birthday again. I have to hang up, but before I do I have to tell you that your Uncle George said to tell you he misses you and so do I. Try to come back to see us soon, please?"

"I miss you, too, and tell Uncle George I sent him a letter with yours. Will you take it to him?"

"Yes, I will. I have to go now. Good-bye, Corey."

"Good-bye, Tommy, and thanks again."

Corey smiled as she hung up the phone. She was glad Angelique had insisted she go back to see her friend before they left Naples. It had been a much better visit and he got to meet Andy. Afterward, his letters had kept their friendship going and he kept her informed about what was going on back there. Perhaps, one day, she would go back to visit, but now the pain was still too fresh.

Angelique helped Corey into her new white dress and tied its blue sash about her waist. She brushed Corey's dark hair, which had grown long again, away from her face and placed two blue satin ribbons on either side.

"I want you to look especially nice for the photographer, Corey, so try to keep from mussing your hair until he has finished." She opened the case on her brooch, looking at the tiny watch inside. "One-fifteen. He should be here anytime."

Corey stood in front of the mirror after Angelique left, studying her reflection. She would have been more comfortable in her regular clothes, but there was something about the way she looked all dressed up…a feeling she could not explain stirred within her. But there was no time to dwell on it, the photographer would soon be here, and Corey wanted to check to see if Andy had arrived.

Harvey was escorting a man into the parlor when Corey came down the stairs. She eased her way through the photographer's equipment stacked in the hallway.

"Harvey, has Andy come yet?"

"No, Miss Corey, I haven't seen him," and, seeing the dismay on her face, he added, "But it is early yet, so don't you worry."

Corey went into the parlor and watched as the camera was set up. Chairs had been brought in and placed around the room to accommodate her guests, and flowers from the garden had been arranged in vases, filling the room with their fragrance. The chair Corey was to occupy sat apart from the others by the window.

The guests arrived, pictures were taken, and all the while Corey kept a vigil near the window. Mechanically, she took part in the games and opened her gifts, trying to show the proper enthusiasm. Then it was time to move to the dining room for cake and ice cream.

Streamers were hung about the room and a large banner proclaimed a brightly painted wish for a happy birthday. The lights were lowered as the last child took her place and Cook wheeled a cart through the door carrying the large cake. Eleven candles stood firmly in the pink sugar roses around the perimeter of the cake and the tiny flames danced with the movement of the cart.

"Make a wish, Corey, and blow out all the candles," Angelique instructed while the children sang happy birthday.

Corey took a deep breath, closed her eyes, and blew until there was no breath left in her, extinguishing all the candles. Slowly, she opened her eyes and breathed a sigh of relief when she saw the deed was accomplished. It was a silly superstition, but deep down she truly believed that had one candle remained lit, her wish would not be granted. Now that they were all out, Andy had to come today.

🍁   🍁   🍁

Angelique bent over Corey and shook her gently. A tear glistened in the corner of her eye, breaking loose and trickling down her cheek as she stirred from her sleep.

"Is he here?" Corey asked drowsily, rubbing her eyes.

"No, dear, not yet, but it is way past your bedtime and you've had a busy day."

"Couldn't I wait a few more minutes? I know he will be here. I just know he will. Please, Angelique?"

"I'll make a deal with you, you go to bed and I promise to wake you the minute he gets here. Okay?"

"You promise?" Corey asked hesitantly.

"Cross my heart."

Corey sank into a fitful sleep, tossing about the bed and dreaming crazy dreams. Suddenly she sat upright in her bed. "He's here. Andy is here," she sang aloud.

"You betcha I'm here, kid. Ain't nuthin' gonna keep me from my lil hobo on her birthday," a voice answered in the darkness.

"Andy!" Corey cried, groping blindly until she found him and threw her arms around his neck. "Tell me you are not another one of my dreams."

"You ain't dreamin', kid, it's me right enough, but you'd best loosen your grip or you'll make me into a ghost," he laughed. "Whut say we git a little light on th' subject here? I can't see a blasted thing."

Corey fumbled until she found the chain on her bedside lamp and both blinked against the sudden burst of light. Andy was in the same state of disorder as when Corey had first met him and she scolded him for not taking better care of himself.

"I ain't had much time fer thet nonsense th' past few days, kid. I been tryin' to git here on yer birthday. Now don't you be givin' me none o' your sass. I know'd it'd been awful peaceful whilst I was away fer some reason," he laughed and shook his head at Corey. "Why don't you git yourself outta thet bed and come downstairs whilst I have some o' thet cake o' your'n. I might jest have a surprise fer you."

Corey grabbed her robe and trotted anxiously down to the kitchen with Andy, prodding him all the way to reveal the surprise. When they opened the door, Injun and Lord Mayor grinned sheepishly at her from the table.

"Happy birthday, Corey," they greeted in unison.

"Injun, Lord Mayor! How...oh, this is the best surprise. Where did you find them, Andy?"

"Can't git shed o' bad pennies. They jest keep on turnin' up. I heard they was lookin' fer help at this here mine in Arizony and when I went thar, who do

I see but them two. They didn't go to Floridy after all. So's when we finished at th' mine they jest kinda tagged along with me here."

"I'm glad they did," Corey beamed, hugging them tightly. "Are you going with us to see Gus? Oh, please say you will, I know you will love it there, won't they, Andy?"

"Whoa, kid, you be talkin' so fast a feller can't git a word in edgeways. I rekin it be up to them if'n they wanna go or not."

"Is someone going somewhere?" Angelique asked, coming through the door as Andy finished speaking.

"When Andy left he promised to come back when school was out and take me to see Gus and Nanette. It will be like old times, Angelique, riding the rails and cooking over an open fire again…I can go, can't I, please, Angelique?"

Angelique sat quietly for a minute, looking from Andy to Corey. Her stomach churned at the thought of Corey tramping across the countryside and meeting up with…heaven only knew what. She was remembering the meeting Corey had had with the tramps and her narrow escape. Her first inclination was to say no, but how could she disappoint Corey when the child had so eagerly awaited Andy's return and probably for this very reason.

"Let me think about it, Corey, it's somewhat of a shock to me right now. In the meantime I think you should get back to bed and try to get some sleep, or you will be worthless in the morning. I should say, this morning," she added, looking at her watch. "It's one-thirty, so off to bed with you."

Corey unwillingly shuffled off to bed and Andy stood to leave, but a sharp glance from Angelique caused him to ease back into the chair.

Angelique listened for Corey's footsteps on the stairs, and then she turned to Andy, "Why didn't you tell me you were going to promise this trip to Corey?"

"It jest slipped out whilst I was talking to her thet day. I figgered it'd cheer her up some and it did."

"Why didn't you discuss it with me before you left? At least I would have been prepared for it better than just having it thrown at me," Angelique glared at Andy. "You know I can't allow her to just wander across country like that…"

"Why not? Thet be th' way we come here, if'n you 'member. 'Sides, Corey's a big girl," Andy interrupted.

"Precisely why I can't allow it. If she was a boy it might be different, but you know what kind of lunatics are running around out there."

"Now, Angel, you know we ain't gonna let nuthin' happen to Corey. They be three o' us to keep her from gettin' in trouble," Andy soothed while Injun and Lord Mayor nodded in agreement.

Angelique studied the situation carefully before giving her final comment. "The only way I will consider this trip is to purchase a ticket to Flagstaff on the train and that way I know she will get there safely. That cabin in the mountains will afford her all the camping out she wants."

"Aw, Angel, thet ain't the idee. She wants to be a 'bo again liken her friends here. It'll probab'ly be the last time fer her. Come on, what you say?"

"Andy, I lost one child I loved dearly and I can't afford to take the chance on losing another. Please do it my way?" She begged, tears filling her eyes.

Injun and Lord Mayor shifted uncomfortably in their chairs while Andy put his arm around Angelique's shoulders, assuring her they would do as she asked. "Come on, Angel, dry them purty eyes o' your'n. Ain't nothin' gonna take Corey from you. Hesh now." When she had composed herself he said, "Time fer turnin' in, too. Me'n the boys gonna camp in the woods the rest o' the night. Tell Corey we'll see her in the mornin'."

Corey was distraught at the idea of having to take the train the regular way, but Angelique stood firm. To make matters worse, they were told at the train depot that Muffin would have to be confined in a box in the baggage compartment. It was only after Corey was convinced she would be able to check on her dog whenever she wanted that she finally agreed, but she vowed the trip back would be different.

They arrived in Flagstaff early the third day and began the trek to the cabin immediately. By the time they reached the general store, Corey was much too excited to eat and kept after the men until they gulped down the can of beans they had bought. Again they traveled until just at sunset they reached that bend in the trail that obscured the cabin. Corey remembered that bend when she had lost sight of Gus standing on the porch waving to them as they left. Now she ran ahead feeling a sudden burst of energy, only to stop in her tracks as she turned the bend.

The cabin door stood open, a gaping hole that seemed to be crying out in protest against the emptiness. Everything was in a state of disrepair. The corral on which Andy and Gus had worked so hard now stood vacant with parts of it lying on the ground. Everywhere there was an abundance of overgrown weeds.

What had happened to Gus? Where had the animals gone, and Nanette? Something was terribly wrong. Gus would never give up this place otherwise. Perhaps they would know at the general store, Corey thought, and turned to find Andy standing behind her he, too, in a stunned silence.

"We have to go back to the store and find out what has happened here, Andy," Corey cried.

"It'll be dark soon, Corey girl, and mebbe we oughta stay here fer th' night. We can start out at first light…one more night ain't gonna hurt."

Corey looked at the cabin and said, "I can't sleep here, Andy. Couldn't we start back and when it gets too dark we could camp on the trail?"

"I suppose," Andy relented and the others silently agreed with him.

The next morning they were waiting on the porch when the store opened.

"Mister, can you tell me what happened to Mr. Gus Thatcher…th' feller thet lives 'bout four miles back a ways? Useta pick up his mail here," Andy asked the man behind the counter.

"Thatcher…Thatcher," the man repeated, rubbing his chin. "Oh yes, his family came and got him eight, maybe nine months ago. He took sick one day, right here in the store. His daughter took him back with her."

"D'ya know how we can git in touch with this here daughter?"

The man eyed Andy suspiciously. "Are you friends of Mr. Thatcher?"

"We stayed with him last summer fer a while and we come all th' way from Oregon to see him. Th' child was brokenhearted when we found th' place empty."

"Well, they did leave an address so I could forward his mail. Just a minute and I will find it for you."

"Mister, do you know what happened to his animals?" Corey asked.

"No, don't rightly know about that," he answered and, finding the address, he wrote it on a piece of paper for them.

"Do you know where this here town be?"

"It's about forty or fifty miles northwest of here. I'll show you on the map."

🍁 🍁 🍁

"This is it, Andy. It's the same address, but it doesn't look as though anyone is at home," Corey said, trying to keep the disappointment out of her voice as she compared the numbers on the small white cottage with those on the paper she held.

"Best way to find out is to go knock on the door," Andy answered, then turned to Lord Mayor and Injun. "Mebbe you'd best wait here till we find out. Ain't no sense scarin' anybody with all o' us traipsin' to th' door."

Corey knocked timidly on the wooden screen door while Andy stood behind her. There was no sound except for the humming of bees round the morning glory vine draped across the front porch. Again she knocked, this time more boldly and the clatter started a dog barking behind the house. Other dogs joined in, causing the neighbors to pull back their curtains and peer at the intruders suspiciously.

"No one is home. Maybe we..." Corey was stopped by the sound of footsteps inside the house and turned back as the door opened.

"Yes?" the young woman called irritably and, seeing Andy, she closed the door until she could barely see around it. "What do you want?"

"We're lookin' fer Gus Thatcher, ma'am. This be whar he lives, ain't it?"

"Who are you and how do you know my father?"

"My name's Andy and this here be Corey. We stayed with your pa fer a while last summer in th' mountains."

The woman was silent for a moment while she thought about what he said. A glimmer of recognition crossed her face and she opened the door wider. "Yes, I remember Father writing about your visit. Please forgive me, but I have been up most of the night with the baby. Won't you come in?"

Corey and Andy stood awkwardly in the middle of the parlor watching the woman flit around the room picking up a newspaper strewn on the sofa and a half-filled cup of coffee from the table in front of it.

"I'm afraid I haven't had time to tidy up since my husband left for work," she apologized. "Have a seat and I'll make a fresh pot of coffee."

"We don't aim to put you out none, ma'am..." Andy started.

"It's no problem, really. Just make yourselves comfortable and I'll be right back. Would you like something to drink, Corey?"

"No, ma'am," Corey answered politely.

When the woman returned, she had hastily changed from her robe into an ill-fitting dress which strained across the rounded little stomach still left after the birth of her child. Her rich, brown hair had been tied securely behind her head with a yellow ribbon to match her dress. Semicircles of blue shadows lay beneath the crisp, gray eyes, attesting to her sleepless night.

"I didn't even introduce myself...I'm Nora Cummings." She offered her hand to Andy.

"How do, Missus Cummings," Andy nodded, "Now about your pa..."

"He'll be sorry to have missed you," she began, her eyes darting nervously around the room. "He talked about you often, how you helped him with the cabin and the way Corey took to the animals." Then she frowned as she looked at Corey. "You know, I could have sworn he said Corey was a boy."

"When d'ya expect your pa'll be back?" Andy asked, avoiding the explanation of Corey's gender.

Nora walked to the window and pulled the curtains back, looking across the street at the two men there. "Are they waiting for you?"

Something was wrong here. Every time the conversation came back to Gus's whereabouts or his possible return, Nora either changed the subject or evaded it. Perhaps Gus had died and she didn't want to break the news in front of Corey, Andy surmised.

"Yeah, mebbe Corey'd better go tell them we'll be thar directly, eh, Corey?"

"But…" Corey started to object and seeing the stern look on Andy's face, she muttered, "Okay, Andy."

Andy waited until Corey had left the house. "Whut's wrong, Missus Cummin's? Whar's yore pa?"

"What makes you think anything is wrong?" Nora tittered nervously, but when Andy waited for her answer, her face went pale and she bowed her head as tears suddenly filled her eyes. She sat down slowly into the chair and, giving a heavy sigh, spoke slowly, painfully.

"I…we had him committed to…um…to a home. I had no choice, Mr….er, Andy. He was very ill and I had no way of taking care of him. When he got better…" her voice broke and she paused long enough to stifle the sob that was choking back her words. "Well, we had no room and with the children, I mean, if he got sick again and…and died…can't you see, I didn't want the children to see that."

"It ain't my place to jedge anybody's doin's, Missus Cummin's. You done what you felt you had to do. Now what be th' problem with Gus? Is he allowed to have comp'ny?"

"The doctor said it was a blood disease, I forget the name, it's so long and hard to pronounce. He said there was no cure and that it was just a matter of time. Just how long he couldn't be sure," she said as new tears filled her eyes. Drying them with the back of her hand, she continued, "I'm sure he would enjoy seeing you again and he is allowed visitors. I haven't been able to see him since the baby came a month ago, but the home would have gotten in touch with me had his condition changed."

"If you'll jest tell me whar this home is, we'll be a goin'. I don't wanna keep grievin' you."

❧   ❧   ❧

Pine Haven Home for Men sat at the foot of mountains surrounded by trees and shrubs giving it the seclusion of a prison rather than a rest home. Deep shadows were falling around it and lights were beginning to show from the windows. Andy and his companions approached the front door in a silent procession and rang the ornate bell marked "for visitor's use." The porch light blinked on and a robust woman in her early fifties opened the door.

"May I help you?" she asked uncertainly as her eyes took in the motley foursome.

"We come to see Mr. Thatcher," Andy announced.

"Visiting hours are almost over. Perhaps it would be better if you came back tomorrow," she suggested, looking over her shoulder to make sure an orderly was still in the foyer with her.

"But, madam, 'tis for sure we've traveled a great distance to see our friend, it is, and 'tis not for certain we'll be stayin' in your fair city another day," intervened Lord Mayor in his lilting Irish brogue.

"Well…I don't suppose it will hurt, but the child will have to wait elsewhere, our rules prohibit children."

"Couldn't she be after stayin' just inside here with yerself? Tis gettin' dark outside for a little one to stay alone," Lord Mayor spoke again, turning on more charm.

"Why don't one of you stay with her, then?" the nurse replied.

This time Andy took up the quest, "Thar wouldn't be time fer all o' us to visit, ma'am. You said yerself visitin' hours was 'most over."

Injun opened his mouth to offer staying behind with Corey only to close again after a quick jab in the ribs from Andy.

The nurse looked at the orderly and back again. The few visitors were now gone, along with most of the staff, and the patients were in their rooms preparing for bed. Poor Mr. Thatcher had not received one visitor in months; perhaps a few minutes wouldn't hurt. "Ten minutes," she agreed, "but if the child causes any problems out she goes immediately." She summoned the orderly who had been leaning against the wall watching the whole scene with a hint of amusement. "Jordan will take you to Mr. Thatcher's room and please stay with him so that you do not disturb the other patients."

Gus lay upon his bed, his back to the door when the men entered the room. He made no effort to move until the orderly closed the door again; then he raised his bedcovers with a sigh and turned on his back, still not seeing his visitors until Andy cleared his throat.

"What…who's there?" he asked. Suddenly, his eyes widened and he jerked the covers back. "Do my old eyes deceive me or is that really you, Andy?" he roared happily.

"It be me awright, Gus." Andy clapped him on the shoulder firmly.

"How on earth did you find me? Is Corey with you?"

"Hold up that," Andy laughed pointing to the bedspread, "I got me a plan and we don't have much time. Is he sleepin'?" he asked, indicating the old man in the next bed.

"Yeah, he's out like a light. What's up, Andy?"

"I want you to change clothes with Lord Mayor here and don't ask no questions. By th' way, this here's Lord Mayor and Injun, friends o' mine. Now, hurry up and do whut I say."

Lord Mayor pulled on Gus' nightshirt and climbed up on the bed, probing the mattress with his fingers. He grinned, "Tis been a long while since I have been after sleepin' in a real bed."

"Well, don't git too comfortable, Lord Mayor, we may hafta skeedaddle outta here in a hurry," warned Andy, "Now, Injun, you come with me and Gus. I'll tell you whut to do whilst we walk."

The halls were empty and the three men made their way easily toward the front desk. As they approached the foyer where the nurse was stationed, Gus lowered his head, covering his face with his hand as Andy had instructed and leaned on Injun. They walked quickly toward the front door leaving Andy to deal with the nurse.

"Pore ole soul, takin' it purty hard. Him'n Gus…Mr. Thatcher, was this close," Andy explained putting one finger over the other. "Had to bring him out afore he broke up. "It'll be awright if'n he goes back to say good-bye after he gits holt of hisself, won't it?"

"Well…sure, I guess, if it doesn't take too long," she whispered, looking after the man with pity showing clearly on her face. "Could I get him a glass of water or something?"

"Naw, he'll be good as new directly. Th' night air'll do him good. 'Scuse me, ma'am, I'll jest go see to him." Andy excused himself before he let go the chuckle fighting to get out and he grabbed Corey by the hand, pulling her out the door with him.

When the group was far enough from the front door to be safe, they unleashed howls of laughter at having accomplished their deception. Corey watched, unsure of what was happening until she saw Gus.

"Gus! Gus!" she cried ecstatically. "I didn't think I was going to see you."

"Ah, Corey, my happiness is complete," Gus crooned, taking Corey in his arms and his eyes sparkled brighter than normal. "Let's have a look at you. Wh…what's this?" he questioned, noticing the long curls.

"It's a long story, Gus. Mebbe we'd best find a place to set down whilst we talk," Andy said and directed the group to a darker corner of the lawn where they would not be disturbed.

Corey and Andy took turns telling Gus of the events leading to their visit in the mountains and those following their departure. Gus listened ardently to their tale, chuckling to himself, and then muttering furiously over the nerve of Lizzie stealing the child's money and accusing Andy of kidnapping. How he would have loved to be there and give the old woman a piece of his mind.

"What became of Nanette, Gus, and the other animals?" Corey asked when the tale was complete.

"I don't know, Corey. After I blacked out in the store, my daughter and her husband took care of everything. I wanted to go back when I started feeling better, but it didn't work out that way. This is my home now," he sighed. "It's not so bad. I have friends here, friends that depend on me. That old man who shares my room? He's been there four years and not one soul has come to see him. It's sad, Andy. His mind has slipped back to the past and he thinks I'm his son. I've given up trying to make him believe I'm not and I take care of him as much as I can," he shook his head slowly, looking off into the darkness.

"Well, my friend, I hate to break this up, but I think mebbe we done stayed past th' proper time. We'd best git you back to yore room afore they lock th' place up fer th' night," Andy broke into the silence.

"Will you be around for a while?" Gus asked as they started back to the home.

"Wish we could stay 'round fer a time, but I gotta git Corey back home afore Angel starts lookin' fer us. Our lil detour took up more time than we'd planned on. You'd best come with us."

"I'd like to, Andy, but my friend wouldn't last long if I deserted him. Besides, I don't really feel up to traveling just yet," he drew a deep breath and stepped aside for Injun to open the door.

"It's locked," Injun whispered over his shoulder as he twisted the knob again. "Now what?"

"Ring th' bell, Injun, someone will answer it."

"I thought you people had left," the nurse scowled through the half-opened door. "You can't come in now, it's been over an hour and I'm afraid you will just have to leave without saying good-bye to Mr. Thatcher. I will inform him in the morning that you came back too late to see him." She closed the door before they could persuade her to break any more rules.

"Maybe we should have told her Gus was with us," Corey lamented.

"And she'd prob'ly called th' cops on us. No, we'll figger another way to git him back. Whut about th' winder, Gus, if'n we give you a boost, could you git in thet way?"

"The windows have bars, Andy," Gus answered, somewhat amused at their predicament. "Some of the men here aren't quite right, if you know what I mean, and to avoid their getting out where they could be hurt, the windows are barred and all the doors are locked at night. The only way to get in is to have someone open the door."

"Mebbe we can git Lord Mayor to open the door fer us. Is thar a back door?"

"Need a key," Gus replied. "looks like you are stuck with me until the morning."

"Will that be a problem for you?" Injun asked. "I mean, will you be needing medicine or anything before bedtime?"

"Good Lord!" Andy exclaimed, "Whut if'n they give your medicine to Lord Mayor thinkin' it's you?"

"The only thing they will be giving me, or rather Lord Mayor, would be a mild sleeping potion and that won't hurt him," laughed Gus.

"But it won't make you sick if'n you stay outside fer th' night, will it"?

"No, I'll be fine. I could even go home, if I had a home to go to. Don't worry, fellows, I'll be okay. In fact, I'm looking forward to this, camping out and all."

Gus, Andy, and Corey talked into the night with Injun listening and adding a statement once in a while. Finally Injun called it a night, and then Corey nodded off. Reluctantly, they all found a spot and curled up on the ground using an assortment of clothes and blankets for covers.

The next morning Gus awakened Andy just as the first rays of the sun filtered through the trees.

"I have to be getting back now, Andy. Pretty soon they will be getting everybody up for their medicine and baths before breakfast. Your friend will surely be discovered then."

"How are you getting back in?" Injun asked. "it's too early for visiting hours."

"There is a door just down from my room that some of the morning help use and it will be unlocked now. I really must hurry, though," Gus answered, peering through the hedges.

Andy cleared his throat noisily, "Well, ole friend, can't rightly say when we'll be back this way…" he began, his eyes taking on a misty brightness as he placed his hand on Gus' shoulder. "You take care o' yourself and if'n you ever need anything jest git holt of Corey at thet address we give you last night."

"You don't know what it has meant to me, Andy, Corey, to see you again. Whenever I get down in the dumps, I'll think about this time and how you busted me out of the home for the night," he paused as if tucking the moment away where it could easily be reached at a later time. "Injun, thank you, too, and I shall never forget my new friends. Now, I must really get back. So long, Andy," he said, taking Andy's hand firmly in his. "Corey," he sniffed and held her close, his body jerking uncontrollably as he wept. Then he was gone through the shrubs and across the sweeping lawn.

CHAPTER 15

"Angel ain't gonna like this none," Andy shook his head thoughtfully. "You was supposed to ride th' train proper like whilst we was gone."

"But, Andy, she won't know until we get home and by then there'll be nothing to worry about. I'll be safe and sound. Please, Andy? What can happen with you, Lord Mayor, and Injun to protect me?"

Andy looked to his friends for help, but they shrugged their shoulders and turned away. This was a decision they wanted no part in making. He looked again at Corey, thinking about what she had said. This trip would take two, maybe three days and what could happen in that short a time? Hadn't they traveled months, just the two of them?

"You know who she's gonna be madder'n a hornet at, don't you?" Andy grinned.

"Oh, Andy, thank you!" Corey exclaimed, throwing her arms around his neck. "This may be the last time ever I will get to do this and I did so much want it to be like old times for us. Besides, Angelique won't stay mad at you for long."

"We'd best git goin' afore I change my mind," Andy muttered, gathering his belongings and stowing them in his knapsack.

Ash Fork, Arizona, was five miles away and by the time they had covered that distance it would be dusk. Easy enough to hop in a boxcar unnoticed since it was a small community, but they would have to be quick because the train would be stopping only long enough to pick up mail and a passenger or two.

"Now, Corey, I want you to go cash in your ticket and see if'n they be a train comin' in directly. Lord Mayor'll go with you whilst Injun and me wait at the mercantile. Wouldn't do to git anybody askin' a bunch o' questions whut with all o' us goin' in," Andy instructed as they filed into town.

"Then can we get something to eat?" Corey asked, her stomach rumbling angrily. "I don't think I can go all night without eating and poor Muffin hasn't had anything all day."

Andy dug into his pocket and brought out two crumpled dollar bills. "You jest go on like'n I told you and I'll see what I can git in here. Hurry up now!" Andy wanted to get this trip over with as soon as possible. He didn't like going against Angelique's wishes, yet he didn't want to disappoint Corey either. If only he didn't have that uneasy feeling.

The clerk behind the counter jumped at the sound of the bell above the door when Injun and Andy entered. He made a quick mental note of their description before breathing a sigh of relief.

"You fellows gave me quite a start there," he laughed nervously. "The whole town's a bit edgy what with those bank robbers loose. I was just getting ready to go home."

"Whut's thet you say 'bout bank robbers?" Andy asked.

"The police were just here and said two men held up the bank in Flagstaff. They killed a man, too. Seems they may be headed in this direction. I…hey, where are you going?" he called as Andy whirled around and ran out the door with Injun at his heels.

"We gotta stop Corey afore she turns in her ticket. Ain't no way I'm gonna let her ride th' rails now," Andy called over his shoulder to Injun, but before they could get to th' depot, they spotted Corey and Lord Mayor hurrying toward them.

"Andy, there's a policeman at the train station," Corey gasped, trying to catch her breath. "We won't be able to get on the train while he is there."

"I know. Did you cash in your ticket?"

"Yeah, and there's a train due in twenty minutes."

"Damn!" he swore under his breath, "whut're we gonna do now? You can't go back and tell him you changed your mind agin."

"'Tis no problem, Andy, we'll just be after catchin' the next one. It'll not be comin' for a good while yet," Lord Mayor said.

"It ain't gonna be thet way. We gotta find us some place to stay fer th' night and first thing in th' mornin' Corey's gonna buy a ticket fer home," Andy scowled. "I shoulda never listened to her in th' first place, then we wouldn't be in this here mess." He explained the problem to Corey and Lord Mayor.

"There is no hotel and it's for sure no one is going to open up their houses to the likes of us tonight," Injun stated. "Got any ideas?"

"We got no choice but to set up camp jest outside town here. We gotta stay close enough to be safe, but fur enough thet no law-'biding citizen shoots first then asks questions," Andy sighed.

After they set up camp, Injun volunteered the first watch. Those men would not venture this close to town until some of the commotion died down, but they wanted to be prepared just in case.

Corey lay on the ground listening to every sound. The noises seemed to be amplified by the seriousness of their situation. She held on to Muffin, knowing if someone was out there he would be the first to hear them. Andy lay on one side of her and Lord Mayor on the other and she felt, rather than saw, Injun leaning against the tree near her head. There was no fire for fear of attracting attention.

"Andy, do you think those men are really around here?" she whispered.

"Naw, they prob'ly made a wide circle 'round th' town. We be too close to be bothered by them. Now, you git some shet eye and afore you know it, it'll be daylight."

Sleep did not come easily to Corey and she was still awake when the shift for the watch changed. She heard Injun groan as he lay down on the old blanket vacated by Andy and she raised her head, propping it in the palm of her hand, leaning on her elbow.

"What's the matter, Corey, can't sleep?" Injun asked. "You know, I'd be almost willing to bet those men are long gone by now. This is too close to town for them. It'll be daylight soon and we'll be heading back into town, so you better get some sleep." He shifted around trying to find a comfortable position on the ground and within minutes was breathing the deep, even breaths of a sound sleep.

Corey's eyes grew heavy, but when she closed them, pictures of her nightmarish encounter with the tramps came back to her. That same fear washed over her now and she pulled Muffin even closer in hopes the warmth of his little body next to hers would help push back those fears, but Muffin clambered away from her. He sat up to listen to a sound only he could hear and a growl rumbled within him, finally escaping with a menacing sound. Injun stirred, listened briefly before easing himself from the blanket.

"Corey, I'm gonna put you up in this tree and I want you to climb as high as you can. Don't make a sound until I tell you it's all clear." Injun whispered and picked Corey up, pushing her within reach of the tree branch.

Andy and Lord Mayor quickly gathered up their gear and pushed it beneath the bushes. They wouldn't have time to climb into the trees because the crackling of footsteps on dead leaves was almost upon them. Andy grabbed Muffin, holding his hand firmly over his muzzle and followed Lord Mayor into the thicket while Injun disappeared into the woods.

The footsteps stopped just short of the camp and one of the men struck a match against his pant leg. A flame burst forth, illuminating his face as he lit a cigarette and sat heavily on a nearby log.

"I gotta catch my breath, Virgil. We been walking for hours. Don't you never get tired?"

"Be careful with that match, you fool! All we need is to start a fire and lead the cops right to us," the one called Virgil growled.

"You worry too much, Virg," the first man sneered. "They probably quit looking for us last night when we didn't show up."

The strangers were so close that Muffin began struggling furiously in Andy's arms trying to break free. Andy tried to get the dog pinned between his knees and in the process broke a dead branch from one of the bushes. He jumped at the loud sound as it broke the silence, loosening his grip on Muffin just long enough for the little dog to break free.

"Who's there?" a startled Virgil called, pointing his gun into the darkness of the predawn. "Come out where I can see you or I'll start shooting!"

Muffin had reached the men and was biting angrily at one, then the other's leg. The men kicked frantically at the dog until one connected with Muffin's head, bringing forth a sharp yelp, then silence. Once again the blaze of a match lit the darkness as the men examined the unconscious, furry form on the ground. A high-pitched scream echoed through the woods, causing the hair to rise on the frightened men's necks.

"C-come out or I'll shoot," Virgil shakily repeated his warning.

Andy's heart quickened its beat. If the men started shooting into the trees there was a good chance Corey would be hit and he was sure they had probably figured out from where the scream had come. He would reveal himself and draw the attention in his direction. He could only hope Corey would have the good sense to stay put. He motioned for Lord Mayor to stay where he was and slowly crawled out of the bushes, making enough noise for the men to hear him.

"Don't shoot, fellers, I'm a comin' out," Andy called, his hands above his head.

A soft gray light was beginning to creep into the horizon and Andy could barely make out the two men as he shuffled toward them. One started forward to meet him only to stop short at the sound of Corey scrambling down from her hiding place.

"No, Corey!" Andy yelled, "Stay where you are!"

"I wouldn't listen to him if I was you, Corey. I have a gun pointed at the old man's head and if you don't show yourself, I'll blow his brains out," commanded Virgil's companion.

"Don't hurt him, I'm coming," she begged as she slid down the tree trunk.

"Well, well, well, if it ain't a kid." Virgil's laugh came out as a deep-throated guttural sound.

Corey ignored him, running passed his clutching hand and knelt beside Muffin's still form. She stroked his fur, sobbing uncontrollably, then stood up and whirled upon the men, attacking them with her fists.

"You killed my dog!" she screamed and kicked at them.

Andy tried to grab Corey, but one of the men pushed her into him and they went sprawling onto the ground. Muffin had regained consciousness and, upon seeing the attack on his master, lunged at Virgil. A gunshot rang out, dropping Muffin to the ground again, but this time a dark crimson circle spread quickly on his fur.

"Saints preserve us!" Lord Mayor exclaimed aloud. "I can't be after hidin' me unworthy self when me friends are in trouble." Besides, he thought, between Andy and himself they could keep the men busy enough to allow Injun to sneak up on them. He would be close enough to disarm one of them. Yes, that was the best way.

"What, another one? Who else is hiding out there?" Virgil growled.

"Tis just meself 'n no one else," Lord Mayor said slyly, winking at Andy. He looked at Corey and his brow knotted with concern, for the child was clearly in a state of shock. She sat silently staring, oblivious to everything around her, an ashen hue coloring her face. Andy moved to her side and Lord Mayor took the place on her other side.

"What're we going to do with all these people, Virg? Half the town is going to be breathing down our necks soon's they figger out where the shot came from," the man wailed.

"Shut up, Grover, and let me think a minute. We can't take them with us, that's for sure," he scratched his chin and motioned to Andy and Lord Mayor. "Empty out your pockets and go sit with your backs against that tree over yonder," he ordered.

Lord Mayor caught a slight movement in the bushes behind the men, but he didn't dare look closer for fear of alerting his captors. He couldn't even let Andy know what he suspected, so it was up to him to be ready when Injun made his move. He moved more slowly toward the tree indicated by Virgil, giving Injun a chance to get closer. Suddenly, in a blur, Injun was on top of Virgil and Lord Mayor leaped at Grover. Another shot rang out, this time hitting Lord Mayor. Andy ran to his side and for a fraction of a second Injun took his attention off the robbers. Both men scrambled to their feet and disappeared into the woods. Injun jumped up and started to pursue them, but Andy stopped him.

"Let them be, Injun, they won't bother us no more. Whut we gotta worry about now is Lord Mayor. It looks bad," he moaned.

The sound of the gunshot had snapped Corey back to reality and she began screaming hysterically. Injun walked over to her, slapped her soundly across the cheek and caught her in both arms as she crumpled toward the ground.

"Can you handle things here while I go for help?" Injun asked Andy.

"I got no choice. Jest git a doctor here, even if'n you hafta shackle him. Don't stand there, man, get goin'!"

🍁 🍁 🍁

Injun had just emerged from the woods and started across the field for town when a police car came barreling toward him.

"Hold it right there, mister!" ordered one of the deputies, his gun pointed at Injun.

"Please, can you get a doctor? My friend has been shot by one of the men you have been looking for."

"Where's your friend?" the driver asked, eyeing Injun suspiciously.

"Just back there in the woods. Please, he's bleeding bad."

"Tom, see if you can help his friend, then try to pick up the suspects' trail. I'll take this fella back to town with me and round up more help," the officer instructed as Injun hopped into the car.

The car whirled around, slipping on the grassy meadow and fishtailing while Injun clung desperately to the open window frame as they bumped across the uneven ground.

"What's your name?" the deputy asked when they had reached the highway.

"Folks call me Injun," he answered, looking anxiously ahead. "How much further is it to the doctor's?"

"Couple more minutes," the deputy cast a long sideways glance at his passenger. *Hobo or tramp,* he thought scornfully, *useless no-good people.* "Doc'll take you back out there," he said, stopping in front of a small white frame house. "I'll want to talk to you later. You will be around?" It was an order more than a question.

"Yeah," Injun called back as he jumped from the car and ran to the house.

Andy left the deputy with Lord Mayor and walked over to Corey, sitting down on the ground beside her. He put his arm over her shivering shoulders and pulled the tattered blanket more securely around her.

"It's gonna be awright, Corey girl," he soothed, "th' doc'll be here right quick, now."

Corey looked at Andy through eyes swollen from the torrent of tears she had shed. Now, there was none left. "What about Mu—Muffin? Poor Muffin, why did they have to kill him? He was just a little dog," she moaned, her chin quivering as she looked at the small lifeless form a short distance away.

Andy put his hand against her face, turning it gently away from the vision of the dog. "They were killers, Corey. Don't make no never mind who or whut. If'n it gets in th' way, they'll kill it. Try not to think on it, child."

"I can't help it, Andy. I keep seeing it over and over again,' she cried. "And Lord Mayor and all that blood. He isn't going to die, too, is he, Andy?" Panic strained at her voice.

"There, there, Lord Mayor's a tough ole bird and he ain't ready to check outta this here world just yet," Andy reassured her. He hoped he was right. If only Injun would get back with the doctor…

"Your friend is still out, but I made him as comfortable as possible under the circumstances," the deputy interrupted. "I wonder if you could give me a little more information. We don't have much to go on."

"Lemme see, th' one called Virgil was a lil feller, five-four mebbe five-five. Th' other one was taller. Couldn't tell much else, warn't enough light and they was wearin' caps. They both had guns, too."

"Do you happen to know the other man's name? Did they mention where they were headed?"

"Grover was th' other feller's name. Didn't say whar they was headed, just took off through yonder liken th' devil was after them," Andy answered, pointing through the trees in the direction the men had disappeared.

"Anything else you can think of that might help us?"

"Nary a thing, sorry. How much longer d'ya think it'll be afore the doc gits here?"

"Any minute now," the deputy muttered, focusing his attention on the scrap of paper where he was writing down the information Andy had given him.

There was a sound of the bushes being swept aside and voices.

"Here he is, Doc, right over here," Injun was shouting to the short, rotund man struggling to keep up with his long-legged guide.

Corey and Andy moved to Lord Mayor's side as the doctor took scissors from his bag and began cutting the shirt away from the wound.

"How bad is it, Doc?" they both echoed in unison.

The doctor slipped his hand gently under Lord Mayor, examining his back. "The bullet's still in him. I'll patch him up as best I can out here, but we'll have to get him to my office to get the bullet out. He's lost a lot of blood, too," he noted, again reaching into the bag. He cleansed the area around the wound thoroughly and applied a bandage, then signaled the men to bring the stretcher.

While Lord Mayor was being placed on the backseat, Injun went around to the passenger's side and picked up a shovel from the floorboard in the front.

"I'm glad you thought o' that, Injun," Andy whispered, taking the shovel from him. "It's best I do this whilst Corey ain't around. I'll foller you in a bit."

Injun nodded, and then joined Corey and the doctor in the front seat. He explained to Corey that Andy was going to get their gear, but she knew what he was going to do even though Andy kept the shovel out of her sight. As the car pulled away Corey's eyes filled with tears and she stared out the window ahead of them.

The ground was soft in the shade of the pine trees where the sun had not baked it. As Andy dug, the odor of the fresh-turned earth, along with the pungent smell of pine needles, stirred him deeply. Seemingly forgotten memories, transported him to a long-ago time and place. He was a young boy again, standing at the foot of the grave where his father had just been buried. Sounds of the wind moaning through the trees filled his head and he was unable to discern if it was from that time or this.

His young eyes looked through the trees down to the cabin that had been their home. How could it stand there totally unaffected when his world had just come to an end? Why had it not fallen to the ground in utter ruins as he felt his life had? Perhaps it was just a nightmare and if he ran to the door calling for his father, he would appear, smiling that calming smile he always had when Andy awakened from a nightmare.

"Pa! Pa!" the young boy was calling as he ran toward the cabin. He threw open the door and the emptiness was like the deep hole under the trees, swallowing him. "Pa," he whispered, then felt a hand on his shoulder. One of the neighbors had followed him.

"Are you all right there?" someone was asking, but it was not the neighbor and Andy was no longer the little boy in the cabin.

"Yeah, Deputy, I be fine," he sighed.

Andy wrapped Muffin in his old blanket and lowered the bundle into the hole, covering it with the fresh dirt until there was a firm little mound.

"Well, old friend, our tracks be leadin' in different directions now, and I'm sure gonna miss you. You made a fine 'bo even if'n you was jest a dog and I was right proud of you. S'long, lil one."

*   *   *

Andy paced nervously up and down the platform, glancing occasionally down the tracks for a sign of the train. How he hated calling Angelique about his failure to keep Corey from harm, but having to face her was even worse. Maybe she had had time to settle down some. He grinned wryly, knowing, if anything, she would be worse. She would have worked up a full head of steam by now.

A train whistle cut sharply into the morning air, causing Andy to wince. *Right on time, too, wouldn't you know,* he thought. *Only time it'd be late was if'n I was lookin forward to meetin' her.*

Angelique stepped from the train assisted by the porter, her eyes scanning the few faces in front of her. Slowly, Andy edged toward her.

"Hullo, Angel," he greeted meekly.

Angelique's eyes narrowed, and she opened her mouth to speak but decided against unleashing her anger in the presence of strangers. She nodded curtly, her gaze shifting from his and sweeping the platform.

"Corey ain't with me, Angel. She be waitin' over to th' doc's place. I figgered you'd wanna talk to me alone first," again he winced.

"How is your friend?" her voice was cool and polite.

"He's doin' good. Doc says he'll be fit as a fiddle in 'nother two or three days. Lord Mayor's a tough ole coot," he laughed uncomfortably, waiting for the storm.

"What in God's name..." she sputtered, "How could you put Corey in a situation like that? I told you when you left no more wandering around the country like this. You promised me, Andy!"

"I know I did, Angel, but Corey jest wanted to do it one last time. I didn't wanna ruin her trip none. 'Sides, it weren't gonna be fer long…goin' back."

"Well, you couldn't have made it much worse," she glared.

"Aw, Angel, that ain't fair. You make it sound liken it was all my fault. You know thet child means a lot to me, too," he moaned.

"All I know is that you did exactly what I told you not to do and we both know the results, don't we?" Her words were harsh and she stopped to look him right in the eyes, "Now, I intend to take Corey home on the next train out of here and I will appreciate it if you would just go your own way and stay out of our lives. You have caused me enough grief in my life and, quite frankly, I don't need anymore." She blinked fiercely against the stinging tears.

The words stunned Andy and he sucked in his breath sharply as if someone had thrown cold water in his face. For a moment he stood rooted to the spot, staring unbelieving at Angelique. "You don't mean thet, Angel…?"

"I'm afraid I have never been more serious. Now, if you'll take me to Corey, I will attend to the business at hand so we can be on our way."

Andy turned silently and headed down the street with Angelique following behind. Anger kept Andy from speaking for he knew he would only say something he would later regret. His only hope was that Angelique's reactions had been from the pressure of the situation and that, given time, she would not uphold the words she had just spoken.

Corey had been watching from the window, and when she saw Angelique coming toward the house with Andy, she bolted through the door to meet them. Burying her face in Angelique's shoulder, she sobbed freely as the fear and grief she had suppressed the past three days finally erupted.

"That's good, honey, get it all out," Angelique soothed. "You're going to be fine, now, I'm taking you home."

Later that evening Angelique unhooked the laces on her shoes and heaved a sigh of relief as she slipped them from her aching feet. How fortunate it was that the rooming house had a vacancy. She disliked staying with strangers and had declined the doctor's invitation to stay at his place, after learning it would be the next day before another train passed this way. She prodded the mattress with her fingers and shrugged, not exactly like sleeping in your own bed. She reached to turn the covers back when she was interrupted by a knock at her door. The sound exploded in the quiet, tiny room.

"Who's there?"

"It's me…Andy," the answer was as sharp as the knock.

"I have nothing more to say to you, Mister Curruthers," she retorted through the closed door.

"I ain't leavin' 'til you open this here door."

Angelique unlocked the door brusquely, intending to reprimand Andy for his rudeness, but he pushed past her into the room.

"We don't need none o' yore charity," he scowled, his face dark with anger. "Me'n Injun was fixin' to git us a job to take care o' th' doc's bill. I don't take handouts and especially not from you. You know thet, Angel."

There was that stubborn pride again, Angelique thought, how could she have forgotten? It had taken him from her so long ago and still stood between them when he finally came back into her life. No, it had not diminished with time and separation. Something stirred within her, a feeling perhaps from long ago, or was it…? She didn't know what it was, nor was she going to pursue it, not at the expense of more grief.

"Look, Andy, your friend is under the doctor's care because he was protecting someone who is very dear to me. For that I am truly grateful and paying for his care was one way I could repay him. Don't take that from me, please," Angelique sighed, suddenly very tired. Her anger had passed after the confrontation with Andy earlier and now her emotions were spent, her defenses down.

"Yeah, but if'n it wasn't fer me it wouldn't have happened, ain't thet right?"

"I guess I shouldn't have put the blame entirely on you. It's just that…well, that's neither here nor there, now. What's done is done. I just want to take Corey home."

"Nope, it ain't done. I'll git me thet job and send the money to you 'til it's all paid," Andy answered. "Nother thing, I was plannin' to see Corey off in th' mornin'. I hope thet's awright."

"That is fine, but please don't tell her of our earlier conversation. I don't think she needs to be upset any more than she already is."

"Then you still aim to go through with it…I can't see her no more?"

"I think that will be best for her, Andy. I don't want her getting any more ideas about chasing all over. She was lucky this time, next time who knows?"

Andy stood quietly deliberating her words, feeling much older than his years. What she said was true, but what would he tell Corey? How could he hide the despair he felt when she was able to sense his mood? He felt a gentle tug at this heart as he pictured Corey, her face aglow seeing the ocean and picking an orange off the tree for the first time. There were other such discoveries out there he wanted to share with her, but not at the expense of her happiness or safety. Perhaps, if his life had been different, but it was not, nor was it going to be.

"Well, Angel," he finally spoke," you're right as usual. Ain't no place in her life fer th' likes o' me. When that thar train pulls out in th' mornin', you can rest easy 'cuz it'll be th' last you see of me." He glanced around the room, avoiding her eyes and, seeing her shoes on the floor, realized she had been getting ready to retire for the night. "S'pose I'd best git outta her and let you git some sleep. Guess I didn't think on how late it was. 'Night, Angel." And he was gone.

The next morning Andy rushed along the street toward the boarding house where Corey was waiting. He had promised to take her to Muffin's grave before she left for home and if he didn't hurry there wouldn't be enough time. The sheriff had taken longer than he had allowed with all those questions.

"You ready, Corey girl?" He called softly, knocking on her door.

"I thought you had forgotten, Andy," Corey pouted as she opened the door. "We don't have much time left."

"I know, let's git goin'. Durn sheriff helt me up." He handed her the small bouquet of flowers Doc had picked from his garden.

Andy took Corey's hand as they approached the spot where Muffin was buried, giving it a reassuring squeeze. He heard her heavy sigh and saw the quiver in her chin as they reached the little mound. Corey knelt on her knees, placing the flowers gently on the grave.

"You know, Andy, he was a good dog and an even better friend. If it hadn't been for him I don't know how I could have made it all those months with Aunt Lizzie," she sniffed loudly and tenderly caressed the mound of earth. There was silence while Corey gathered strength, then she continued, "Do you think there is a heaven for dogs, Andy?"

"Oh, I'm sure of it, jest as sure as I know he's a sittin' up there this very minute lookin' down on us. He's got it made, Corey girl. He ain't never gonna want fer nothin'. They won't be no pain or growin' old and feeble. Why he's prob'ly so happy up thar with all them other dogs, runnin' 'round and th' like, thet he prob'ly feels sorry fer us down here," Andy answered thickly.

Corey smiled through her tears taking comfort in Andy's words. Yes. that is how she would think of Muffin, running and playing with new friends. She could accept that.

"I hate to say this, but it's gettin' 'bout thet time…"

"I know, I'm ready now," she whispered.

The train bumped noisily to a stop, releasing a hissing sigh of steam. Angelique stood up and moved slowly down the platform, giving Andy an opportunity to say good-bye to Corey.

"Well, Corey, I guess this is it," he began to fumble for the right words to say. "You won't be...uh, it's gonna be some time afore I see you...uh, I got me this here chanct out East. I mean, it's a chanct to make money fer a good stake," Andy lied. He squinted against the bright morning and, turning his face away, he caught a glimpse of Angelique watching. "You see, Corey," he continued, "I ain't gittin' any younger and afore you know it I won't be able to keep up with this kinda life. So's I hafta git ready for thet day whilst I can."

"But, Andy, you could come back with us and work at Angelique's mill."

"Nope, can't do thet, child, leastways not fer a while. Gotta make it on my own. I know you can't understand thet right now." He was going to have to get tougher if he was to make the break Angelique had forced upon him. This was not working. "Now thet I got you off'n my hands I can do what I hafta." He ached inside as she winced at his words, but it had to be done. He had known it would not be easy, yet the pain at this moment seemed more than he could bear. He bent over, quickly brushing his lips against her forehead and uttered hoarsely, "S'long, Corey. Be a good kid fer Angel and remember whut I said 'bout listenin' to th' music, it'll make you a fine woman." Then he was gone without even a backward glance, for to look back at the small, heartbroken girl was more than he could manage.

CHAPTER 16

Corey's stomach churned nervously as she stood with Francie and her parents waiting for Phillipe Bernard to step from the train. She wondered if he had changed much in the three years since his return to France. His letters had sounded much the same, but people do change. She had been a gangling, boisterous fourteen-year-old when he left, and now she found herself slipping into a more subdued womanhood at seventeen, at least she would be in two more weeks.

Phillipe had entered her life at a time when she sorely needed male companionship, Andy having abruptly left her. Perhaps because Phillipe was two years older than she, Corey valued his opinions on the many problems she took to him. He was like a brother to her until shortly before he left. At some point, she was not exactly sure when or why, her feelings toward Phillipe had changed. Had it been a girlish crush, or the beginning of something stronger? Maybe now she would find out and it was this thought that gave her an uneasy, awkward feeling.

"Phillipe! Phillipe!" shouted Francie over the noise, waving frantically to catch her brother's attention. "Over her, *mon frere!*" Francie reached her brother and squealed with delight as she threw her arms around his neck, her feet dangling above the platform. She grinned lovingly, "You have gotten much taller, *mon frere,*" she appraised as he gently released her. "It is good to have you home again, Phillipe, I have so much to tell you—"

"Not now, Francoise. We'd like the opportunity to welcome your brother home, also," Mr. Bernard interrupted, slapping Phillipe soundly on the back.

Corey stood watching the scene, suddenly wishing she had not come. This was not the Phillipe she remembered, but a handsome nineteen-year-old man.

Polished and refined, he was now almost a stranger to her. She glanced down at her clothes and scolded herself for not having taken more care in dressing for the occasion. Brushing a strand of long, dark hair from her forehead, she smiled weakly as Francie rejoined her.

"Come over and say hello, Corey."

Before Corey could answer, Phillipe and his parents approached. He took Corey's hands in his and holding her at arms' length, examined her approvingly.

"This can't be Corey?" He asked in mock disbelief. "Why, it's the proverbial butterfly all over again. You have emerged a beautiful young woman, *ma ami*," then he laughed at the blushing Corey, his blue eyes twinkling mischievously. He had always enjoyed catching her off-guard, and in that, he had not changed.

"Hello, Phillipe," she answered softly, hoping her voice did not betray the turmoil she felt. There were unknown feelings awakening inside her like little sparks of electricity. She felt the flush in her face and pulled her hands from his. "I see you haven't changed much. You are still as impudent as ever. I must say I enjoyed the peace and quiet while you were away."

Why had she been so childishly rude? she wondered. Surely the women he met in France would have been more clever and perhaps a little flirtatious. She felt the sting of jealousy at the thought of other women in his life and quickly lowered her eyes under his steady gaze, afraid he would guess what she was thinking. Again the warmth of a blush rose upward from her neck.

Phillipe bowed, laughing once again, before following his parents from the station, leaving a bewildered Corey to bring up the rear behind Francie.

The next two days Corey avoided seeing Phillipe. She was frustrated at these new feelings he aroused in her and was angry at not having more control in his presence. Therefore, when Francie called to remind her of their shopping trip she was hesitant about going. They were to pick out dresses to wear to Francie's graduation party. Only when Francie pleaded that they only had three days left, the party being this Saturday, did she relent.

Hot and tired, but successful, they decided to stop at Jordan's Ice Cream Parlor for a tall cool phosphate before going home. They paused at the counter briefly to look at the menu on the wall. Morgan Connor was perched on a stool at the counter and greeted them. Corey nodded at Morgan, then glanced around the room looking for a table when she saw Phillipe in a booth toward the back of the room. He waved cheerfully and motioned for them to join him.

There was that flutter in the pit of her stomach again and the dryness in her mouth.

"Did you two get your shopping done already? I did not expect to see you until the town had closed its doors for the night," he laughed. He stood to allow Francie to slip into the booth beside him. Corey took the seat across the table.

"Be nice, *mon frere*," Francie smiled. "Did you find something suitable to wear to my party?"

When Corey had word of Phillipe's return from France, she hoped he would ask her to be his date for the party and had turned down all other invitations. Now she was unsure of the idea and shifted uneasily at the mention of the party. What would it feel like to be in his arms, dancing to a dreamy waltz?

"Who was that gorgeous creature you were talking with, Francie?" Phillipe was asking.

"You mean Morgan? She's just one of the girls we go to school with."

"Will she be at your party?"

"Yes, she'll be there," Francie grinned. "Well, well, do I detect a spark of interest there?"

Phillipe ignored the remark, "Do you know if she has a date?"

"I think she was coming with Corey and two other girls, why?"

"Could you introduce me to her and perhaps I will extend an invitation," he winked. Then addressing Corey he said, "You wouldn't be too upset if she came with me instead, would you?"

Humiliation and jealousy flared within Corey at the same time and she wanted to flee, but it was too late. Morgan was sliding in beside Corey, blocking her escape.

"Morgan, I would like you to meet my brother, Phillipe. Phillipe, this is Morgan Connor."

"*Enchante, mademoiselle...*" Phillipe began, but Corey interrupted.

"I really am sorry, but I have to leave. I promised Angelique I would be home by three and it's already ten past. You will excuse me, won't you?" Corey apologized, edging Morgan out of the seat. "Morgan, dear, don't let him trick you. The first time I saw Phillipe he pretended not to speak English, and then listened to what I said to Francie about him." Turning to Phillipe she cooed, "Phillipe, you weren't planning that same old trick on Morgan, were you?" And smiling sarcastically, she looked directly into his eyes, "*Bon jour*, everyone."

Corey flew through the front doorway and up the stairs to her room. She was angry at herself for acting such a fool back at the ice cream parlor and at Phillipe for causing her to behave so. How could she go to the party now and watch Phillipe and Morgan laughing and dancing? The very thought was more than she could bear and she buried her face in the pillow, trying to shut out the painful vision.

Angelique knocked softly at the door and stuck her head into the room. "I thought that blur going up the stairs looked familiar. What's wrong, dear, couldn't you find a dress?"

"I found one all right, for all the good it will do," Corey pouted. "I am not going to the party, Angelique. In fact, I'm going to return the dress tomorrow." She picked up the box and hurled it onto a chair.

"Did you have a misunderstanding with Francie?" Angelique asked, putting her arms around Corey. "Don't be hasty, dear, I'm sure you will have it all worked out by the time of the party."

"No, it's not Francie, it's Phillipe. Oh, Angelique, I hate him!" she moaned.

Angelique studied the girl closely. "Those are mighty strong words, young lady. Whatever did he do?"

Corey told her about the incident and the terrible manner in which she had behaved. Angelique chuckled softly to herself. Ah, my little Corey, hate him? I think not.

"You know, Corey, Phillipe still thinks of you as the little playmate of yesterday, not the young woman you have become. It's going to be up to you to change that. You can't do it by staying home or avoiding him anywhere else," she soothed.

"What am I supposed to do…flaunt myself? I don't think I care anymore whether he notices me or not!" Corey wailed.

"Oh, pooh! Go to the party and enjoy yourself. Be polite to Phillipe, and should the occasion present itself, dance with him. Oh, I'm not saying he will change his thinking about you overnight, but there are subtle ways of chasing a man and bringing him around. With your ingenuity, I am sure you will come up with a way; in fact, I'm counting on it. Now, no more talk of not going. Dry your eyes and let's go down for a cup of tea."

❦ ❦ ❦

"Corey, you sure look spiffy," called Francie, bouncing down the stairs at her friend's entrance. "Turn around, let's have a look. *Oo-oo,* I like your hair."

Corey patted the waves. "Do you really think it looks okay? I haven't had time to get used to it being so short yet, and I feel silly." A snug-fitting cap, dotted with rhinestones, covered much of her head, but the short haircut wasn't completely hidden.

"Well, don't. I'd tell you if it didn't look right, wouldn't I? Wow, and that dress is a knockout. Let me look at you." She took Corey's hands and spun her around. The blue dress was the exact color of her eyes and the sheer material seemed to float around her as she moved. "Come on, the band has already started and wait till the boys get a load of you." They both entered the ballroom laughing merrily.

"What about Sally? I was supposed to wait for her," Corey asked, suddenly remembering her promise to wait.

"She's already here. I told her I would watch for you."

The ballroom was a long hall, lighted by a chandelier on either end. A row of chairs was placed along the walls, broken at one point by a small alcove where a table had been set with punch and cake. At one end of the room, french doors opened onto a terrace, while at the other end, a raised platform held the band.

Corey looked around the room for Sally and, not seeing her, slipped easily through the mingling guests toward the punch bowl. The anxiety of her entrance had left her mouth dry and the punch would be a welcome relief.

"Hullo, Corey," Chad Gorman waved. "You just getting here?"

"Yes, Chad," she cringed as he moved toward her. She had hoped to remain inconspicuous for a while longer, at least long enough to gather more self-confidence. If only she had stuck to her decision to stay home…

"How's about a dance?" he grinned, bowing dramatically.

"Well, I…" she began, but from the corner of her eye she saw Phillipe and Morgan heading in their direction. "I would like to dance with you, Chad," she answered quickly and started onto the dance floor before Phillipe could reach the alcove.

Corey was only half listening to what Chad was saying as they danced. Her attention was directed at Morgan, who was now standing with a group of girls talking and laughing as they watched Philippe disappearing into the crowd. Even Corey had to admit Morgan was beautiful this evening. Her reddish-gold hair shimmered as she stood beneath a string of lights. The green gown she wore reached to her ankles and the jagged hemline fluttered in the breeze blowing through the open doors. One of the girls had just whispered something to Morgan and a blush crept across the creamy skin. Corey could imagine she was teasing her about Phillipe. After all, he was the talk of the party among the females. Corey had noticed more than a few heads turn as he walked past, followed by huddled whispers.

The music stopped and Corey suddenly realized Chad had asked her a question and was waiting for a reply.

"I'm sorry, Chad. What did you say?"

"Let's go out on the terrace and get some air. It's beginning to get stuffy in here."

"Okay," she answered simply, thinking it would be nice to get away from the preening Morgan Connor.

"I'll just grab some punch first. Wait here for me," he winked.

Out on the terrace Chad produced a small silver flask from under his coat and poured a ration of its contents into his cup.

"Want some?" He asked with a sly grin. "Spice up your evening a little and I must say, you could sure use it."

"What on earth are you doing with *that* at this party?" she demanded. "You're a fool, Chad Gorman."

Chad moved closer to her, putting his arm around her waist. "Aw, c'mon, Corey, loosen up a little. Everybody takes a nip once in a while. It's the in thing," he murmured, leaning even closer, his breath heavy with the odor of whiskey.

Corey put her hands against his chest and gave a determined push. She was furious with herself for being so preoccupied she had failed to notice he had been drinking.

"Take your hands from me this very minute," she said through clenched teeth.

"Gimme a kiss first, then I'll let you go. Just one little one."

There was a slight movement from the corner of the terrace just as Corey raised her hand to give Chad a slap across his face.

"*Ma ami,* there you are. My poor sister has been looking everywhere for you. Come, let me take you to her," Phillipe scolded, stepping from the shadows and, slipping his arm around her, he guided her back inside. "You really should be more careful who you go out into the moonlight with, *ma ami,*" he whispered in her ear, grinning broadly.

Corey whirled around to face him and snapped, "I am quite capable of taking care of myself, thank you. Why don't you run along back to your date where your attention is more needed and appreciated." She hurried across the room, leaving Phillipe staring after her.

"Corey, over here," Sally called from the alcove. "I'm sorry I didn't see you come in. Did you get rid of that creep? He's really ossified, you know."

"Yes. I found that out," Corey answered, her voice tinged with annoyance. Changing the subject, she asked, "Have you seen Francie?"

"She was here a moment ago...oh, there she is now."

"Will you excuse me, Sally? I need to talk to her." Corey wanted to go home. Her head was throbbing and so far the evening had been disastrous.

"Are you all right, Corey? I mean...he didn't do anything to you..."

"No, I'm fine, I just have a splitting headache. I should have stayed home as I had planned, but I thought it would pass. Excuse me, please?"

Phillipe took Francie by the arm and pulled her to him. He whispered something in her ear, then strode across the dance floor and out onto the terrace.

"*M'seur*," he addressed Chad, resting a hand firmly on his shoulder. "I believe it is time for you to say good night. We simply will not tolerate your behavior here tonight, nor at any other time. So, if you will come with me, I will see that you find your way out..."

Chad jerked his shoulder from Phillipe's grasp and leered, "I don't see that this is any of your business, Frenchie, and I will thank you to keep your nose out of it."

"Ah, but you are wrong. This is my home, too, and you have insulted one of our guests. To make matters worse, you chose someone I look on as a sister. Now, you can go quietly or otherwise, but make no mistake about it, you will go." He looked long and hard into Chad's eyes, his scowl darkening as he waited for the next move.

"Awright, awright, your party is a real bore, anyway." Chad whirled around and stomped out across the lawn.

"Corey, I am so sorry you were exposed to such dreadful behavior...at my party, too," Francie soothed, "Please do not let such a thing ruin your evening. He won't bother you anymore. Phillipe has sent him home.

"There was no damage done, Francie, but I really think I am going to have to go home," Corey assured her, explaining about her headache.

"You are sure it has nothing to do with Chad?"

"No, that's not it, I promise. This started long before your party. Now, quit worrying about me and get back to your guests. We'll get together in a day or so and you can fill me in on what I missed. Okay?"

"If you are sure, *ma ami*," Francie said hesitantly.

"I am sure. Now get going, that's an order," Corey smiled to reassure her and Francie turned, casting an uncertain look back at her friend.

Corey stepped out the front door into the night air, breathing deeply the freshness. She would get Phillipe out of her thoughts and try desperately to put their relationship back where it belonged. There would be nothing to gain if she pursued a different course. *Face reality*, she thought, climbing into the roadster Angelique had given her for graduation.

❦ ❦ ❦

Two days had passed since the party and Corey felt she had gotten the problem with Phillipe worked out quite well. She bore no ill feelings toward Morgan, and she felt the next time she saw Phillipe her emotions would be in their proper place. She could now venture outside the confines of her home without fear of facing him. Besides, she had no intentions of joining the ranks of girls swooning at his feet.

Corey picked up the telephone to call Francie. There was little more than a week before her birthday party and she wanted her friend to help with some errands in town.

"Dear, there's a letter here for you," Angelique summoned.

"Who is it from?"

"Tommy Rice."

Although they had kept up their correspondence through the years, it had been two years since she had heard from Tommy. Now, she wondered about her old friend. What kind of person had he become? Did he still go fishing in that pond he liked so well? She smiled to herself at the memory. She could only picture him as a little boy, the little boy who had helped her escape from Aunt Lizzie. How long ago that seemed!

May 28, 1927

Dear Corey,

I know you must be wondering why you are hearing from me after so long a time, but first things first. I would like to congratulate you on your graduation. I know it was an exciting day for you and I know it was eagerly anticipated as mine was for me.

Now, the reason I am writing. My grandparents, who live in Washington, have extended an invitation to visit their ranch for the summer and, for my graduation gift, have sent me a train ticket. My parents think it would be a good idea, since I have not been more than ten miles from home and will soon be going off to college. (They seem to think I will be less of a hick if I do some traveling. Ha!)

Since I have to travel through your neck of the woods, your uncle has asked if I might stop by and see you. Corey, he talks about you often and I am sure he would come himself but, as you know, he is getting on in years, or so he says. Between you and me I think he feels you haven't forgiven all that happened.

I shall be leaving on the night of June 6, and reach your city on Friday, June 9th. I know this is short notice and if it is inconvenient please call me or send a wire as there is no time for a letter. My phone number is Parkview 243.

Unless I hear from you to the contrary, I will be seeing you soon.

Your friend,

Tommy Rice

Corey put the letter down with mixed emotions. In one way it would be exciting to see Tommy again, but she couldn't help remembering their last reunion and the disappointment she had felt at first. They had both grown up now and perhaps there would not be the childish expectations as before.
"Are you asking my permission?" Angelique asked after Corey told her about the letter. "You don't need to, this is your home, too. I think it would be nice for you to see him again. After all, he was a close friend."
"It's just that I'm not sure..."
"Nonsense, it will be good for you. Call up the boy and tell him you'd be delighted to have him," Angelique scolded.
Corey gave the number to the long-distance operator. "Mr. Tommy Rice, please," she requested of the man on the other end of the line.
"This is Tom Rice, and to whom am I speaking?"
"Tommy, you don't sound like you. Oh, I'm sorry, this is Corey," she laughed excitedly into the phone.
"Corey!" he exclaimed. There was a moment of silence; then he continued, disappointment clearly showing in his voice, "I knew I should have given you

more warning about this trip, Corey, but your uncle approached me a few days ago. I could always stop on my way back home."

"Don't be silly, Tommy. That isn't why I called. I am looking forward to your visit and it couldn't come at a better time. Angelique is giving me a birthday party the day after your arrival and I would like nothing better than to have you as my escort."

"Very good. My train gets in there around six-thirty and I would like to take you and Angelique to dinner, if that is okay with the two of you."

"Yes. She will come with me and it would be our pleasure to accompany you to dinner afterward," Corey repeated for Angelique, making sure there were no objections. "See you then, Tommy…er, Tom."

Corey hung up the phone and happily hugged Angelique. "I'm glad you talked me into it," she sang. "I have to tell Francie the good news. She will be so excited, getting to meet Tommy."

🍁 🍁 🍁

"Well, hello, stranger," Phillipe greeted mischievously. "I was beginning to think you had forgotten your way to our door."

"Don't be silly, Phillipe, it has only been two days. Is Francie home?" she quipped, ignoring the flutter in her stomach.

"*Oui*, she is here. Won't you come in while I find her?"

"That won't be necessary. I'm right here," Francie announced. "Corey, you look so happy. I see you recovered from your headache quite well, that is good. But there is something else…"

"I noticed that, too, Corey," agreed Phillipe. "I thought perhaps it was seeing me again," he teased.

"Well, you were wrong, Phillipe. I'd like to speak to Francie alone, if you don't mind."

"*Tsk, tsk,* just as in the old days trying to get rid of me. Well, I can take a hint," he grinned as the two girls went into the parlor.

"I brought your invitation to my party," Corey began.

"Am I invited, also?" Phillipe asked, sticking his head into the room.

"Phillipe!" Francie scolded.

"I'm going, but there had better be an invitation there for me, too."

After Phillipe left Corey turned to Francie again. "Guess what? I'm having a house guest next week," she squealed. "Remember the boy I told you about who loaned me his clothes when I ran away? He's coming to visit me and will be here for my party!"

"Oh, Corey, how wonderful for you! How exciting that an old boyfriend would travel such a distance to see you again. I mean, that is so romantic."

"Well, hardly that. I'll admit when we were children we talked of getting married when we grew up, but that was long ago and I hardly know him now," she laughed.

"Still and all, you never know. Maybe he will turn out to be your Prince Charming," Francie grinned slyly. "I am pleased for you and look forward to meeting him. Now, why have I not heard from you these past two days?"

"I have really been busy with this party, getting the invitations ready and all. I could ask you the same question, you know."

"I am sorry, Corey, but it seems there is always someone here and I haven't had time to think properly. Which reminds me, why don't we go to the ice cream parlor and have a soda? If we stay around here we won't have a chance to visit and, frankly, all these so-called friends are starting to bore me. I have begun calling Phillipe down when the girls come over. That seems to be why they are here anyway," she sighed.

"Can I give you girls a lift somewhere," Phillipe offered when Francie and Corey emerged from the house. "I have to go to Father's office."

"You can drop us off in town, brother dear," Francie cooed, tweaking him on the cheek.

Morgan had just arrived at the ice cream parlor as Phillipe dropped the girls off. "I'll pick you up here afterward if you like," he stated and as Morgan approached the car, "Good morning, Morgan."

"Good morning, Phillipe. You haven't forgotten we have a date tonight, have you?" she smiled sweetly, taking note that Corey heard, as had been her intention.

Phillipe laughed, "I haven't forgotten. S'long all," he waved cheerily.

"Well, Corey, I see you have been added to the growing list of my competition," Morgan smirked.

"I wouldn't worry about it, Morgan. Phillipe has been more like a brother to me for many years," Corey retorted. "If you will excuse us, Francie and I were going to have a soda."

"You wouldn't mind if I join you?"

"Of course not," Corey answered icily. It was becoming increasingly more difficult for Corey to be polite with Morgan, especially when she behaved this way, but she was determined to overcome her ill feelings. Morgan had never been a close friend, but she had run around with the same group as Corey.

Corey and Francie spent the next half-hour listening to Morgan talk about Phillipe until Francie finally said she had to be getting home.

"Are you coming, Corey?"

"No, Francie, I have a few things to take care of while I'm in town. I will see you later, though."

"Do you mind if I tag along, Corey?" Morgan asked. "I'd like to talk to you about your party."

"Sure, Morgan, but I have to warn you the errands are boring. I have to stop by the caterer and approve the menu, pick up the place cards for the table and…"

"That's okay, I don't mind," Morgan interrupted.

The printer's shop was located in a seedy part of town and Corey grinned at Morgan's displeasure over being there. She wanted to tag along, so she did not say anything, but Corey could tell she wished she were somewhere else. Corey didn't mind the neighborhood. She had done some volunteer work for a doctor not far from here, in a small clinic for the poor. She had become quite familiar with the area and used the merchants here when possible.

"Help! Please, someone help my friend," a voice called.

Corey looked down the street and saw an old, bedraggled man bending over another one lying on the sidewalk. People scurried out of the way as he reached out trying to stop someone to help him. Corey hurried to him while Morgan rushed to keep up.

"What is the trouble?" Corey asked.

"I don't know, I can't seem to get my friend awake," the man cried frantically.

Corey knelt beside the man's still form and put her hand to his cheek. It felt warm to her touch, so she knew he wasn't dead. She gently prodded his shoulder a few times but got no response. His face was an ashen gray and he seemed barely breathing.

"Corey, what on earth? You are liable to catch something from that bum," Morgan wailed.

"Morgan, the man needs help. Would you have me just leave him here as everyone else seems to be doing? And as far as catching something, I can wash my hands more easily than my conscience. You go get Doc Winslow. His office is just around that corner there. Be quick!"

The man's eyes fluttered momentarily and he stared at Corey before closing them again. She found something very familiar about those eyes. The look...oh, my god! It was Pete, from the hobo camp. She would never forget that haunting look when she awoke and found him hovering over her.

"Pete, Pete, can you hear me? It's Corey." But he had slipped back into unconsciousness. Poor Pete, he was so frail and old-looking now. It was clear he had never found his family. Corey brushed the thinning, unkempt hair from his forehead and tenderly stroked his cheek. How terribly sad she felt for him.

"Move back and give the man some air," Doc Winslow ordered, pushing his way through the crowd now gathered around. He went quickly to work on Pete and shook his head slowly.

"He isn't...dead, is he, Doc?" Corey asked.

"No, Corey, but...come over here," he instructed, leading her aside. "It's only a matter of time, though. I've seen several cases like this one. He is suffering from malnutrition and rotgut alcohol. It's common with these tramps, I'm afraid."

"He's a hobo, not a tramp," Corey corrected. "Can you help him?"

"Temporarily, but I'm afraid the damage is irreparable. Besides, he will just go back to doing the same thing, drinking whatever he can get his hands on and not eating properly." The doctor answered, an eyebrow quirked as he noted her correction. He would let his curiosity lie until she was ready to explain how she knew the difference.

"Do what you can. I'll round up some clean clothes for him and I'll be around later," Corey suggested, "and don't list him as a John Doe. His name is Pete. At least he will have that much."

"Corey," Morgan gasped, "you know this...this Pete?"

"Yes."

"But how...where?"

"It's a long story. One day perhaps I will tell you all about it, but right now I have a lot to do."

Morgan looked at Pete with disgust on her face, then back to Corey. It seemed there might be something shady in Corey's past and she could hardly stand the dismissal. Little Miss Goody-Goody might not be all she was cracked up to be, Morgan sneered,

Corey noted the look of disgust and she faced Morgan sternly, "I wouldn't be so quick to judge. You don't know anything about this man or why he is the way he is." Corey checked herself; it wouldn't help matters to try and explain anything to Morgan and she didn't have the time, anyway. "I'll see you later," she tossed over her shoulder and left a startled Morgan standing on the sidewalk.

Corey never got to talk to Pete. The few times she visited him he was sleeping and two days later he simply walked out of the hospital as the late shift was changing. She suspected he had been assisted by his friend. She faced the empty bed forlornly, wishing there had been more she could do. What would become of him? Turning to leave, she caught sight of a crumpled piece of paper on the floor and she bent down to retrieve it. As she smoothed out the wrinkles, a hastily scrawled name appeared. Had he finally found his wife and been rejected once again? Was this the reason he ended up unconscious in the street? Should she try to find this person whose name was on the paper and plead for Pete? But she remembered the look on Morgan's face when she looked at Pete. Perhaps that was the look on the face of this woman he sought. Maybe things would be best left as they were, the humiliation poor Pete would have to endure. Evidently Pete had thought better of going any further with this person for he had discarded the piece of paper and, presumably his past as well. No, she would not interfere; it would be better all the way around.

🍁   🍁   🍁

Corey glanced nervously at the clock. Ten more minutes and Tommy's train would be arriving. Angelique patted her on the hand, sensing her stress.

"You are going to be a nervous wreck, Corey. Everything is going to be fine. Relax and just let things come naturally. You'll see, everything will fall into place."

"I wish I could be sure of that," Corey groaned. Then a train pulled into the station and she exclaimed, "It's early!"

"They watched anxiously as four people got off, none being a young man alone. When no one else appeared, Corey looked down the platform at the other end of the train.

"There he is," Angelique nodded. "It has to be. He is about the right age and there is no one with him."

Corey waited to be sure, watching the tall, young man brush a lock of brown hair off his forehead. His gaze calmly swept the people until it rested on Corey and Angelique. A smile lit up his face as he hurried toward them. He picked Corey up, whirling her around. "I hope you are Corey or I am going to be terribly embarrassed!"

"You have the right person," she laughed.

"And you must be Angelique. Please forgive me for being so personal as to use your first name, but I don't remember ever hearing your last name," he apologized, taking her hand warmly in his and shaking it.

"Angelique will do nicely, Tommy. I don't stand much on formality among friends," Angelique replied. "How as your trip?"

"Fine, fine. Saw a lot of beautiful country and met some nice people," he grinned. "I thought Texas was the only place with beautiful country, but I had never seen real mountains before. We have hills, some of them pretty tall, but nothing like what I have seen the past two days. What a sight for these bumpkin eyes of mine."

Corey smiled appreciatively, for she knew the feeling well. She had been equally amazed when she left home and saw all kinds of new and exciting things. It would be fun to compare notes with Tommy, reliving that excitement again. Suddenly she was thinking even more strongly of Andy and she felt sadthat she had let her life become so involved with the little everyday events that she had shut him out so easily. Why hadn't he tried to contact her? Had he forgotten her? Had something happened to him that kept him away? He was not dead, she felt sure of that, but how was she so certain? Was it an intuition or simply because she would not think otherwise?

"Corey," Angelique's voice broke into her reverie, "are you coming with us, dear, or were you planning to stay here?" she laughed.

"I'm sorry, Angelique, Tommy. I guess I was daydreaming," Corey apologized. "Are we ready to go to dinner now?"

The dinner crowd was in full swing when they reached Latimer's, but their wait for a table was a short one. Tommy helped the women take their seats and eased into a chair between them. He picked up the menu left by the waiter, and his eyes came to rest on the fish. A slow grin crossed his tan face and he turned to Corey.

"Remember that old fishing hole of mine? Well, I bought the property it sits on. Trouble is I haven't had time to go fishing for almost the whole year. I bought me a farm just outside town and I've been trying to get it in shape. I got the land cleared for the house and the stakes laid out before I left. It'll be next spring before we can plant anything, and I have hired a man to take care of the place and the few animals I've managed to acquire so far," Tommy beamed.

"How are you going to manage the place and go to college, too?"

"That's one of the reasons I hired this fellow, plus I'll be coming home for the holidays. I'll get the house started before I leave and my father will supervise the rest. After it's finished, my folks will move in. You know, my father is planning to retire next summer and he has some good offers on his farm equipment store."

"I am amazed, Tommy. How did you…where did th…"

"Money come from?" He finished the question for Corey. "Between my folks and grandparents, they had set aside a little nest egg to get me started after I got out of school. This property was a one-in-a-million opportunity and I got it for a song. Of course, I have been working, too, after school and summers since I was fourteen. And I must say, I've been very frugal."

The waiter had been standing idly by their table waiting for them to decide what to order. Discreetly, he cleared his throat making them aware of his presence. Without further ado, Tommy ordered their meals and was about to continue when again they were interrupted.

"Why, Corey, it's been days since I last saw you. Where on earth have you been keeping yourself?" Morgan purred as she approached the table, her arm securely looped through Phillipe's as if she were to relax her hold he would slip away.

"Why, Morgan, it was only last Wednesday," Corey mimicked Morgan's tone. Dating Phillipe had changed her into somewhat of a snob and Corey found her more intolerable to be around. "Morgan, Phillipe, I'd like you to meet Tommy Rice," she introduced him when it was evident Morgan was not leaving until she had done so.

"Tommy, it's a pleasure," Morgan smiled sweetly. "I don't recall seeing you around here before. Is this another one of Corey's little well kept secrets?"

"Morgan, the pleasure is all mine," Tommy returned, standing to acknowledge the introduction and he extended his hand to Phillipe. "I am just a visitor to your fair city. I just arrived from Texas this afternoon."

Phillipe shook Tommy's hand as he made a quick appraisal of the young man from Corey's past. Admittedly he had been curious about Tommy after overhearing Corey and his sister talking about him, but he would just as soon the meeting had taken place under different circumstances, when he had been better prepared.

"I believe we have intruded on your reunion," Phillipe stated, a hint of annoyance creeping into his voice. "I'm sure we will be seeing you again before you leave, Tommy." He bowed ceremoniously to Corey and Angelique. "Bon appetit, ladies."

Corey watched in amusement as Phillipe ushered the pouting Morgan from the restaurant. Knowing Morgan, Phillipe would certainly get an earful once they were outside, as this had obviously not been the exit she had planned.

CHAPTER 17

Corey stood by the window in her darkened room looking out across the moonlit gardens below. Soon her guests would be arriving, but, for the moment, she felt an overwhelming desire for this short quiet time to herself.

The scent of roses and jasmine permeated the still air outside her open window. Leaning closer to capture the scent, Corey could hear the faint strains of music as the band went over the selections they would play at the party. It was truly a night of which dreams were made and it played upon her senses, filling her to a point she wanted to cry out to relieve the pressure. A vision crept into her consciousness…a vision of dancing alone with Phillipe in the garden. She could almost feel his arms around her, his eyes looking into hers. Suddenly, the vision changed. It was no longer she and Phillipe, but another couple. It was a young Andy and Angelique in the moonlight, she in the dress Andy had described that long ago night and he in his hobo clothes. Startled, she blinked her eyes and the vision was gone. At the same time, the sound of someone knocking at the door summoned her to the present.

"Corey, is everything all right?" Angelique called.

"Yes, Angelique, everything is fine," she answered, gazing uneasily into the garden.

"It's getting late and we were beginning to worry about you."

"I'll be right there." Corey sighed, turning from the window and in so doing caught a slight movement in the garden. She turned back and peered into the darkness, but whatever it had been was gone. Probably her imagination, she shrugged. It certainly seemed to be working overtime tonight.

❦ ❦ ❦

Andy stepped farther back into the shadows where he would not be seen. Still, he wanted to have a good vantage point of the house, hoping to be able to pick Corey out of the crowd.

He sat down slowly, pushing back the weariness that had been with him for several weeks and reflected on the events that had taken place since he last saw Corey. He had traveled with Injun and Lord Mayor, being unable to face the emptiness in his life. They had traveled across the country extensively, working when they could find a job. When he worked, he attacked his job with a vengeance to keep from thinking about the child. When he traveled, he pushed himself and others fiercely.

Time had, of course, softened the pain, but it had also taken its toll. He wasn't as agile as he used to be and it was getting more difficult to catch the trains and continue the life he had been leading. Realizing this he was overcome with an obsession to see Corey again and visit the place of his beginnings while he could still make the trip. Perhaps with the help of Injun and Lord Mayor, he would rebuild the old place; then Corey could come and visit him there. He smiled comfortably at the thought and settled back, waiting for the party to end.

Corey stood in the foyer with Tommy greeting her guests as they arrived and making the proper introductions. A festive mood had replaced the uneasiness she had felt before and she fairly beamed beneath the huge crystal chandelier, its myriad of sparkling lights playing upon her dark, bobbing head. Her cheeks held a faint blush from the warm evening, and occasionally she flicked open a small fan with the slightest movement from her wrist, waving it in front of her face.

A small group had arrived together and Corey rushed through the introductions, grinning at the forlorn Tommy as he tried to remember all the names. One of the girls bent forward to whisper something to her, but she never heard it. Phillipe had just walked in with Morgan and suddenly Corey's heart was pulsating wildly, filling her head with the sound. Briefly their eyes met and Corey felt the blush deepen in her cheeks and she fought to control her emotions.

"Happy birthday, *ma ami*," Phillipe smiled and bending toward her, brushed his lips against her cheek. "You look absolutely smashing this evening and I must say, birthdays definitely agree with you."

"You are always so gallant, Phillipe," Corey answered, trying to remain unaffected by his performance. She took a deep breath and turned to Tommy, hoping he would say something to Phillipe and rescue her before she made a complete fool of herself, but he was engaged in conversation with Morgan.

"Now, Corey, is that anyway to accept a sincere compliment?" Phillipe laughed. He started to move away, then turned back to her. "You will save a dance for me this time, won't you?" He winked mischievously, and then spoke briefly with Tommy before escorting Morgan into the ballroom.

"I think I have some competition for your attention this evening," Tommy teased when they were alone again.

"What do you mean, Tommy?" She asked absently.

"That fellow Phillipe," Tommy answered, "More than a friend?"

"What makes you think that?" she asked cautiously.

"You fairly sparkle when he is around. I noticed it in the restaurant yesterday and now, tonight."

"Is it that obvious?" she sighed, "Oh, Tommy, I feel so foolish." She bowed her head under his direct gaze.

Tommy put his hand beneath her chin, lifting it slowly. "Do you think it is safe to abandon our post here and join the party?"

She nodded and smiled in spite of herself. "I think everybody who is coming is already here."

He lifted her arm and slipped it through his then led her into the ballroom. Just inside the door he bowed theatrically and asked, "May I have the first dance, beautiful lady?"

They danced around the floor in silence for a while, and then Tommy whispered in her ear, "What are you going to do about Phillipe? I mean, are you going to let him know how you feel about him?"

"Absolutely not. As you can see he already has someone. Besides, I simply do not wish to add myself to the list of moonstruck young ladies chasing after Phillipe Bernard. I'm sure I will get over it, given time," she chided. "Now, if you don't mind, I'd like to change the subject."

"Of course, Corey," he smiled down at her. "But if you ever need a sympathetic ear…"

"Thank you, Tommy, you are a dear friend," Corey replied and kissed him affectionately on the cheek.

Meanwhile, Phillipe had been watching Corey across the room, somewhat confused. He could not figure out why she had become so hostile since his return when they had been all but inseparable before. She avoided him, and when she spoke it was always sharply. This had him so puzzled he could not keep her out of his mind and the sight of her friendliness with Tommy caused him great concern. A dark frown creased his brow as he watched her kiss this young man and he took Morgan's hand firmly, leading her out onto the dance floor, determined he would dismiss this matter from his thoughts.

Tommy watched over Corey's shoulder as Phillipe and Morgan moved to the center of the floor and maneuvered Corey toward them. When they moved alongside, he deftly switched partners with Phillipe. "You don't mind, do you, old man?" and he whisked Morgan to the other end of the room.

For a moment neither spoke, but eased into step with the music. Phillipe could feel the tension in her body and asked, "Would you prefer to sit this one out?"

"No, it's…it's all right," her voice almost a whisper. She could feel the trembling begin in her body as Phillipe tightened his arm around her waist, and again she fought to contain herself. She could feel the warmth of his body against hers and his breath against her hair and it was almost too much to bear.

"Corey, might I talk to you?" Phillipe's voice broke into her struggle and he released his hold.

"Sure," she breathed gratefully.

"Would you mind if we went outside where it is quieter?"

"Do you think that wise? After all, you did come with Morgan and she might take offense," she snapped, having regained some of her composure.

"Morgan will be fine. She seems quite taken with your…houseguest, is it?" his voice edged with annoyance and the frown played upon his brow again.

Corey's heart sank as she noticed his irritation. He was actually jealous of Tommy and Morgan, and all the while she thought their dating had been more casual than…she would not let that thought go any further. Instead, she followed Phillipe through the open doors onto the balcony.

Phillipe took a cigarette from its pack and tapped it gently against the railing before placing it in his mouth. He struck a match, holding it away from him until the burst of flame softened and he gazed across the moonlit gardens.

"Oh, Phillipe, when did you start that?" Corey scolded.

Phillipe touched the match to his cigarette and filled his lungs with smoke, then released it slowly watching it hang on the still air. "While I was in France," he answered, turning to face Corey. "everyone else was doing it so I decided to give it a try. That is what I was doing on the terrace the night I came to your rescue at Francie's party." His eyes twinkled remembering Corey's anger when he had taken her inside, her cheeks aflame and her eyes sparkling as they always did when she was angry.

"I didn't need your help, Mr. Bernard," she bristled, "as I told you then I was quite capable of handling it."

"Corey, I didn't bring you out here to start an argument, in fact, I want to declare a truce. Whatever I have done to make you so angry at me, I apologize. Ever since I returned, you have been nothing but uncivil toward me. Why? Where is the Corey I knew before?"

"People change, Phillipe. Feelings change. Perhaps that is what you have failed to notice," her voice strained above the loud beating of her heart. How could she tell him what was really wrong? Especially now that Morgan…Again she stopped the thought. She turned away from him, staring into the night and once again the vision stole her mind, the vision of she and Phillipe dancing in the garden. She became so totally consumed by it she did not realize Phillipe was talking until he took her by the shoulders.

"Corey, Corey," he said, shaking her gently. "Is something wrong?"

She was looking into his eyes, his face so close to hers she could almost feel his touch. Breathing was difficult for her and the warm night was making her dizzy. She was aware Phillipe's mouth was moving and strained to hear what he was saying all the while watching his mouth, getting lost in it.

"Corey, *ma petite*," he murmured thickly, "please don't be angry with me anymore," and he bent even closer, his lips reaching for hers.

"Well, well, what are you two doing out here?" Morgan purred.

Phillipe stiffened and without taking his eyes from Corey, he answered sharply, "I was about to wish Corey a happy birthday, Morgan," and he placed a quick kiss on Corey's lips. "Happy birthday, *ma ami*, and don't forget what I said." he winked wickedly and grinned slowly at her before Morgan took him by the arm, leading him back into the house.

"I'm sorry, Corey, old friend. I tried my best," Tommy shrugged, stepping onto the balcony.

"Oh, Tommy, what am I going to do?" she asked helplessly and he put his arm around her as the tears began.

"Hey, no tears on your birthday," Tommy scolded as he took a handkerchief from his pocket. "Now, dry your eyes and listen to me. From what I saw, Phillipe has more than a friendly interest in you, maybe he just doesn't know it yet. I think it is going to be up to you to open his eyes and if it hadn't been for the interruption I think you would have done just that."

"You're wrong, Tommy. What you saw was a friendly birthday kiss and nothing more," she sighed. "It's Morgan who holds his interest. Why, he got so jealous when you took her away in there! Do you suppose he was using me to make her jealous?" she sniffed scornfully. "And fool that I am, I played right along with him. *Oooh,* that…that…" she sputtered.

"Corey, Corey, what am I going to do with you?" Tommy shook his head slowly. He knew it was no use pursuing this. He would not be able to convince her otherwise. "Come on back in and finish the dance we started a while ago."

"In a minute, I have to pull myself together first. Be a dear, Tommy, and let me have a few minutes alone," she smiled behind the tears. "I'll be fine, really I will."

❦   ❦   ❦

Corey slipped out of her clothes and tossed them carelessly onto a chair. She pulled her nightgown absently over her head and reflected on the party. In spite of the moment with Phillipe, the evening had gone well with everyone having such a good time they had been late in leaving. She had managed to put Phillipe somewhat out of her mind and enjoy what was left of the evening. She had decided to give him what he wanted and that was to be friends, nothing more and she could handle that. Yes, she smiled wryly, she was in complete control of her emotions again and she was determined not to ever let that control slip again.

She picked up the cup of hot chocolate and finished it, making a face at the bitter dregs in the bottom of the cup. Poor, dear Harvey. He knew how she looked forward to a cup of hot chocolate before going to bed and, even though climbing the stairs was a real chore for him now, he personally saw to it she had a cup waiting. She would miss him when he retired next month.

Corey sat the cup down and stretched laboriously. The bed was going to feel so good after the long day and she reached for the switch on the lamp when a sharp click against her window stopped her. She listened closely, but there was no further sound, so shrugging it off to her imagination, she switched off the lamp. Again the sound of a click against her window, but this time a small stone found its way through the half-open window and bounced with a clatter on the floor.

Corey eased toward the window and looked to the ground below, taking care to keep behind the curtains. While the moon still lit the night, it had moved across the heavens to the other side of the house and deep shadows kept her from seeing who had tossed the rocks. A slight movement caught her attention and she called softly, "Who's there?"

"A tired old 'bo with a hankerin' to see his growed up girl," Andy whispered back.

"Andy! Oh, Andy!" Corey squealed. Then, "Wait there, I'll be right down."

Corey was halfway down the hall when she realized she was in her nightgown and she ran back to her room, pulled on her robe and bounded down the stairs. She flew into Andy's arms almost knocking both of them to the ground and clung to him, weeping joyously. When she had spent her tears and found her voice, questions poured from her mouth.

"Where have you been? Why did you stay away so long? How is Lord Mayor...and Injun? Did they come with you?"

"Whoa, girl," Andy laughed. "Let me catch my breath. You durn near jostled me into next week."

"I'm sorry, Andy. I seem to have forgotten my manners. Come, let's go into the kitchen and I'll make some coffee. It won't be as good as the campfire coffee, but we can pretend," she laughed.

Once inside the kitchen, Corey made a pot of coffee while Andy settled himself at the table.

"You sure growed into a right purty woman, Corey. Bet you broke lots o' hearts a'ready. Tell ole Andy whutcha been doin' all these years," his eyes twinkled merrily as he reached across the table and patted her hand.

"You first, Andy. I want to know all about where you have been and what you have been doing."

"Ain't much to tell. Been travelin' all over, workin' when I could find it. Can't stay fer very long in one place," he paused long enough to pour some coffee into the saucer, blowing it gently before sipping it. "Leastways, I useta keep movin'. This here ole body's slowin' down on me, though, and I'm afraid my travelin's 'most over."

Corey looked at Andy closely and for the first time since his arrival, noticed the deep weariness in her friend and she grew worried. "Nonsense," she scoffed, trying to keep the concern from her voice, "all you need is some rest and tender loving care. Why I bet you haven't had a decent meal in ages."

"Naw, Corey girl, it ain't thet. I know it's time to give up chasin' after trains and settle some'ers."

"Well, you've come to the right place," Corey said excitedly. "We're going to have such fun, Andy. We can go fishing and you can help Angelique with the mill…I found this place about four miles from here and wait until you see the bass in it."

"Mebbe later. You see, I got me this hankerin' to see the ole place agin and I thought mebbe I might spend some time thar."

Corey bowed her head to hide the disappointment from him. Her chin quivered as she asked, "You are going to stay a while before you leave again, aren't you?"

"I ain't leavin' right this minute, if'n thet be whut you mean," he laughed. "Now, whut about this feller I saw you smoochin' with earlier?"

"You mean you were here during my party and didn't let me know?"

"If'n you ain't the durndest…ever'time I ask you a question, you answer with one. Whut's it gonna take to git you to tell me about yourself?" He shook his head as he scolded her.

"Okay, he's a friend, an old friend and we weren't smooching. He was giving me a birthday kiss," she answered, her mouth tightening and her eyebrows knotting over the bridge of her nose.

"This here's old Andy you be talkin' to, child," he scoffed. He grasped her under the chin, forcing her to look directly into his eyes. "Th' truth, Corey girl."

After Corey told Andy all about Phillipe and the way she felt toward him, Andy took her by the shoulders and asked, "Whut happened to thet spunky kid I know'd long time ago who wuz gonna hop on thet train in the middle of daylight?"

"Are you saying I should chase after him?" she asked in disbelief.

"I'm a sayin' give him a chanct. Feel him out. I'd be willing to bet he be taken with you. If'n it don't work out, it's cuz they be some'un else fer you."

Corey thought about what Andy said. She wasn't sure she wanted to pursue the relationship, what with Phillipe's obvious affection for Morgan. That was something she had not mentioned to Andy. She opened her mouth to explain to her friend, but the visible weariness in Andy stopped her.

"If we are to get some fishing in tomorrow, I think we'd better get some sleep. It's been a long day for both of us," she smiled at the old man instead.

🍁　　🍁　　🍁

The aroma of coffee filled the morning air as Corey stepped from her car at the spot she was to meet Andy. Independent cuss that he was, he had insisted he stay in camp rather than at the house. She cupped her hands around her mouth and called, "Hullo in camp!"

"Corey, me darlin'," an excited Lord Mayor shrilled, suddenly appearing through the trees. "Tis a fine sight ye are for these tired ol' eyes," he beamed, dancing a little jig in the clearing.

"Lord Mayor!" Corey screamed in delight. "Andy didn't tell me you were with him."

"Was after surprisin' you we were. Come, coffee's ready 'n I'll be wantin' to hear all about your fine self," he chuckled, releasing her from a hearty hug.

"Whut did Angel say when you told her whar you wuz goin'?" Andy asked.

"Everyone was still asleep, but I left a note in case she was looking for me." Then, seeing the relief on his face, she probed, "That must have been some argument you two had. I don't remember you being so concerned about Angelique's reactions to you before."

"Jest don't wanna git in dutch, thet's all," he mumbled, taking a slow sip of coffee and tossing the rest on the fire. "We'd best be gittin' our hooks in th' water afore them fish find something else fer breakfast."

After they had selected a spot most likely to assure a catch, Corey sat down on the bank and dropped her hook into the murky water. Water bugs skimmed across the surface, leaving tiny wakes behind in their dangerous games. Presently, the sound of a plop in the water ended the flirtation with death for one as it was devoured by a fish. Still others came, undaunted by their predecessor's fate, like miniature ships setting out for distant shores.

Corey lay back, propping her head on one hand, and watched in fascination until she felt a persistent tug on her line. She sat up quickly, taking care to hold the fishing pole securely against the battling fish.

"It must be a whopper the way it's fighting," she called to Andy.

"Easy now or he'll git away. Don't let him git in them weeds over thar," he cautioned, pointing to the bar extending into the water.

"I got him…" but she had spoken too soon. Just as the fish came out of the water he flopped off the hook and was gone. Corey shook her head and laughed at its size. "For such a little guy, he sure put up a big fight."

"Them lil perch fight liken that. Now, you take ole gran'daddy cat, hardly know he wuz 'round till he swims right off with the hook," Andy mused, all the while his gaze surveying the water. "Fling your line easy like over yonder and mind them weeds."

Corey lifted her cane pole in the air and gently swung the line behind her to get enough leverage to send it to the appointed spot. As the line came around it was caught in an abrupt puff of wind, entangling the hook in Corey's sleeve and the sharp tip pierced her skin.

"Here, let me help you, girl," Andy said, shaking his head comically when he saw she was in no danger. "Been fishin' a long time, have you?" and grinning at her exasperated sigh, went about releasing the hook.

It was at this point Phillipe appeared through the trees and, seeing the scene, assumed Corey was under attack. He began running in their direction and yelling. "Hey, you leave that woman alone! Take your hands off her right now or I'll beat you within an inch of your life."

Corey and Andy turned, not sure what was going on for the moment while a frightened Lord Mayor scrambled to their side. As Phillipe reached them and was about to grab Andy, Corey had regained her senses enough to speak.

"Phillipe, what are you doing?" she asked, stepping between the two of them. "What is the matter with you, attacking my friend like that?"

"I thought…well, it looked like…" Phillipe sputtered.

"Well, you thought wrong as usual. When are you going to get it through your thick head that I can take care of myself? Who appointed you my protector anyway?"

"Corey, I really am sorry. If you would look at it from my viewpoint you can see how the mistake was made. After all, I thought he was a…"

"Bum?" she finished angrily. "He's a hobo, for your information and there is a difference. Anyway, you really shouldn't pre-judge people." Corey jerked up her fishing pole and stomped off toward the car.

"Leave her be, son. Let her cool down some," Andy winked at Phillipe, taking him by the arm when he started after Corey. "It'll give us a chanct to talk. Th' name's Andy," he said, extending his hand to Phillipe.

"Of course, you are the friend that brought Corey to Oregon. I should have known right away. My deepest apologies, sir. It's just that…well, Corey drives me to the point of distraction at times and I always seem to do the wrong thing."

"We all do thet onct in a while when it comes to wimen. AIn't no sense ponderin' on it," Andy grinned, following Phillipe's gaze toward Corey.

Corey sat in the car watching the men talk, her vanity bruised. *What a time for Phillipe to show up*, she fumed. She pulled the scarf from her head and took a mirror from her handbag on the seat. She tried to restore some semblance of order to her hairdo. *What could those two be talking about?* she wondered, her mind darting from her appearance to Phillipe and Andy. If Andy said anything to Phillipe about…At the thought, she hurried from the car.

Lord Mayor had joined the group and they were laughing when Corey approached the group. If only Injun had come instead of going on that job, the picture would be complete. Her favorite men would all be together. Of course, she couldn't leave Tommy out, but at least he would be with them later.

"Ah, Corey, it's no wonder you sing this man's praises. He's truly fascinating," Phillipe remarked at Corey's approach. "I could sit here all day and listen to his stories, but, alas, I must be going," he sighed and stood up.

"Since you so obviously have pressing business elsewhere, why is it you came here?" she asked crisply, trying to keep from sounding disappointed. He probably has to meet Morgan, she thought bitterly.

"My father is leaving for New York this morning on business and I am going with him. I called your house to let you know and also to tell you I have something very important to discuss with you when I return. I...well, when I return, I'll tell you. I don't want to ruin the surprise. Anyway, Angelique told me you were down here fishing, but she neglected to tell me you had company."

Corey wanted to pursue Phillipe's surprise, but something told her it would be best if she waited. Maybe it was something she did not want to hear at all. "How long will you be gone?"

"A week and a half. Two weeks at the most." He turned to Andy and extended his hand. "I guess I'll say good-bye to you, since you'll be leaving soon. I wish you would stick around until I get back. I would really like to talk to you some more."

"Cain't do thet, son, but mebbe we'll see each other agin, never can tell. You take care o' yourself in th' meantime and my girl here," he grinned, putting his arm around Corey.

"Don't encourage Phillipe, Andy. You saw what happened today," Corey tried to smile.

"Now, Corey girl, you mind your manners and tell this feller bye whilst Lord Mayor and me head back to camp." He leaned over to Corey and whispered in her ear, "I like thet young feller o' yours."

After Phillipe left, Corey talked Andy into going back to the house with her. It had always been her dream to get Angelique and Andy together again with the hopes they might marry at long last. However slim the chances were, she had to give it one last try. If neither she nor Angelique could keep him from leaving, then she would be content with that.

Andy peeked around the door. "Mebbe I oughta pitch my hat in first, if'n I had a hat, huh, Angel? You ain't gonna throw a old feller out on his ear, are you?"

Angelique tried to remain cool at Andy's return, but her eyes sparkled and danced, giving her away. "Come in, you old fool. I have a bone to pick with you," she scorned teasingly, her arms folded across her chest and her toe tapping dramatically. As he entered the kitchen, she threw her arms around him, tears welling in her eyes. "Why in the world didn't you let us know where you were? I know you thought I would still be angry with you, but you should know better than anyone else that I can't hold a grudge for long." She released him and wiped the tears with her ever-present handkerchief.

"Mebbe you're right, but I wuzn't takin' no chances," he answered sheepishly. "You was purty durn mad th' last time I seen you."

"Let's not talk about that," Angelique interrupted, glancing at Corey. "Sit yourself down and tell me about all those years."

Corey nudged Tommy, who had joined the reunion only moments earlier and led him out the back door.

🍁   🍁   🍁

The afternoon sunlight filtered through the trees, illuminating patchy areas and giving a hazy look to the woods. Occasionally an animal darted into the undergrowth, frightened by their approach. Corey loved the woods at this time of the day, when all the animals came out to feed. Many times she would come out here and sit quietly watching them.

She moved to the creek bank, motioning for Tommy to sit beside her. For a time they sat watching the easy flow of the water, broken now and then as a fish darted to the surface.

"It's everything you said, Corey," Tommy finally spoke. "Beautiful and peaceful. It's even like back home. I wish you had been there longer, and I could have taken you to some of the lakes around Naples." He turned and studied her face as he asked, "Do you think you'll ever go back? I mean, to visit your uncle. He would really like to see you again, you know."

Corey picked up a rock and sent it skimming across the surface of the water. She knew the question would come up eventually, but she resented the inflection of painful memories in her special place.

Tommy picked up a rock and deftly flicked it across the water behind Corey's. When the stones had disappeared, he continued, "After you left the last time, when your uncle signed those papers, I really felt sorry for him. I guess I felt guilty helping you run away; he missed you so much. He would come to me and ask if I had heard from you and if so, had you mentioned him. One day he stopped me when I was going fishing and asked if he could come along, too. Afterward, we went fishing quite often." Tommy paused to see if Corey was listening.

"I thought about visiting him," Corey sighed, "But as long as Aunt Lizzie is there, I can't. Tommy, I just can't face that terrible woman again."

"I know, Corey. She was mean and you hated her, but maybe after I tell you something about her you may be able to understand a little better.

"After all the trouble your uncle finally blew up and really laid the law down. Your aunt weakened and for the first time in their marriage, they finally began talking to one another. I mean really discussing things. Over a period of time things came out about Lizzie's past." He looked directly into Corey's eyes, "Did you know that her mother died when she was ten and it became Lizzie's responsibility to see after the house and her five younger sisters and brothers?"

"Yes, Aunt Lizzie pounded it into my head how she was taking care of a house and children when she was my age."

"But she didn't tell you everything…how her father began drinking and would come home drunk at night. He would beat Lizzie and curse her and the children, blaming them for his wife's death. You see, she died in childbirth and the doctor said she had had too many children without time to regain her strength. Rather than admit his own feelings of guilt, he turned to the bottle and lashed out at the children.

"Lizzie literally took her mother's place with the children, so much so that she eventually began to think of them as her own. Then one day her father came home with a new wife. Lizzie was stripped of her self importance. She was no longer mistress of the house and, even worse, her self-imposed motherhood was taken from her. Of course she was jealous of the woman, but as the children turned more and more to the stepmother, a deep resentment grew between them. The woman was not a patient person and rather than try to understand Lizzie, she decided the only way to get through to her was to "beat some sense into her."

Tommy threw another stone across the water and watched it until it disappeared. He glanced sideways at Corey before continuing.

"Those were lean years for the family, yet the stepmother wanted for nothing and finally Lizzie was fed up. By now she was old enough to go out on her own, so she left. She barely existed for the next few years, working in sweat shops at the textile mills and sleeping wherever she could find shelter. Your uncle met her while he was keeping books at one of the places she worked. After a time they were married, but she never discussed her background. She had blocked it out of her mind."

Corey analyzed the story and came to some conclusions about the abuse she had suffered. Lizzie had probably looked upon her as another intruder, someone who would likely interrupt her life again. Her greed probably stemmed from a combination of insecurity and the hard times she had been through. Lizzie had been afraid Corey would take her husband's attention, too, leaving nothing for her. Did she possibly love Uncle George, in her own way, or had he been just security for her?

"I'll need time, Tommy," Corey answered at last. "I'll need time to overcome the hatred. At least, I think I can overcome it."

"I think your uncle will understand that. After all, he's had a lot to overcome, too," Tommy smiled. "Now, what say we go back to the house while we can still find our way." He indicated the growing darkness around them.

"I've had a great time, Corey, and I hope you'll have me back again some day."

"I'm so glad you came, Tommy, I feel we've recaptured some of the old days. I'm going to miss you when you leave. Please say that you will keep in touch until we meet again."

"And you do the same," he hesitated for a minute. Clearing his throat he opened his mouth to say something, then decided against it.

"Okay, Tommy, what is it?"

"Pretty obvious, aren't I?" he grinned. "Do you think Miss Francie would mind if I kept in touch with her, too?"

"Do I detect a note of interest?" Corey stopped him and looked directly into his eyes. "Are you a bit smitten?"

"Maybe," he laughed. "What do you think?"

"Why don't you ask her yourself? Go over there tonight and take her for a soda or something."

"I believe I will do that. Thanks, my little friend."

Andy had not relented in his decision to leave, saying he had a lot to do and the sooner he got started the sooner Corey could come and visit him at his own place. He left the day after Phillipe, followed by Tommy. Francie had even been out of town, having just returned last night. It had been two weeks and Corey paced the floors, an emptiness growing inside her. If only Phillipe would return, it would at least give her morale a boost.

She picked up the phone and dialed Francie's number. She needed to get out of the house and away from the emptiness. It would be a good time to find out about Francie and Tommy. Wouldn't it be great if they got together, she thought. Neither one had mentioned if they had an interest in the other, at least not to her. Perhaps they thought it would be out of line.

"Francie," Corey greeted, hearing her friend's voice on the other end of the line. "I was wondering if you would like to meet me in town. I'm afraid the walls are closing in on me here and I've missed you terribly."

"I missed you, too, and I know how you feel," she answered. "This place feels like a morgue with Phillipe and Father away. Mother went to visit one of her friends."

"Shall we meet in half an hour at our usual place?"

"Yes, see you then."

Corey slid into the booth and picked up the menu from the table. She knew the contents by memory, but occasionally there was a new ice cream flavor.

"Well, Corey," cooed a familiar voice.

"Hello, Morgan," Corey answered, not taking her gaze from the paper, perhaps if she did not encourage Morgan, she would go away. But that was not to be the case. When she made no effort to leave, Corey lifted her eyes hesitantly to see a radiant Morgan slip into the seat across from her.

"Aren't you going to ask me why I'm so happy?"

"But, of course, Morgan, I can hardly wait to hear."

"I have reason to believe Phillipe is going to ask me to marry him when he returns from New York," she whispered excitedly.

Corey gathered her strength before speaking. "What makes you think that?" she asked shakily.

I got a note from him this morning saying he would be back in the middle of next week and he had something important to discuss with me," she breathed dramatically. "As you know we have been a steady item since his return from France. Well, what else could that important thing be?"

"Of course, you're probably right and my congratulations to you," Corey choked out the words. "Will you excuse me, Morgan, I just remembered something I have to do."

"Sure, Corey," she smiled sardonically, knowing why the sudden departure and loving every minute of Corey's distress. At last she had taken the mighty Corey down a peg or two.

Corey stumbled from the ice cream parlor, forgetting completely about Francie and got home as quickly as she could. By the time she reached her room, she was sobbing uncontrollably and flung herself across the bed, lying there until nothing was left. No tears, no feeling, nothing.

Angelique heard Corey come in and started up he stairs clutching the letter from Lord Mayor.

"Corey," Angelique called softly as she knocked at the door, "may I come in, dear?" She hesitated and, hearing no answer, went on in. Seeing the forlorn girl stretched out across the bed, she exclaimed, "My poor child, whatever is wrong?"

When Corey was able to speak the words came out thickly, "I…I can't talk about it just yet, Angelique."

"I have something that just might perk you up a bit. It's a letter from Lord Mayor. That dear man, I don't know how we would hear from Andy if it weren't for him writing the letters," she sighed.

"Put it on the dresser. I'll read it in a while."

What on earth could have happened? Angelique wondered. Ordinarily Corey would have grabbed the letter eagerly. *Oh well, when she is ready she will tell me*, she thought. Then aloud, she said, "I'll be in the library if you need me and, please dear, try not to upset yourself anymore over this…whatever it is." She laid the letter on the dresser and, giving Corey a kiss on the cheek, left the room.

CHAPTER 18

After a restless night of much deliberation, Corey awakened with a new determination. She would no longer dwell on Morgan and Phillipe. What was done was done and Andy had said, 'if it didn't work out, it wasn't meant to be'. It wouldn't be easy, but then a lot of things that had to be overcome were not easy. Then she remembered Andy. Angelique said there was a letter from Lord Mayor.

She went to the dresser and picked up the envelope. It was postmarked Minnesota. Then Andy had made it home again. She tore open the envelope and quickly unfolded the sheet of paper.

> Dear Corey,
>
> It is with heavy heart I pen this letter to you, for our friend, Andy, has passed on to his final reward. His passing was a peaceful one as he was asleep when his Master called.

Corey read the sentence again and still could not believe what she had read. It was like a nightmare and it didn't touch her. She moved as in a dream, walking across the room with the letter in hand. She finished reading:

> This information will be somewhat a comfort, I know, that he suffered no pain, but went peacefully and quickly.

Andy gone? As though from far away she heard a scream, then darkness settled over her. She was floating, drifting through the warm darkness, while somewhere in the distance someone was sobbing. She tried to see who it was and why that sobbing voice was calling her name.

"Corey, Corey, answer me," Angelique cried, slapping Corey's cheeks.

"I think she is coming around, madam," Harvey observed. "Let me take over now, you are in no condition."

"I'll be fine, Harvey. You go call the train station and find out when the next train leaves for…whatever that place is in Minnesota. It's on the envelope."

"Yes, madam," Harvey replied and took the envelope with him.

Angelique picked up the letter and read again.

> The reason, dear Corey, that I write to you instead of calling is that Andy made me promise some time ago, should this happen, he did not want me to notify you until it was all over. He wanted to spare you the tortures of the finality of it all.
>
> I will be staying here for a while and Injun will be joining me soon, so if you want to get in touch, below is the address.

Angelique summoned Harvey once again and instructed him to send a telegram to the general delivery address with the information when they would be arriving.

🍁   🍁   🍁

Corey stared out the train window at the vast rolling plains. The hot sun had washed all the color from the landscape and there was not a tree for miles to add a contrast to the barren land. It was all like something in a bad dream and she kept hoping she would wake up in her bed with everything as it had been two weeks earlier.

Finally, three days later, when they pulled into the station Corey saw the sad little figure of Lord Mayor, she realized it was no dream, but so very real.

"Hullo, Corey me darlin'. Miss Angelique," the old Irishman greeted somberly. "Tis sorrowful I am that ye be havin' to make such a trip under these circumstances. Ye must be all done in. I'll be after gettin' your bags and we can go right to the hotel."

"Can't we have them sent over? I'd like to go see Andy first," Corey objected.

Lord Mayor glanced at Angelique helplessly. "But, me darlin', tis about five miles th' other side o' town and ye really should be after havin' a rest first." Lord Mayor's eyes sought Angelique's, silently pleading with her to intervene on his behalf. He was afraid the visit to the grave would be too much for the already pale and drawn girl, especially after the long trip. From the deep blue shadows beneath her eyes, Lord Mayor could tell she had not been able to sleep the whole way and Angelique did not look any better.

"He's right, dear. By the time we get unpacked and changed, it will be dinnertime. We'll make it an early night and get a fresh start in the morning," Angelique soothed.

"At least tell me where he is...buried." There, she had said it. Buried. That word she had refused to think about and she swallowed hard, fighting back the choking sob.

Lord Mayor shot a glance at Angelique and when she nodded for him to answer, he told the story.

The town officials had wanted to bury Andy in the section of land reserved for the poor in the community graveyard, but Lord Mayor was determined Andy should be laid to rest on the old homestead, beside his parents. The farm had been sold a long time ago to cover the mortgage and he had to find the owners to get their permission.

"They be fine people, the Jensens. Couldn't seem to do enough for me after I told them about Andy and his family. Ye'll be meetin' them in th' mornin cause they will be after bringing ye out there. Wouldn't have it any other way," Lord Mayor concluded.

Corey spoke with great difficulty, "I can't tell you how grateful I am, Lord Mayor. I wouldn't rest knowing Andy was with strangers. It was so fortunate you were with him..." but Corey could manage no more and covered her mouth with her hand as if to stop the rush of new tears.

Angelique put her arm around Corey and spoke gently to the troubled Lord Mayor, "She'll be okay. If you tell me what time the Jensens will call for us in the morning, I think we shall get settled in the hotel."

While Angelique unpacked, Corey stood at the open window watching Lord Mayor until he disappeared down the street. In the distance she heard a low, mournful train whistle echoing in the quiet evening air. There was a tightening around her heart and chills crept across her skin as it did when the church bells in their town tolled the passing of one of its own.

How could her beloved Andy be gone? There was so much she had not said to him and now she would never have the chance. She had even forgotten to tell him about Pete and she hadn't had the time to tell him how much, how very much she loved him. If only she had made him stay with her. But she guessed there were always the '*ifs*' and '*I should haves*' you had to face at a time such as this, especially when you took for granted loved ones would always be there.

Corey turned from the window, her shoulders sagging heavily under the weight of her grief and she sank onto the bed.

"Corey, would you rather have dinner sent up?" Angelique asked gently.

"I think I'll just try and get some sleep. I'm not very hungry. Thanks anyway, Angelique."

The next morning on their way to Andy's old homestead, Corey surveyed the countryside. Like Oregon, there was an abundance of trees and rolling green hills. Occasionally, a small dirt lane cut through the fields from the main road, punctuated by a mailbox silently announcing the farmer's name. Overhead, puffy white clouds drifted across the skies, building for the rainfall she could feel in the air. Mr. Jensen and Angelique kept a steady conversation going in the front seat, but their words escaped Corey. She was trying to picture Andy, the young boy, roaming the farmland or working by his father's side in the fields.

The countless stories Andy had told her of his childhood sprang vividly to mind, and she wondered if this had been the route his father had taken that winter day so long ago in search of help for his mother. A neighbor had helped him that day. What had been his name? Jensen! Could it be their host was a relative of that long-ago neighbor? The name was very common in this part of the country; she had seen it on quite a few mailboxes.

"Mr. Jensen, how long has your family been here? I mean, living in this particular area?" Corey interrupted.

"We go way back to the early 1800's, Miss James."

"Would you possibly know anything about the Curruthers…Andy's family?"

"No, my father does, though. He was a boy when they lived here, maybe eleven or twelve, but I've heard him talk about them, so I know he remembers. Was there something you would like for me to ask him?"

"Would it be possible for me to talk to him sometime?" Corey asked eagerly. "There is so much I'd like to find out about Andy's people. Do you think he would mind telling me about them?"

"He would love it," Mr. Jensen laughed. "He's in his glory when he can talk about the 'good old days' before we were all corrupted with the 'new fangled' inventions and evil ways of this society." He eased the car to a stop and announced, "Well, here we are."

Corey stepped from the car reverently as though she was stepping on hallowed ground. The old cabin lay in partial ruin amidst building materials someone was using to restore it. To the right of the cabin, the land inclined gently upward to a grove of trees standing sentry over a small graveyard. In the near distance, Corey could see two weathered headstones protruding from the ground beside a new wooden one. Momentarily their images swam in the pool forming in Corey's eyes.

Mr. Jensen cleared his throat awkwardly as his mood changed to a somber one. "If you will excuse me, I'll wait in the car for you," he spoke quietly to Angelique.

"I hate to tie up your day like this, Mr. Jensen. Couldn't you come back later for us? I'm sure Corey will want to stay here for a while and there really is no sense in your staying."

Mr. Jensen pulled the watch from his pocket and looking at it said, "It's ten o'clock now. What if I come back around noon? Perhaps you and Miss James will have lunch with my family?"

"That would be nice, but somewhat an imposition on Mrs. Jensen…"

"Nonsense. She wouldn't have it any other way, Mrs. Martin. Until noon then?" Touching the brim of his hat, Mr. Jensen got back into his car.

Corey climbed the hill to the graveyard, her attention affixed on the new mound of dirt with its simple wooden marker. She sat upon the ground, her fingers caressing the earth under which Andy rested. At first it seemed more than she could bear, yet as she sat there calm settled over her. She found herself remembering when they had gone to Muffin's grave. The wind picked up as the storm grew closer and the pine trees whispered above her. Listening closely she could almost hear his voice. *"He's got it made, Corey girl. He ain't gonna want fer nuthin'. Won't be no pain."*

How wise Andy had been, she thought, even at the end. Had she come here for his funeral, seeing him in a state of eternal sleep, she would have always remembered him that way, but now she had better memories to draw on. Those memories would keep him alive for her.

"Corey, I hate to intrude, but it's starting to rain. Come back down to the cabin with me," Angelique said and her hands lifted Corey from the ground.

Corey turned to face Angelique and seeing the solemn concern on her face put her arms around the woman and spoke with a new tenacity, "I'm going to be fine now. Really I am."

Lord Mayor had arrived at the cabin with Injun when Corey and Angelique came back down the hill. Coffee was brewing in the old stone fireplace and the aroma filled the damp room. Abruptly the coffee boiled over, hissing as it hit the dancing flames. Lord Mayor plucked the rag from a worn table in the center of the room and lifted the pot from its hook.

"Thought ye might be after havin' a cup to take off th' chill."

"Oh, yes, that would be nice." Corey shivered, feeling the dampness of her clothes. She turned to give Injun a hug as Lord Mayor poured each of them a cup of the hot mahogany liquid. "It's so good to see you again, Injun," she smiled warmly at the tall man.

Lord Mayor eyed the roof with pride as they listened to the rain beat down on the tin roof. He carefully watched for leaks and when there were none, he announced, "We fixed the roof first 'cause of the summer storms, me and Andy…" the words slipped from his mouth before he thought and he bowed his head regretfully.

"It's all right, Lord Mayor, go ahead," she smiled and patted the old man's hand tenderly.

"Well, 'twas Andy's dream to fix up th' place and spend the rest o' his days here. We didn't think about th' place being someone else's, ye understand, and he never knew." Lord Mayor paused wistfully. "Anyways, we put th' tin on th' roof 'til we could be after gettin' th' real stuff whilst we worked on the rest of the cabin." He sighed heavily, staring out the open frame of the window.

No one spoke for a minute, each reflecting on the plan Lord Mayor had shared with them. Corey was getting an idea and she turned sharply to Angelique.

"Do you think we could get the Jensens to sell this place to us? They aren't living on it and it appears they aren't using it for anything."

"We could discuss that when we have lunch with them, but," she cautioned, "don't get your hopes built up too much."

Corey paid no attention. Instead, she began making plans. "We could finish the house and maybe put in a small garden and get some animals. Oh, we have to have a goat, too, one like Nanette. Remember me telling you about Nanette?"

"Corey," Angelique interrupted, "what are you going to do with it once you have finished? All these things require constant care. Are you planning to live here? What about your friends in Oregon?"

"I don't know, Angelique. I have to take a closer look at my life, get it in some kind of order, then I'll know where to go from there. With the work and isolation here, more or less, I think I'll be able to iron everything out. Even if I decide not to stay here, perhaps Lord Mayor and Injun would consider making this their home for a while."

Angelique knew Corey was referring to Phillipe. She had gotten the story from her on the train. She knew only too well what the girl was going through. Hadn't she gone to Europe after Andy left her so long ago, seeking the same solace? But she would miss Corey terribly should she stay here and she could only hope it wouldn't take too long for her to sort out her problems. What if Corey should decide to remain in Minnesota? She shook the idea from her head. No, Corey's life was with her in Oregon. She would have to believe that.

The rain was over almost as quickly as it began, and Angelique left Corey talking with the men while she paid her respects at the graveside. She climbed the hill with some effort, the dampness bringing a twinge of pain to the arthritis in her knee. She circled the grave slowly. Then, looking down on it she spoke in a clear, tender voice. "You old fool, you have left me again, but I'll see you eventually and there will be no getting away from me then, so you had better be ready." She wiped a tear from her cheek with the heel of her hand and her gaze drifted down to the cabin.

"Andy, ole dear, our little Corey is troubled. Watch over her while she is here. Time heals all wounds, well, almost as we both know, but I hope she will find comfort here while that healing process is going on."

Angelique leaned against the tree while her mind flashed images from the past. She was a young girl again, willful, headstrong and very much in love. Perhaps, at first, it had been fascination meeting someone who had traveled recklessly about the country, living on his wits and not much more, but there had been a special quality about Andy. That quality had reached out to her and filled her very being. Oh, the ignorance of youth, she mourned. Had she had any common sense at that time she would have tracked him to the ends of the earth, told him it made no difference what kind of life they would have had, as long as it was together.

She stood quietly breathing in the fresh, rain-washed air and the smells of the wet earth. How lovely it was after a rain! Sparkling droplets of water clung to the leaves, catching the sunlight and sending tiny myriads of light and color in every direction. It was a moment to be spent with someone special, a moment when emotions built to overflowing, drawing them even closer at having shared it. Now, it was loneliness instead that welled within her. Angelique pressed her cheek against the rough bark of the tree and wept.

🍁   🍁   🍁

Once the proposition was put to them it took very little time for the Jensens to agree to sell the Curruthers' old homestead to Corey and Angelique. Hard-pressed finances not to mention the generous profit were factors in their decision. In fact, they said, it was only a matter of time before they would have been forced to put it on the market.

So it was that the next few days were busy ones for Angelique. She had to arrange the transfer of funds from her bank to cover the sale and to set up a small account to draw upon for the repairs to the cabin. Also, there was the paperwork requiring her signature for the transfer of ownership. Only after all this was done did Angelique finally make preparations for her return home. She had been negligent of her own business long enough.

Corey attacked the restoration on the cabin with a vengeance, leaving little time to think about Angelique's return, or Phillipe and Morgan. Lord Mayor and Injun were hard-pressed to keep up with her and finally gave up, settling on a pace they could handle. By the end of the first week, enough had been done that Corey could move from her hotel room into the small, refurbished bedroom Andy's father had added to the main part of the house.

As she unpacked the groceries and put them on the shelves, she tried to capture the feelings of Andy's mother as she had moved in after working long and hard next to her husband building the cabin. Perhaps her feelings had been those of relief. The work was much harder in those days. There would have been trees to chop down and the backbreaking chore of getting them hewn and put into place.

There must have been an intense pride, too, seeing it completed and knowing they had done it themselves. The depth of this pride of accomplishment would escape Corey's generation with all the conveniences at their fingertips. But then, her young romantic fantasies made much more of those times than could possibly have been there. They didn't extend to the harsh, sometimes deadly existence of day-to-day life.

After lunch Corey climbed the hill, paint bucket in hand, to put the finishing touches to the picket fence Lord Mayor had built around the graveyard.

Capably, she slapped the white paint on the bare slats and smiled in the knowledge of how far she had progressed in such a short time. Two weeks ago she would have had more paint on her than the object she was painting, and the very thought of hammering nails into something and having it come out as it was supposed to would have been more than she could realize.

Corey moved steadily along the fence until the last piece of wood was covered and straightened slowly, shaking the kinks out of her legs. She carefully inspected her handiwork. *Not bad, Corey my girl, there's hope for you yet,* she praised herself, *and even time to catch your breath before supper had to be started.*

She laid her brush carefully on top of the paint bucket and walked to the slope of the hill, looking down on the cabin and the field beyond. This had been the spot Jed Curruthers had taken his son and told him about the music of life, that beautiful speech Andy had shared with her a few years back. She listened closely and heard the laughter of the brook as it spilled across the rocks, the wind singing through the trees and the birds calling across the distant meadows. How long had it been since she had stopped and listened to that music? Too much time, she thought, and so much had slipped away.

Suddenly she was thinking about her uncle and, yes, even Aunt Lizzie. Time had healed the terror she had felt and now there was only pity left. She realized she must go back and bridge that gap between them, to bring back that one link she had with her family. After that she could move forward with her life and put the pieces back together again.

A slight movement from the corner of her vision caught Corey's attention. Thinking Lord Mayor or Injun had come for her, she turned hesitantly, savoring the moment. When she turned, she took a sharp breath before clasping her hand over her mouth. There, in the shadows, Phillipe stood. Phillipe, hat in hand and that irrepressible grin upon his face.

"I did not mean to frighten you, *ma petit,*" Phillipe apologized. Further words escaped him as he drank in the vision of Corey. The golden-red sunlight of the late afternoon cast a warm glow about her. Ringlets of dark hair had escaped the knot tied securely at the back of her head and floated gently around her face, caught by the breeze. He had never seen her look more lovely. He cleared his throat, trying to relieve the tightness before speaking again.

"Mr. O'Reilly told me where to find you," he said, pointing toward the cabin at the figure in the doorway.

"Mr. O'Reilly? Oh, you mean Lord Mayor," she acknowledged, still not completely sure he was really there. Perhaps her mood had influenced her imagination, but the next moment she knew it was no dream. Phillipe was at her side, his arms encircled her waist and he lifted her off the ground.

"*Mon Dieu,* but I thought I had lost you when Angelique came home alone and said you were planning to stay here," he moaned desperately in her ear. "She told me about your confrontation with Morgan. I am so sorry about that. I would have told you the day at the lake that I wanted to marry you, but I wanted to get the ring first." He paused and reached into his pocket, taking out a small red-velvet box. Tenderly, he took the ring from its slot and slipped the box back into his pocket. Drawing a deep breath he asked, "*Ma amour,* would you do me the honor of becoming my wife?"

Corey looked up at him through the prism reflected in her tears and whispered, "Yes, yes, I will." She was unable to give more than a breathy answer over the tightness in her throat.

Phillipe bent down, placing a kiss on her mouth. Her heart was pounding, her head reeled with happiness, and she didn't know whether to laugh or cry. When he released her, they walked hand in hand through the woods, talking and planning.

"Corey, *ma petit,* I have much sorrow at the loss of your dear friend and even more that I did not get to really know him," Phillipe offered. Looking around him he continued, "I can see why you would want to stay here. It is so peaceful, but could you truly be happy here? We could make this our home if you wish?"

"Perhaps, one day, Phillipe, we shall return here, but for now I am ready to go back to my life in Oregon. That is, after I have done something I feel I must do at this time. I really have the urge to go home again…that is, back to Texas to make amends with my aunt and uncle. I can't explain why to you, only that I must."

"I understand. At least, I think I do. It will be difficult returning to Oregon without you, but I know it won't be for long." Then, grinning, he added, "Will it?"

Corey knew Phillipe had not offered to go with her, realizing this was something she must do by herself and she loved him even more for the consideration. She slipped comfortably into his arms and whispered, "No, not for long, so take heed when you see Morgan again that I won't be far behind," she teased. "By the way, that note you sent her…did you tell her you were marrying me?"

"No, but I felt I should have a talk with her, tell her we were no longer an item, as she put it. We had been seeing each other regularly and I am afraid she had assumed it was more serious than intended. I had to put things in order with her." Phillipe held her at arms' length, a mock frown on his face and then he grinned, "Do I detect a note of jealousy there?"

Laughing, she put her arm around his waist, drawing him close to her again. She felt alive once more, being here with Phillipe. Resting her head against his shoulder, she closed her eyes, recording the happiness she felt at this moment. Briefly, the vision of a man standing with his small son on this hillside floated through her consciousness, while high above her the wind whispered through the trees, echoing words from long ago. These words she knew would touch generations to come:

"Listen, son, can you hear the music?"

0-595-30268-8

Made in the USA
Las Vegas, NV
25 August 2024